22

C,K T

God's Pocket

Also by Ken Hodgson
in Large Print:

Hard Bounty

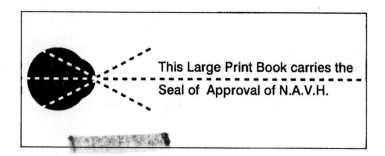

This Large Print Book carries the
Seal of Approval of N.A.V.H.

God's Pocket

A Western Story

KEN HODGSON

WHEELER
PUBLISHING

Published in 2005 by arrangement with
Golden West Literary Agency.

Wheeler Large Print Western.

The text of this Large Print edition is unabridged.
Other aspects of the book may vary from the original edition.

Set in 16 pt. Plantin by Al Chase.

Printed in the United States on permanent paper.

Library of Congress Cataloging-in-Publication Data

Hodgson, Ken.
    God's pocket : a western story / by Ken Hodgson.
        p. cm. — (Wheeler Publishing large print western)
    ISBN 1-59722-123-6 (lg. print : sc : alk. paper)
    1. Large type books.   I. Title.   II. Wheeler large print
western series.
PS3558.O34346G63 2005
    813'.6—dc22   2005021709

This book is dedicated to
Elmer Kelton,
who writes wonderful stories of the West,
and Myron C. Woodley, who lives them.

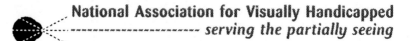

Introduction

Jarbidge, Nevada
November 1st, 2001

Computers are absolutely, without a doubt, instruments of the devil. She caused them to be put on this earth to frustrate good and honest people into drinking too much, then sinning away their immortal souls.

I thought my year-old IBM had crashed and lost my story. When you're 102 years old, you don't need that kind of excitement. Thankfully I managed to hit the save button in time.

Now that the crappy power company has brought me out of my story, I guess we can visit for a spell.

When I started out in life, automobiles were a novelty. Airplanes were rare as a virgin in Hollywood. If you're wondering why a 102-year-old man living in an end-of-the-road-near-ghost town like Jarbidge, Nevada has a blasted computer, let me tell you. The government doesn't care how old you are. I've got to fill out oodles of forms for income taxes, liquor licenses, and, of course, the state of Nevada's curse to business folks, the sales tax. All of this is one hell of a lot easier with a dang' computer, even if I do think about shooting the thing full of holes on occasion.

For a lot of years, friends have been telling me I ought to write down what it was like living in the last of the Old West. An awful lot of history has happened around these parts. It's a fact that the last stagecoach robbery in the United States happened here in 1916.

Jarbidge also hosted the last big gold rush. There were shootings, robberies, hangings, thieves, pimps, whores, and bunco artists galore. Kind of like Las Vegas is today.

I got to thinking my friends might be right, so I decided to go ahead and write about those times before I get too old.

The fact that I was there and you wasn't should make my story interesting, at least.

Chapter One

Pa blew up himself and everyone in my family except me on the fifteenth day of April, 1916. Things like this cause a young man to grow up awfully fast.

It was the first warm days of spring and he wanted to go sturgeon fishing in the Snake River. A bundle of dynamite dropped into a deep hole of water is one quick way to get a mess. In those days, this was just a means to fill the cupboard. Nowadays, I reckon they'd throw a person in jail for even *thinking* about such a thing.

I had just turned seventeen at the time, having been born into this world on April 1st, 1899. They call that "All Fools' Day." The fact that I would later go off looking for a lost gold mine and wind up living in Jarbidge, Nevada proves that at least one philosopher knew shit from Shinola.

My name is Milo Theodore Goodman. I was given my middle name because Teddy

Roosevelt made that charge up San Juan Hill and became famous. My folks were so taken by what Roosevelt had done, they went and wrote the name "Theodore" on my birth certificate. I've always been proud of that. The fact that Teddy dropped out of law school and never became a practicing shyster earned him a lot of my respect.

At the time, we lived on a 160-acre farm nine miles northwest of Buhl, Idaho. My grandfather on Mom's side had died a few years earlier. Eunice, my mother, was his only child. When the estate was settled, she inherited a considerable sum of money.

Dad, his name was Thomas, always had a hankering to come out West and farm. To this day, I don't know what possessed him to buy a dairy, but he did. So in 1910 my two younger brothers, Bill and Leonard, along with myself were hauled out to Idaho, and introduced to the dubious joys of living in the country and milking cows twice a day.

Twenty-five Guernsey milkers might not sound like a very big herd these days, but back then you had to milk them by hand. After the first dozen or so, your hands cramp up something fierce. By the time you're done, you really don't have a lot of love for cows.

Every day, seven days a week, we got up at

four in the morning. After the last milking, we still had chores to do. It was dark when we started working and dark when we finished. The worst part of it was, every year the family got a little more broke.

That fateful afternoon of the 14th, Lem McElroy came by to pay us a call. He raised alfalfa hay and sold it to fools who owned dairies, so Lem had plenty of time to visit. It seemed he had this box of dynamite he wanted to get rid of.

After we were done with milking the next morning, we took our Model T pickup over to get the dynamite. I did the driving as usual. Pa had bought that truck with some of Mom's inheritance money but he never learned to drive it without hitting something or running off the road.

Lem brought out that wood box of dynamite and set it in the back of our pickup. I noticed that crate of powder was covered with patches of sparkling white crystals but didn't pay it any mind. At the time I didn't know dynamite could go bad with age. Those crystals I saw were pure nitroglycerine.

Pa was afraid to leave the dynamite where it would freeze, so he had me stop in the yard. Then he grabbed up that crate of crys-

11

tallized nitroglycerine to his chest and headed for the fruit cellar. Now the cellar I'm talking about was right under our house. Mom was inside, probably cooking, and my two brothers were with her.

I'll never know whether Pa dropped that case of dynamite or what. I was just pulling the Model T into the barn when the whole back wall blew in.

Four days later I woke up in the Buhl Hospital. Steve Williams, the young Presbyterian minister who preached to us on Sundays, was the first person I laid eyes on. He looked like he'd slept in his clothes. And he had. I found he'd been with me the entire time I'd been laying in that bed.

"Where's my Ma?" I remember asking the preacher.

He pursed his lips and looked at the floor. "You're the only one in your family that didn't go to be with Jesus."

His words hit me harder than the crossbeam from the barn had. I found out later it had flattened the cab of the Model T on top of me and fractured my skull.

"You mean my mother and my brothers were blown up?" I asked, not really wanting an answer.

"Son," the preacher said as soothing as he could, "this was a terrible disaster. I'm afraid the explosion completely blew your house apart. We weren't sure for a couple of days if you were going to make it or not."

"*All* of them?" I asked again. I was too shook to cry. All I recollect of those days was just being numb.

The preacher took hold of my hand. "We had their funeral yesterday. When you're up to it, I'll take you to the cemetery and show you where they're buried."

Then some doctor wearing a white coat came in and gave me a shot. The room started spinning, and the next thing I knew it was two days later. This time, when the fog cleared from my head, I was alone.

I finally sweet-talked a nurse into bringing me a copy of the local newspaper. One thing my pa had been set on was me getting a good education. Still, I sort of wish I hadn't been able to read that newspaper. Back in those days reporters didn't gloss over any details.

FAMILY OF FOUR BLOWN TO BITS IN EXPLOSION, the headlines glared. SOLE SURVIVOR NOT EXPECTED TO LIVE, the next caption read. That reporter might have been wrong about the last part, but he wasn't about the first. I read a few lines about them trying to identify the body parts they found scattered around, then I wadded up that paper and threw it on the floor. I never asked for any more details.

They kept me in the hospital for a month. The doctor kept telling me he wanted to make sure my skull had healed up. I think the biggest reason for him keeping me that long was because I didn't have anywhere else to stay.

A few of the neighbors came by to see me. From their visits, I learned that Fred McAllister, another fool who owned a dairy, had taken the Guernsey cows to his place. Everyone felt sorry for me and offered to put me up for a while, but the last thing I wanted was to be around a lot of people.

I sent word for Edward Tichenor, the president of the bank, to come by and see me. It didn't take him long to show up, and I was shocked to find there was nearly $1,000 in that bank.

Tichenor told me, since I was the sole surviving heir, the money was mine. Also, he offered to negotiate the sale of the cows to McAllister. I was more than happy to take him up on that one. Ever since then, I've loved eating a good steak. I wouldn't drink a glass of milk if someone held a gun to my head.

When I got out of the hospital, I took a

room in the hotel. It only cost me ten dollars a week for room and board, so there was no hurry for me to do much. I hung around town, finding any excuse I could to keep from going to see what was left of our farm.

After a few days of laying around the hotel, I went to see Frank Haskins. He owned a combination garage and livery stable in Buhl. In those days, folks weren't real sure what the future was going to hold for either cars or horses. Frank and others like him hedged their bets by catering to both.

I paid Frank and one of his hired hands to go out to the farm and tow back the Model T. When I got a good look at it, I knew I was lucky to have survived with just a cracked head. The cab of that little truck was flattened even with the bed. The first thing I did was cut off the old top and throw it away. Then I bolted some two-by-fours to the body and made a wood framework where the old cab had been. After wiring pieces of tin on top for a roof and putting on a new windshield, that old truck — while it wasn't much on looks — was drivable.

Tichenor surprised me by saying he had a buyer for the farm if I wanted to sell it. I didn't haggle. I took the offer. The last thing I wanted was to own that dairy farm.

For the entire month of June, I kicked around Buhl. I had well over $3,000 in the bank and a pickup to drive, but had absolutely no idea what I was going to do with my life.

I took out enough money to have the undertaker put up stone monuments in the cemetery. When they were in place and engraved, I drove out to see how they had turned out. This was my first trip to the cemetery, but I didn't need a preacher to point out my family's graves. Some folks, neighbors I guess, had cut big bouquets of flowers, pink peonies mostly, and put them on each of those plots. The stones were right well done. Everyone's name was spelled out correct and chiseled deep into gray granite.

I said my sad good byes to everyone that afternoon, then I went to the bank and took out $200 in cash.

It was the first day of July when I climbed into that old Model T and headed off. At seventeen years of age, I pointed that old truck toward Twin Falls, Idaho where they were having a big 4th of July celebration. I thought that might cheer me up some. I reckon if I'd had any idea at the time what that decision would bring me, I'd have gone to California instead.

Chapter Two

Calvin McVey's dog got run over by a Stanley Steamer during the 4th of July parade that summer of 1916. The car had a full head of steam built up and was decorated to the hilt. I was paying especial attention to the Steamer because it was carrying the parade queen. She was voted Miss Dairy Farm, or something like that. They don't have much to celebrate in Idaho that doesn't have either a potato or a cow involved somewhere.

I was nursing a bottle of beer and trying to get a good look at the girl in that chugging Steamer. Then this big brainless mutt starts yapping its fool head off and runs past me to start biting at the wheels on that Stanley. They had wrapped burlap sacks through the spokes and someone had sewn white stars to them. I guess that dog took a real dislike to seeing them spin around like they were.

When a dog bites into a gunny sack, his

teeth get hung up and he can't let go. That mutt let out a real puzzled yelp and was flipped under a wheel. The Steamer raised up in the air as it ran over the dog and came down with such a crash the wheel broke.

I chugged the last of my beer and ran out to make sure the parade queen was all right. This galoot nearly knocks me over skittering toward that flattened mutt blubbering: "Nugget, ole Nugget, are you OK?"

It didn't take him but a short look to figure out ole Nugget had yapped his last yap.

"He caught what he was chasing," I remarked to him, being a little sore that he'd kept me from helping the girl out before a half dozen other guys showed up to do it.

"He was the best darn' lion dog in Idaho!" the man yelled at me. "I've had him since he was a pup."

"If there's any more from the same litter, they'd come in mighty handy at stopping runaway Stanley Steamers," I said before he popped me in the jaw.

It wasn't much of a fight and we didn't attract a lot of attention. Most everybody's thoughts were directed on getting the parade started up again. We rolled around in the dirt pounding on each other for a spell, neither one doing a lot of damage to the other. Finally I just got tired of fighting, and said: "Hey, I'm sorry about what happened to your dog and I apologize for saying anything."

This guy blinked his eyes, and we looked each other over. He was a gangly sort of fellow, not much older than me, with long blond hair draped over his shirt collar. He also had the biggest set of ears I'd ever seen on another human being. One of them was dripping blood from where I'd bit into it.

"Nugget was a good dog," he said one more time. He was determined to make that point.

"Yeah," I answered not too enthusiastically. I still thought that mutt was as dumb as a sack full of hammers, but it was too hot for any more fighting. "I'm sorry he got run over. Let's go have a beer."

He looked at me for a while trying to figure out if I meant what I said or if I was going to hit him again. Finally a little grin crossed his face and he held out his hand. "McVey's the name, Calvin McVey. Most folks call me Cal. I reckon you didn't do much but say what others were thinking. Nugget had a lot of sense when it came to chasing lions, but it sort of failed him when he got around automobiles."

I shook his hand and introduced myself,

19

then we headed for the nearest bar. Once Cal's ear quit bleeding, his attitude improved, and by that evening we'd become pretty fair friends. He had eight brothers and sisters. The whole family, including his ma, pa, and both sets of grandparents lived on a potato farm south of Twin Falls. I could see why he liked to go lion hunting all by himself, that many relations hanging around would cause a preacher to drink.

It turned out Cal was only a year older than me. I suppose farming potatoes added age to his looks. He was fascinated by the fact that I had my own Model T pickup. When I told him how I came to own it, he grew silent for a long while. Then he said he was sorry about punching me and, to change the subject, tossed out a rough-looking piece of rock onto the table top.

I picked it up and saw it was white quartz with some yellow metal streaks running through it. "Is that gold?" I asked.

"It sure is," Cal answered proudly. "A few tons of high grade like that would set a man up for life."

"Where'd it come from?"

"That's the problem. This is the only piece I found when Nugget and me was hunting lions last year above Jarbidge. My guess is it's a chunk of ore that broke off a vein higher up the mountain. I was in the area where the Lost Sheepherder's Mine's supposed to be."

"Couldn't you just follow the little chunks up the slope of the mountain until you come to the mother lode?" I questioned simply.

"That's not how you go about it," he said, looking at me like I was some rube. "Have you ever heard of looking for a needle in a haystack? Those mountains back of Jarbidge are as rugged as anything you ever laid eyes on. There's maybe little teaser pieces of high grade scattered all over the side of that peak. The only person whoever came out of that area of God's Pocket with chunks of gold from the outcrop was an old sheepherder named Ishman. He died before he could ever get back to his diggings."

I took a swig of beer and decided I'd better get all of the information I could while Cal was willing to part with it. I also thought we'd best start with particulars. "What's a Jarbidge?" I asked him.

"It's only the richest gold rush town in Nevada, that's what," Cal spouted. "A man by the name of Dave Bourne found high grade there five years ago. I'd reckon there must be over a thousand people living in that little cañon nowadays."

"With all those folks looking for gold, wouldn't you suppose they'd have found that Lost Sheepherder's Mine by now?"

Cal gave me a serious look over the top of his beer bottle. "What I'm telling you is, they're all looking in the wrong place. God's Pocket Peak, where I found my ore, is miles to the southeast. You've got to remember, I was tracking lions, not looking for gold. They're skittish critters and avoid being around people. I had gone up the east fork of the Jarbidge River, and finally caught track of a big male near Slide Creek. From there, I followed that cat clear up God's Pocket Creek durn' near to the top of the mountain. That's where I lost him. I was searching for cat sign when I found that gold."

Now I got pretty worked up by Cal's story. I'd been wondering what I was going to do with my life. Finding a lost gold mine and making myself a millionaire seemed like a mighty good plan.

The whole thing seemed so simple. It couldn't take more than a few weeks. Any idiot should be able to pick up chunks of gold from the top of the ground and head up a hill until he found the mother lode. Looking back on the situation, I should have taken an idiot with me.

Cal was getting fairly drunk and kept ranting on about how much he wanted to go after that mine. I bought us another round and made him a proposition: if he'd come along, we would go partners.

"I can't do it," he blubbered. "There's too much to do at the farm."

If growing potatoes was as much work as running a dairy, I knew he had a point. "Once we have the gold, you can hire all the help you need."

"No, I can't do that to my folks, they're depending on me," he replied. "I was lucky to get a week off to go lion hunting. Now I can't even do that . . . I've got no lion dog."

He was getting all teary-eyed. Too much beer does that to some folks.

"You made fun of ole Nugget," Cal sobbed. "Any man who makes fun of a good lion dog getting run over ain't fit to be a partner."

We'd made a circle and come back to where we'd met. Cal jumped up, dumping the table over. When he drew back to throw a punch, he hit his own ear, the one I'd bit a chunk out of, and started it bleeding again.

This time he never got to punch me. The big guy who owned the place had him in an arm lock before he knew it. That was the last time I ever saw Cal McVey. The bartender dragged him to the door; all the while he was blubbering and crying about ole Nugget getting killed, and his ear spurting blood onto the wood floor.

I stood the table back up and picked up the spilled bottles. This made a good impression on the bartender, so he let me stay. The more I thought about that Lost Sheepherder's Mine, the more I wanted to go after it. Later, when I left to walk back to the hotel, I felt that it had been a really good day. At least for everyone but ole Nugget.

The next morning I was a little slow getting started. I've never been one for getting in a dither just because the sun came up. I took my breakfast in the hotel, then I went shopping.

I sure spent a bunch of money, but, when I was done, I had that Model T loaded with everything a man needs to find a lost mine. I'd bought a heavy felt coat, several changes of warm clothes, a new fedora hat and rain slicker, along with a pick and shovel.

Before I left Twin Falls, I stopped by a gas station, filled an extra five-gallon can, and bought a couple of extra tires and wheels for the Model T. Then I went to a hardware store and picked up a .30-30 Winchester rifle, along with several boxes of shells.

It was nearly noontime and black clouds were building in the west when I left Twin Falls. I'd inquired of several people about how to get to Jarbidge. Most folks I asked said the road was "pretty bad."

Being born on the 1st of April, I paid little heed to what folks said. Heading south on that dirt road, trying to outrun a rainstorm, my heart was high for the first time in a long while.

I was going to find a lost gold mine, right after I spent the night at a place called Kitty's Hot Hole.

Chapter Three

There was no problem finding the road to Jarbidge. There were plenty of people coming and going from the place. All of this traveling had rutted the road considerable, making for slow going. I had plenty of time to enjoy the view, which I would have done if there had been any. One sagebrush looks pretty much like the other.

I did manage to outrun that thunderstorm. This was a stroke of luck for that road turned into a quagmire any time it rained. I noticed some jagged snow-capped mountains jutting up in the distance. The fact that it was the first week of July and there was still snow on those peaks should have told me something. All I thought of when I saw them was that lost mine. I knew for sure it was on one of them.

The terrain was generally flat, covered with nothing but sagebrush. Occasionally a creek wound its way across that expanse, marked by a line of green trees. A few home-steaders were trying to make a go of it where there was water. Most of those folks were raising alfalfa hay. I sure felt sorry for them, working so hard on a farm just to make a few dollars, when there was gold lying on top of the ground above Jarbidge.

A red sunset was beginning to form in the west when I came to a god-awful steep cañon. The road just took a dive off into its shadowy depths. Down in that tree-lined gorge, the Bruneau River was running high and roily.

I stretched my neck, looking to make sure there weren't any freight wagons coming or going. The road that snaked along the cañon wall to the river wasn't much wider than my Model T. I put the truck in low gear and headed down, nice and slow. Model Ts had brakes only on the two back wheels, so it didn't pay to get in a hurry de-scending a steep hill.

Thankfully I didn't meet anyone, and it wasn't long until I was down and driving along the river. I worried some about having to return up that hill, finally deciding I'd have to back up it. My truck's lowest gear was reverse. When you come to a steep hill with a Model T, the best way up was to go in reverse. There wasn't any fuel pump for the engine; the fuel ran to the motor by gravity. When you headed up a steep hill, the gasoline ran to the back of the tank and not to your engine, starving it out. It was a better plan all around to back up any precipitous road.

Kitty's Hot Hole was in the bottom of that cañon next to the river. The place consisted of one big log cabin with a sign on the door saying **Meals served anytime** and a bunch of lodgepole corrals filled with mustangs. I pulled that Model T to a stop in front of the joint and killed the engine.

When I climbed out to stretch my legs before going inside, I noticed steam rising from below a steep rim rock across the Bruneau River. A hot spring spurting out boiling water helped give the place its name. Kitty Wilkins, the lady who owned both the hot spring and business, completed the moniker. Preachers and prudes referred to this stopover as the Wilkins Ranch. Everyone else called it Kitty's Hot Hole.

There were four tables inside. One of them held a couple of rough-looking cowboys. Both frowned and glared at me like they'd rather shoot me than say hello.

"And just who might you be?" the older cowboy with a graying beard said gruffly.

I started to answer that he could call me

gone when a female voice yelled from the back room. "Reece, for Pete's sake, not everyone who stops by here works for Logan."

I spun around to see who was talking. This big woman, wearing an apron, was headed toward me, holding a bloody butcher knife. I was trying to decide between running for the door or simply making a mess in my pants, when this lady gives me a warm smile and said: "Take a seat, son. I'll rustle you up some supper in a bit. We've butchered a pig. I'll have some fresh pork chops pretty soon."

The fact that this woman hadn't been using that butcher knife to chop up the last fool who stopped by relaxed me some. She was built like a pickle barrel and really old. I figured her to be maybe forty or so. What I remember most about her was her eyes. They were the deepest turquoise blue. When she smiled, they made her look close to pretty. Too much sun had etched deep lines in her face and her long blonde hair was streaked with gray.

"If there's a problem, ma'am, I can be moving on," I told her politely.

"Oh, there's a problem all right," she said in a sad voice. "A man by the name of Logan is trying to take away my ranch. He has a lawsuit against me. Once in a while, some of his toughs come around trying to make trouble."

"But we take care of 'em," the man called Reece added firmly.

"These are my hands, Reece Morgan and Billy McGraw," the lady said, nodding toward the cowboys. "I'm Kitty Wilkins."

I introduced myself and sat down at a table. Kitty brought me a cup of coffee to sip on while she finished butchering the pig. After a spell of silence, the cowboy called Billy looked at me and said: "Sorry about being so gruff when you showed up. The last guy who came through here, driving a car, was a lawyer. The biggest mistake we made was not shooting him when we had the chance. He had a law paper with him."

"That's a lawsuit," Reece corrected. "But Billy's right about the fact we should 'a' shot him. Lawyers are a bigger pain in the ass than Injuns ever were."

"Why's this Logan fellow trying to take a ranch from some lady as nice as Kitty?" I asked.

"She has been catching wild mustangs for years. We round them up, tame them down a mite, and sell them to the government. Miss Wilkins never got around to filing a paper claim to the land. A while back, this guy named Logan found that out and laid out a homestead over Kitty's ranch."

"From what you've told me, I'd think you ought to shoot *him* instead of the lawyer," I said, trying to be agreeable. "Generally a lawyer takes off like a scared chicken once they quit getting paid."

Both of those cowboys cracked the first smile, and Reece said: "You've a right smart head on your shoulders. Billy and me would like nothing better than plugging that snake, but Kitty won't let us. She says the law will prove her right."

"At the speed this thing's moving, before it's settled I'll likely be wearing Roebucker teeth, instead of my own pearly whites," Billy remarked, grinning with his mouth wide open to show me how good his teeth were.

I was getting to like these two cowboys. Billy, especially, had a happy smile that shone bright from under a crop of the reddest hair I'd ever seen on anyone. Reece, was the oldest of the two. I figured him to be in his thirties. From the manner he looked at Kitty, I didn't think his interest in her was all financial.

There was a banging of pots and pans from the kitchen, then a sizzling sound as pork chops hit the skillet. Soon the aroma of frying meat began to fill the cabin.

Kitty began carrying in heaping plates of food. Aside from the pork chops, there were mountainous portions of fried potatoes covered with gravy and, surprisingly enough, some fresh asparagus. When we all started eating supper, I saw how Kitty managed to keep her figure. What the cowboys and I didn't grab right off, she ate every speck of, right down to sucking the meat off the bones of those pork chops.

After supper, all of us chipped in and helped clean up the dishes. Then, with cups of steaming black coffee, we sat down at the table nearest the stove. I was beginning to learn about the high country; it can get mighty cold up there, even in the summer time.

"I wish the apples would come on, then we'd have a cobbler," Kitty remarked.

"That'd be good for sure," Reece said, looking at her. "I expect it won't be but a few weeks and we can lay in a supply."

"How long have you been here?" I asked.

"My folks settled this country back in Eighteen Eighty," Kitty replied. "I was just a little girl when we came here. The Indians wintered at the hot spring. It was a nice warm place for them to hole up."

"Why did they leave?" I asked.

Kitty grinned a snaggle-toothed smile and

said: "My folks had better title to it than they did. Judge Colt and Sheriff Winchester were on their side of the matter."

Reece grumbled. "That's how we ought to handle Logan."

I figured this line of conversation had been worn out, so, to change the subject, I said: "I'm heading on over to Jarbidge in the morning. I've heard tell there's quite a gold rush going on."

Kitty beamed. I think she was real proud to talk about something other than her problems. "It's about the richest mining town you'll ever see."

Reece looked at me sternly. "By the way, supper's fifty cents. For a dollar more, you can bunk in here where it's warm and we'll feed you breakfast in the morning to boot."

I thought for a moment about just paying for my food and sleeping on the ground, but that fire felt mighty good. I fished out a dollar and a half. Kitty grabbed up the money, sticking it somewhere into her voluminous overalls.

"Thank you, Milo," she said sweetly. "I hope you strike it rich up there."

This threw me for a curve; I hadn't said anything about going to look for gold. "What makes you think I'm prospecting?"

Kitty and the cowboys grinned, and Billy

remarked: "What for in God's good name would you be going to a place like Jarbidge, if you weren't? You're too nice a fellow to be a drummer, and you ain't brought out any cards, so you're not a gambler. That leaves either a prospector or a pimp."

"Oh, I'm prospecting," I said quickly.

Everyone had a good laugh, then Kitty chilled me to the bone when she said: "Son, you might even get lucky and find the Lost Sheepherder's Mine."

I swallowed hard and I'm sure all the color ran out of my face. "You've heard of the mine?" I asked weakly.

"Oh, hell, boy," Reece said. "Everyone's heard of it. Folks looking for that mine was who first found gold in Jarbidge."

I wished for a moment I'd bitten Cal McVey's ear plumb off. "But no one's found it?"

Kitty looked at me sweetly and said: "No, that mine's still lost. Someone will find it, though. I hope it's you. I really do."

There was little sleep for me that night. I tossed and turned, worrying myself silly that someone would beat me to the Lost Sheepherder's Mine.

Early next morning, Kitty came out dressed in overalls again. She wrapped the same bloody apron she'd worn yesterday around her waist and began fixing breakfast. I used some of the smarts I'd gained from last night and filled my plate with bacon and biscuits before that woman got a shot at them.

I would have hung around and drank coffee for a while, but a couple of freight wagons stopped and the place began filling up. As I walked out the door, Kitty yelled at me: "I hope you find that Sheepherder's Mine, boy!" I thought if Jarbidge had a newspaper, I'd take out an ad telling everyone why I was there.

Even though it was the 6th of July, I could see my breath as I cranked on that Model T. I let the engine run for a while to warm up while I looked over the road going up the other side of the cañon. It was plenty steep, so, once I crossed the bridge over the river, I turned around and backed up it.

My neck was cramping up bad by the time I got to the top of that rim rock. It felt good to be able to turn around and face where you were pointed. A drab sea of sagebrush washed across a flat mesa toward the green mountains in the distance. There's only two kinds of country out there: it's either as flat as a dance floor or so steep a mountain goat's liable to break his neck crossing it.

I hadn't gone two miles when I hit a deep

wagon rut the wrong way and broke a wheel. When I had the Ford jacked up and was unloading the bed to get a spare out, I was startled when a voice said over my shoulder: "You're in the road."

When I spun around, I saw one of the biggest men in the world standing there holding onto the handles of a wheelbarrow. He wore a pair of dirty, patched overalls and had a straggly sand-colored beard.

"There's lots of room to go around," I said.

"Ma tol' me not to leave the road," he answered, and left his mouth open. Right about then, I figured this guy was a biscuit shy of a full breakfast.

"I've got to change this wheel, then I'll be off," I told him.

"OK, mister," he said agreeably. "Ma wants this stuff. My name is Willie. They call me Wheelbarrow Willie."

I smiled when I saw the only thing he had in that barrow was one small box wrapped in oilcloth.

"These are peaches," he said proudly. "They're for my ma. She likes 'em. You got any oil? My wheel won't turn."

When I checked out his wheelbarrow, I found the wheel hadn't been greased for so long it had locked up. From the skid marks in the road, this guy had been pushing that barrow for miles without the wheel turning. I couldn't help but feel sorry for him, so I took the time to pull off that wheel and grease it.

He moved his wheelbarrow back and forth a few times, gave me an open-mouthed grin, and said: "Thanks, mister . . . you're in the road."

I shook my head and went back to fixing my own wheel problem. Right about then, the jack slipped and that Model T crashed to the dirt. I said a few words appropriate to the moment and started trying to fish the jack out from under the truck. All of a sudden that Model T went up in the air. I looked and Willie held it like it was a feather. It was my turn for an open-mouthed stare.

"Does this help you, mister?" he asked.

"Yeah, Willie, you're a big help," I replied. Regaining my wits, I slid a new wheel onto the axle.

"Ma likes peaches," he said again.

"Where did you get them?" I asked while stowing the jack.

"Got 'em in Twin Falls. My ma sure likes 'em. We work a gold mine."

I couldn't believe someone pushing a wheelbarrow for a hundred miles just to bring back a case of canned peaches. "There's room on the back to put your stuff. You can ride into town with me," I told him.

"Ma tol' me to stay on the road. When you get off it, I'll be jus' fine."

I spun the crank and started my truck. When I headed off, I saw Willie following me, pushing that wheelbarrow and grinning like a cat. A little grease had made his day.

Some of the wagon ruts were a foot deep, so I drove slowly and more carefully. I only had one more extra wheel, and I didn't want to block Willie's road again.

Around noontime, those high mountains were no longer in the distance. I pulled over and stopped where the road took a dive into another steep cañon. I saw a stagecoach being pulled by six horses struggling up that steep grade, so I lit up a cigarette and waited for it to top the rise. Those horses were winded and wheezing when the driver stopped the stage by me to give them a breather. I walked over and made my introductions.

"I'm Fred, Fred Searcy," the driver said from his seat. He lit up a cigarette while looking over my truck. "You going prospecting?"

"Yeah, I am," I answered, almost yelling

out that I was also looking for the Lost Sheepherder's Mine just to keep him from asking.

"You want to be careful camping out in these parts," he told me in a concerned voice.

"What do you mean?" I asked.

"Bears are the problem. There's been a killer grizzly dragging prospectors out of tents and eating them. I hear this bear's got a dozen or so already."

I felt a cold chill in my back. "Surely there's folks out hunting a killer bear like that."

"That grizzly soaks up lead like he's a sponge. If I was you, I'd check into the Jarbidge Hotel." With that comment, he flicked the reins and the stagecoach started rumbling toward Kitty's.

When I took another look down into that cañon, it was a lot darker and gloomier. There were groves of trees all along that river where a killer bear could be hiding, just waiting for a juicy prospector to happen by.

Looking for lost gold mines was turning out to be a tougher nut to crack than I'd thought at first. I cranked the engine to life, then laid my rifle across my lap before I slowly headed down into the dark depths of that deep and forbidding cañon.

Chapter Four

Once I dropped off that mesa, the road got steeper than hell. If a bear had jumped out of some trees at me, it would have broken its neck when it fell off the cliff. A few places I got so close to the edge I could look down and see buzzards flying in the breeze below me. Briefly I wondered if they were dining on the last idiot who tried driving a car to Jarbidge.

Between that cliff-side road and a prospector-munching bear, I made a decision. As soon as I found a wide spot where I could turn that car around, I was getting out of here. That rifle I'd bought would come in mighty useful for shooting Cal McVey. I fully intended to do that right after reminding him of just how dumb his dog had been. Then I saw the town of Jarbidge stretched out along the river below me.

Since I'd lived through everything so far, I began feeling lucky. I lit up a cigarette and in a few minutes I was driving into town.

I saw a few small houses with a footbridge over the river connecting them with Main Street. These cabins all had red lanterns hanging above their doors. I took this to be the recreation area for lonely miners.

The second thing I noticed was a knotted hangman's noose dangling from a cross-beam between two huge aspen trees. A sign on the noose said **Reserved for Dave Bourne**. I remembered Cal McVey saying he was the man who first found gold here.

The Jarbidge Hotel was a rambling two-story frame building on the lower end of Main Street. I was flabbergasted when the drunken old biddy who ran the joint demanded three dollars for a night's stay. I only paid her for one night. Bears or not, at prices like that there was no doubt what little money I had left on me wouldn't last long.

After I stowed my gear in that spendy room, I parked the Model T off to one side of the hotel and set out on a walk to see what Jarbidge amounted to.

It was getting late in the afternoon. The sun had set behind a rim rock, washing the town in shadows. During my tour, I counted all of the going businesses. There were six bars, two restaurants and hardware

41

stores. A barbershop, laundry, bank, and a general store filled out my list. I was surprised not to see a single church.

As I headed back down Main Street toward the hotel, I saw a friendly-looking bar called the Miners' Exchange. I decided to drop in and have a beer.

The place was as quiet as a tomb. There weren't a half dozen people inside. I took a seat at the end of the bar next to a skinny man with a long gray beard and ordered a draft.

After a few minutes of silence, the fat bartender came walking over with his fingers tucked into his belt. "You're new in town?"

"Yep," I answered, "just got into town a little bit ago. I've taken a room at the Jarbidge Hotel."

"Spendy place, the hotel is, for sure," the man next to me said with a smirk.

"Better than getting eaten by a killer bear," I replied.

The bartender, this guy next to me, and everyone else in the joint broke out laughing like this was the funniest thing they'd ever heard.

"Pardner," the bartender blurted out between laughs, "you must have talked to Fred Searcy, the stage driver."

"I did. He met me top of the grade and

told me about this bear that had killed a bunch of prospectors."

"And he said to rent a room at the hotel, right?" the man next to me said after a big swallow of beer to clear his throat.

"Well, yeah," I answered not too loudly.

"His ma owns the hotel," the bartender said. "He loves pulling that story on greenhorns."

I realized that I'd been had, so I figured I might as well join in having a laugh, even if it was on me. "I reckon bears aren't a big problem?"

"Nope," the bartender said. "The last guy to be killed by a bear in these parts was years ago, when old Wesley Cristman whacked one with a shovel."

I grinned and told that fat bartender to get everyone a beer on me.

"I'm Jackson Lyman, you can call me Jackson," the man next to me said, offering up his hand. I made my introductions, and Lyman nodded his head toward the bartender who was busy filling up mugs. "The guy hustling beer owns this joint. His name is Dave Bourne."

Right away I thought of that hanging noose with Bourne's name on it. As I hadn't been too successful at reading sign lately, I decided it was best not to say anything.

I plunked a silver dollar down on the bar. Dave Bourne passed the glasses of beer around, then scooped up my money with pudgy fingers. "Glad to see a man with a sense of humor," he grumbled. "Not everyone in Jarbidge has one."

"They're just joshin' about hanging you," Jackson said.

"Nope, they're really gonna hang him," a big man sitting at a table with two others said. "It'll be a shame too, because Jarbidge can't afford to lose bartenders . . . or whores. They're all that makes living up here tolerable."

"Things aren't going so good in Jarbidge?" I ventured.

"Well, it sure as hell ain't *all* my fault," Dave Bourne growled.

"Dave, he just got into town," Jackson interjected with a soothing voice. "He ain't had time to get worked up about hanging you . . . yet."

The fat bartender shrugged his shoulders, let out a belch, and fixed his beady eyes on me. "I reckon I ought to fill you in on why a few misguided folks are upset with me," he said.

"Upset! Hell, they're gonna hang you!" the man at the table yelled.

"Then you can buy the next round,"

44

Dave told him. The guy shut up and humped over his beer, obviously through talking.

"The truth of the matter," the bartender continued, "a short time ago I was the richest man in Nevada. At least on paper I was."

"That's a right true story," Jackson interjected. "Dave came here looking for that Lost Sheepherder's Mine before there even was a town. He found gold, too, right on the hill back of where we're sitting."

I decided then and there I was the only person in this part of the world who *hadn't* made a life study of the Lost Sheepherder's Mine.

"How did you come to grief finding a gold mine?" I inquired.

Dave Bourne said, "When you find gold, it takes a lot of money to get it out of the ground, and then you've got to build a mill to process it.

"To raise money, I sold some stock," he continued. "We finally got the mill built and fired it up a couple of months ago. Big rocks went in one end and little rocks came out the other end. There wasn't a speck of gold to be seen. Then the engineer I'd hired lit out. I was the only one in the company left to explain why things didn't work."

"The outfit *is* called Bourne Mining Corporation," Jackson interjected.

"If anyone needs hanging, it's that damn' engineer by the name of Nyal Bennett," Bourne ranted.

"When word got around there was no gold and the mill didn't work, folks started leaving in droves," Jackson affirmed. "The only ones left are waiting to see if this new company, Elkoro Mines, makes a go of it. Well, that and planning on hanging Dave keeps 'em here."

"Surely the sheriff won't let folks hang you over the fact you lost them money," I said.

Everyone in the bar went quiet and looked at me like they did when I'd brought up that killer grizzly thing.

"The nearest law is in Elko. That's over a hundred miles away as the crow flies," Jackson said, setting down his empty mug. "We had a local constable, but, when the town went bust, they quit paying him. He's still here. You can find him at the Stray Dog Saloon up the street. His name's Ben Kuhl."

Dave Bourne sighed, looked toward the front window, and said: "Kuhl is a low-down skunk. He only bought a hundred shares, and then he goes and makes that hanging rope."

"Ben's mighty handy with a rope, for sure. That's a good noose he made. No one else in Jarbidge knew how to knot one," Jackson said.

"How about it Searcy, you gonna buy that next round or not?" Bourne roared at the big man at the table.

"Searcy, that was the stage driver's name," I said to no one in particular.

"That it is," the big man at the table answered with a grin. "Inman Searcy's the name. These are my friends, Alvin and Rudolph Bruckner. We worked together at Bourne's mill until the roof fell in. Fred runs the stage to Twin Falls under a mail contract. Our ma, Sylvia, runs the hotel. She's also the local postmaster. Right now, all I'm doing is giving Dave Bourne back some of those wages he paid me . . . bring us another round."

As the pudgy bartender began refilling our mugs, the joint grew quiet, giving me time for thought. Since my going to Twin Falls, most folks whose acquaintance I'd made were a bubble off plumb. It seemed the higher the elevation, the more pronounced was their problem. I decided it would be in my best interests to find that lost mine and get to lower altitude *pronto*. As I was born on April Fools' Day, however,

47

things weren't destined to work that way.

"Thanks for the beer," I told Inman.

"I'm the one who should be thanking you," he said, grinning like a cat. "Not everyone buys that bear story. You can stay another night or two . . . no charge. I don't reckon we'll get many more folks up here looking to rent a room until this weekend when there will likely be some show up for the hanging."

Dave Bourne winced. "There's laws against lynching . . . even in Jarbidge. I sent for the sheriff."

"It ain't *us* you need to convince, Dave," Jackson said. "A lot of folks lost a passel of money on that mine of yours."

"I know that," Dave said, looking more worried. "That Bennett fellow had me hornswoggled, too. We raised a million dollars on his phony reports and spent every dime of it building a mill that won't work."

"*He* ain't here and *you* are," Jackson interjected.

"A million dollars?" I blurted out. "I reckon that *is* hanging money."

"Christ on a crutch," Dave Bourne shouted, "he's only been here less than an hour and he's ready to stretch my neck, too!"

"Oh, I'm not for hanging anyone," I quickly answered.

The big bartender sighed heavily and came around the bar. He put a hand on my shoulder and said quietly into my ear: "You come back in the morning and have breakfast with me. We need to have ourselves a little talk." Then he turned from me, looked over everyone in the joint, and boomed: "The last round's on me, then I'm closing the place early. I've got things to do."

"Like writing your will," Jackson quipped.

Dave shot him a look that said if he wanted that free beer he'd best shut his trap. When I left, it was starting to get dark and chilly. I headed for the hotel, when Wheelbarrow Willie came into view. He was pushing that wheelbarrow down the middle of the road, looking straight ahead. I noticed he had acquired a hat somewhere along the way. It was a black bowler about four sizes too small for him. That hat perched on top of his head like a sick chicken, his long sandy hair spilling out around the edges.

"Thanks for fixin' my wheel, mister," he said when he spotted me looking at him. "I found a hat, too. It's been a mighty good day. I've got to get these peaches to Ma."

I watched as he continued on his way up the middle of Main Street until he was just a speck. Across the dusty street from the boardwalk where I was standing, I could see Dave Bourne through the front window of his bar. He flashed a glance at me while putting up a Closed sign.

Most of that night, I laid awake listening to a hoot owl blowing a tune in a tree outside my window and wondering what Dave Bourne, a man who was going to be hung soon, wanted to talk to me about.

Chapter Five

Warming rays of sunlight were beginning to chase away the chill when I left the Jarbidge Hotel to meet with Dave Bourne. My route took me right by that dangling noose. The thing looked far more ominous than it had yesterday.

I made up my mind then and there that, when I found the Lost Sheepherder's Mine, I'd sell out before anyone built a mill that didn't work. I wanted to enjoy owning a gold mine, not get hung for it.

Dave Bourne must have been keeping an eagle eye out for me. I was walking up the boardwalk toward his bar when a voice boomed from the door of a log cabin behind the place. "Come on back here. The coffee's just perked."

That cabin he lived in was a cozy two-room affair nearly hidden in a clump of aspen trees. The Jarbidge River gurgled pleasantly along in the background. When I walked inside, the smell of frying meat was heavy in the air.

"Hope you like your coffee black," he said, wiping out a cup with a dirty dishrag. "I'm plumb out of milk and sugar."

"Black will be fine," I answered.

Dave filled my cup with the blackest, thickest coffee I'd ever seen while looking me over like I'd just sprouted horns. I took a chair and he plunked himself down across the table from me with a grunt. "Why, you're not dry behind the ears. How old are you, boy?"

"I'm seventeen."

He frowned and said: "Hell's bells, I figured you for twenty-one at least. How does a button like you come to be out on his own with an automobile?"

I told him everything.

Dave Bourne said nothing for a long while. Then he got up and moved those sizzling venison steaks to the back of the kitchen stove. He came back carrying that blackened old pot of his and poured more coffee.

"Life don't come with no guarantees, boy," he said seriously, pursing his lips. "My wife, God rest her soul, died of the typhoid fever over six years ago. That's when I came out to these parts. I reckon wherever you go, you take your memories with you, but there's peace in the mountains . . . it's a good place to heal."

"I'm sorry about your wife."

"She was a mighty good woman. There's two rules to living, son. The first one is good folks die. The second rule is you can't change the first one."

Being that I'd had enough philosophy for one day, I asked him outright: "Why did you want me to come by this morning?"

He acted a tad put off by my directness. I'd begun to think Dave was one of those folks who, if you asked them what time it was, told you how to build a watch.

The fat man set down his coffee cup, leaned back in the chair with his thumbs stuck under his belt, and said: "I've got to leave Jarbidge, son. A few toughs like Ben Kuhl and Ed Beck are going to get a mob liquored up and hang me."

"What's all this have to do with me?" I asked again.

"That new mining outfit in town . . . Elkoro Mines . . . is looking over my mine with the intention of buying it. The problem is, it will take a month or two for them to do all their assay work. There *is* gold in that mine. The Elkoro company will have to buy up all of the stock in Bourne Mining to get the property. Then everyone will at least get their money back."

"I really don't have money to buy some of your stock," I blurted out.

"Tarnation, boy! I didn't bring you here to sell you stock. Hell, I'll even *give* you a thousand shares, if you'll trade me that Model T of yours for my bar and this cabin."

I was taken aback. I mulled over what to say to him when he chugged the last of his coffee and continued: "Milo, you can't use that car to prospect with. From here on into the mountains, it's afoot or horseback. I need to get out of Jarbidge . . . fast. They won't be able to catch me, if I've got an automobile."

I noticed all of Dave Bourne's problems hadn't made a dent in his appetite. I judged him to weigh in at over 300 pounds. He was right about not being able to make a fast getaway on a horse. I also realized that Model T had taken me as close to the Lost Sheepherder's Mine as it was going to.

Dave fidgeted around, shifting his weight in that chair; his dark eyes flashed from side to side like a cornered animal. I realized for the first time just how scared he really was.

"Son, I really don't have time for you to think on this. I've got the deed notarized.

Once it's recorded, this place will be yours, free and clear. Those thousand shares of Bourne Mining could bring you a dollar a share. Please, I'm giving you all I can. If I had any money, you could have that, too."

I shook my head and he got pale and started breathing heavy like he was having a heart attack. "OK, it's a deal. I'll trade you," I told him. When he started breathing normal again, he fixed the venison steaks and eggs for breakfast.

After we finished eating, he took the deed to his place from a metal box and gave it to me. It looked a lot like the one Tichenor had made up when I sold the farm, so I assumed it was good. Then he brought out a stock certificate and handed it to me. It was a beautiful work of art, all red and gold embroidered with pictures of miners working and mills puffing smoke etched into the heavy bonded paper. The certificate itself looked like it was worth $1000.

"Do me another favor, will you?" Dave asked. "I'd feel more comfortable if it took a while before anyone knows I'm gone. Back that Model T up to the door here. I'll load up what I'm taking with me. Then I think it'd be a good idea if I rolled up in a canvas and laid in the bed of the truck and let you drive me out of town, at least past Cherry

Flats. It's not a long walk back."

"Cherry Flats?" I questioned.

Dave let out a knowing laugh, "Why you *are* just a sprout. I'm talking about the whorehouses. The Red Fox and Dumb Dora's still working the line down there. If there's a dollar to be spent in a mining town, it's plunked down in a bar or a whorehouse. By the way, a poke costs a dollar and Red's about your age."

All Dave Bourne took with him when he left that day was a couple of suitcases along with a box holding his stock certificates and other papers he thought important. He curled up in the bed of the truck, and I covered him over with my tent. No one paid us any mind when I drove out of town.

When we were past Cherry Flats, I pulled over into a grove of trees and stopped. Dave thanked me profusely while grunting his way into the driver's seat. With a grinding of gears, he shouted out: "Good bye, Milo, I owe you one."

That Model T started off with a jerk just like it used to do when Pa drove it. I watched until Dave Bourne was out of sight. At the time, I thought his luck might have been better with a lynch mob than him driving that truck over the most dangerous road in Nevada. No matter, he was

56

gone and I had a bar.

Walking back to Jarbidge, I was forced to pass close by those few little shacks on the edge of town called Cherry Flats. A young freckle-faced girl with flaming red, waist-length hair was hanging bed sheets on a rope strung between two of the cabins. She was wearing the tightest and shortest print dress I'd ever seen wrapped around a woman. I was admiring the way she filled that dress out when she looked up and called out to me: "Hello, handsome! A good-looking fellow like you should drop by and see me sometime."

Preachers had been telling me for years a man went straight to hell if he messed around with a woman before marrying her. At the time, I was sorely tempted to see if this young lady was worth perdition, but I had other business to attend to. "Uh, yeah, I just might do that," I stammered.

"You come by anytime. Red's the name," she purred in one of those come-on voices a female can get when they want something.

The door on the cabin next to Red's flew open with a crash. A man came flying through the portal to roll across the dirt and come to rest near where I was standing. A woman who looked a lot like a young version of Kitty Wilkins filled the doorway. She was as naked as a plucked chicken, a fact that didn't seem to bother her in the least. She glared at the man, who was getting up brushing the dirt from his clothes, and yelled: "Don't you ever come around here again, unless you've some money on you!"

With that, she slammed the door closed. Then I got a good look at the fellow who just got thrown out. It was Fred Searcy, the stage driver. When he recognized me, his smile fled. "Well, friend, I see you made it into town safely," he said.

"Sure did, *friend,*" I answered. "The Jarbidge Hotel has mighty nice three-dollar rooms. I felt real safe from killer bears there."

"I *told* you, you wouldn't get eaten by a bear if you stayed there," Fred said with his grin back.

I got a good look at him this time. Before, he was wrapped up in a coat sitting on the driver's seat of a stagecoach. He had brown hair and a walrus mustache. I figured him to be maybe a few years older than me. What I noticed most of all was the fact that he took after his brother, Inman, when it came to being big. I dismissed my first plan, which was to kick his ass all the way back to town.

"I reckon you were right about that," I told him, offering up my hand. "In case you forgot, my name's Milo Goodman. I just bought the Miners' Exchange from Dave Bourne."

He shook my hand and with a worried look said: "That's going to upset a bunch of folks, if Dave's gone. They are sure looking forward to hanging him. I hope they don't decide that hanging whoever owns the bar at the time will suffice. Knotting that rope took Kuhl a bunch of work."

I felt a cold chill, then Fred broke into that mischievous grin of his, slapped me on the back, and said: "You *are* a good one to bite on a story. Let's go to your place and I'll buy a beer. It's no more than fair, me being your first customer. After all, you did rent a room at our hotel."

As we walked back to town together, I asked him: "What was that gal so upset about?"

"That's why we call her Dumb Dora." He laughed. "She'll do it with anyone, then ask for the money after it's over."

"That redhead's a looker," I added.

"Yeah, that's a fact, only Red has to be paid up front. Dora's mattress gets more action than Red's."

"There's not a lot of available girls in Jarbidge?" I asked.

Fred looked at me like I was an idiot.

"That depends on what you mean by available. When Bourne Mining was running, there were lots of them on Cherry Flats. Red and Dora's all that's left. If it's marrying-type girls you're referring to, I don't know of a single one."

By the time we got to the Miners' Exchange, I found myself beginning to like Fred Searcy. Now that I knew there weren't killer bears roaming the mountains, I had one less thing to worry about when I went to find that lost gold mine.

We dropped by the cabin first. There, I put a couple of logs in the kitchen stove so I could cook a hot meal later. Using the key Dave had given me earlier, I unlocked the back door to the bar. Fred went straight to where the mugs were, grabbed one, filled it up, then plunked himself onto a stool and watched me while I wandered around the joint, trying to figure out what I had done to myself.

"Dave Bourne sure put you on your feet, I can say that much for him," Fred said with that mischievous grin of his.

"How's that?"

"When you came to Jarbidge, you had a Ford truck, now you're on your feet."

I found a tablet and a pencil beside the big, brass, crank-operated cash register.

Then I began making an inventory of what Bourne had left. I was surprised as all get out when I discovered several full kegs of beer. Later, as I went through the cabin, I grew even more amazed.

Dave's cabin was crammed full of his belongings. A closet in the bedroom held a dozen expensive suits of clothes. This did me no good, for there was no way they could ever be taken in enough to fit my lanky frame. While I was thumbing through his suits, my foot struck another metal box like the one he had taken with him earlier. It wasn't locked, so I looked inside. The contents were letters he'd written to and received from his wife. I examined them just long enough to find out her name had been Hattie. Carefully I replaced the letters and slid the box into a corner of the closet, vowing to keep its contents for Dave Bourne, should he ever return.

Clocks seemed to have been one of Dave's weaknesses. He left behind two of those big oak wall Regulator clocks with a brass pendulum swinging behind glass doors. One was in the bar, the other on the wall of his cabin by the fireplace. I immediately fell in love with them. There was something about their rhythmic ticking that I found soothing.

It was getting late in the afternoon when I quit checking out what was now my cabin. I'd found an envelope along with a two-cent stamp in a kitchen drawer. I wrote my name on the deed that Dave had given me, then folded it and sealed it up.

Fred Searcy was still in the bar, sucking up beer. I started to say something to him about paying for what he drank, then I saw five silver dimes lined up on the counter in front of him. He swiveled around, when I came in, and asked: "Just how old are you anyway, Milo?"

"Seventeen," I answered.

"No, I don't think so . . . not owning a bar. Crumley and Walker, who own the Stray Dog Saloon up the street, will file a complaint the moment they hear of it. I'd say you're a solid twenty-two years old . . . if you get my drift."

It was my bar. What business the government had telling me what I could or couldn't do on my own property, I couldn't fathom. Fred made a lot of sense, however — bending the truth a little is often a good idea. "Now that I think back on it, you know, you're right. I *am* twenty-two."

Fred smiled. "Now you're getting the picture. I expect a good deal of shit's going to hit the fan shortly."

I poured myself a mug while thinking back on how many less problems I'd have had if I'd kept that old Model T with a tin roof. One of the problems I've always had is being too quick to help someone out.

I'd gotten my mug filled when I heard a banging on the front door. Looking through the big windows facing Main Street, I could see over a dozen armed men. Every one of them was looking straight at me with cold, mean eyes.

Chapter Six

"The guy with short, greasy hair sporting ears the size of chamber pots and banging away at your door is Ben Kuhl," Fred said in a concerned tone. "He's one of those natural-born assholes you run across now and again. It gives a body a warm, comfortable feeling toward politicians to think the city council pinned a badge on that turd."

"And when Bourne's mine failed, that put him out of a job," I said.

"Yep, him and a lot of others," Fred replied.

"Now they're mad at me for helping out Dave Bourne."

"I'd venture they're a tad bit riled."

I took a careful look outside and counted nearly twenty armed men glaring back at me. I was just a kid and my experience handling a mob of men who wanted to hang me was definitely limited. All I had really laid plans on was to find that lost gold mine, get filthy rich, and get the hell out of Jarbidge. To this day, I'm not proud of the fact that basically what I did was just stand there trying to decide if I was going to shit or go blind, until the front door crashed in.

"So, you're Bourne's good buddy," Ben Kuhl hissed, while coming for me. I had been so intently watching that mob I hadn't noticed Fred was now standing beside me. Kuhl's icy blue eyes fixed on him as he stopped just a few feet away. "Searcy," Kuhl growled fiercely, "this is none of your affair!"

Fred took a couple of steps toward Kuhl and looked down at him. Searcy was a good foot taller and fifty pounds heavier. "You boys ain't going to hang anyone. If you've got a problem with Dave Bourne, let the law handle it. The sheriff from Elko will be here soon. I reckon he'll deal plenty harsh with those who take the law into their own hands."

Ben Kuhl's eyes narrowed to mere slits. A big blond curly-haired man who I would later know as Ed Beck came up close beside him and cocked the hammer on his pistol, but kept it pointed to the floor.

"You're making mighty big talk for being just one man," Kuhl growled.

I started to get angry. I stepped up beside

Fred, looked over the crowd, and yelled out: "I bought this bar from Dave Bourne fair and square! And from the looks of things, I'd say you folks owe me a new door."

Kuhl started to say something, but a booming voice from the doorway beat him to it. "If you've got a deed to the place, show it to us."

"OK, I will," I said, taking the envelope from my shirt pocket and ripping it open. This guy walked past Kuhl and Beck, grabbed the paper from my hands, and looked it over.

"I'm Farley Walker," he finally said. "I'm co-owner of the Stray Dog Saloon. You're claiming you ain't working for Bourne?"

"Never laid eyes on him until last night. We made the deal for me to buy this place only this morning," I said loudly. "Now if you'll give me my deed back, I'd like to conclude this little meeting."

Farley looked the deed over one more time, and handed it back. I noticed out of the corner of my eye Fred Searcy was grinning like a cat.

"OK, boys," Farley Walker said. "We'll give this guy the benefit of the doubt . . . our gripe is with Dave Bourne."

"I say he's a lying sack of shit," Ben Kuhl said, reaching for his pistol.

Fred Searcy pulled a short length of pipe from the back of his belt and cracked Kuhl up against the side of his head. With a quick backstroke, he also smashed Ed Beck in the mouth with it. Both men fell to the floor. Kuhl was out colder then a wedge. Beck was spurting blood from where his front teeth had been.

"Farley, you really ought to teach these boys some manners," Fred said with a shrug.

"Let's drag them out of here, men!" Farley yelled to the crowd, then looked at me and said: "I'm sorry about this." He reached down to Kuhl's prostrate form, opened one of his pockets, took out a five dollar gold piece, and handed it to me. "This'll pay for fixing your door."

With a lot of grumbling and complaining, the mob dispersed. Beck was able to walk out on his own, dripping a trail of blood. Ben Kuhl had to be carried off by four men. When the place had cleared out, I turned to Fred Searcy and said: "I owe you one . . . where did you come up with that pipe?"

"Oh, Dave kept it behind the bar for times like these. He filled it with lead so it gets folks' attention."

"I can see that," I replied. "But it was still a mighty brave thing you did. There was just the two of us."

"Not really." Fred looked to the side door and shouted: "Come on in, guys, Milo's buying!"

Jackson Lyman and Inman Searcy, both carrying shotguns and wearing pistols, entered the bar. Once they looked the place over, both of them plunked down on stools.

"We figured you might could use help convincing some of those soreheads to leave you be," Fred said to me. "While you was going through Dave's cabin, I went and told them we might need some help."

I really didn't know what to say. The last thing I expected was to have some folks I hardly knew come to my aid like these guys had done. I filled up mugs with beer and told them: "Thanks a lot for helping me out. Why did you do it? Now you're going to have Kuhl and Beck laying for you."

Inman grinned. "Like I told you earlier, Jarbidge can't afford to lose any whores or bartenders."

Later that evening, my new friends pitched in and helped me patch up the front door good enough to last until I could get a new one shipped in. So far, I had only spent one night in Jarbidge. In the short space of time, I'd bought a cabin and a saloon, made some good friends and definitely a couple of enemies. The fact that I'd also stood a fair chance of being hung also made an impression on me.

It was dark as pitch when I left the bar to go spend my first night in Dave Bourne's cabin. There were a few gaslights along Main Street in those days. They cast a multitude of shadows among the trees. In my mind's eye, I could see Ben Kuhl crouching in wait for me. The noose he'd worked so hard knotting was still dangling from that beam. I thought about how I'd look hanging from it the next morning, the sign changed to read: **Reserved for Friends of Dave Bourne.**

I bolted the door behind me and leaned a Winchester by my bed for the night. One thing I'd learned for sure — chasing after lost gold mines isn't for sissies.

The next morning, after I had my coffee and fried up some venison Dave Bourne had left behind, I put my deed back into its envelope and taped it shut.

It was warm that morning, so I headed off to the post office in my shirt sleeves. I was beginning to learn about the high country. Sometimes the temperature can change forty degrees in an hour. Up here you can wake up to a clear blue sky without a cloud in sight and get hailed and snowed on by lunchtime.

From my conversations with the Searcys, I knew the post office their mother ran was in a little cubbyhole of a building alongside the Stray Dog Saloon. Briefly they had voiced concern about her drinking too much since their dad had died.

There were quite a few people milling about. From my Miners' Exchange to the post office was about a four block walk. Jarbidge is just one long street in the floor of a steep cañon. I met a couple of familiar faces from last night's fiasco. I was mildly surprised when they said — " 'Morning, Milo." — and went about their business.

Sylvia Searcy greeted me pleasantly. When I'd checked into the hotel, she'd been so drunk I don't think she remembered who I was. This morning she seemed sober, but, when I got close, I could smell alcohol on her breath. Sylvia assured me the deed would go out with Fred on the noon stage. I visited with her for a few minutes, telling her how much I appreciated her sons' help.

"They're good boys," she said. "You'll find a lot of good folks here. My husband, God rest his soul, believed Jarbidge would be the richest gold producer in the state. That's why we settled here."

"I hope he was right," I said.

"His name was Cody," she continued. "He was named after Buffalo Bill Cody. When we were building the hotel, he smashed his thumb with a hammer. He got lockjaw from it and died. I don't know what I would have done without my sons."

I saw she was about ready to cry. I thanked her for taking care of my letter, walked out the door, and saw Ben Kuhl leaning against the front wall of the Stray Dog Saloon, picking his yellow teeth. He shot me the same icy stare he gave Fred Searcy last night.

"You're a mighty big man when you've got folks backing you up," he growled at me. "How tough are you when you're alone?"

There had been no doubt in my mind this time would come. I simply hadn't expected it to be so soon. One side of Kuhl's face was black and blue where Fred had laid that leaded pipe so efficiently last night. I dropped my hands to my sides and walked over to him.

"Why don't you let it go, Kuhl," I said. "The only quarrel you've got with me is the fact I bought Dave Bourne's bar."

"Don't give me that," he said, straightening up. "I know you're in bed with that fat bastard. If you stick around Jarbidge, you'll find yourself dead."

Right about then, I'd had my fill of being afraid of loudmouths. I took another step toward Kuhl, looked him straight in his bloodshot eyes, and said: "As far as I can tell, the only thing you're good at is shooting off your big mouth."

He drew back and took a swing at me. I ducked it and gave him a good sock. Kuhl plopped down hard, like a dropped sack of flour, and just laid there. I decided I'd been lucky enough to hit him in the same spot where Searcy's lead pipe had. Anyway, he was out cold and drawing a crowd again.

Farley Walker came out of his saloon, looked down at Kuhl for a moment, shook his head sadly, and said: "That boy's a slow learner."

"When he comes around, tell him I'll hold no grudge so long as he stays away from me," I said.

"He'll get the point sooner or later," Farley said, "probably later."

I nodded agreeably and gave everyone a big grin. Then I went back to my cabin and soaked my hand in warm Epsom salts. At the time, I thought I'd cracked a knuckle on Kuhl's hard head.

After lunch, I went over to my bar and swept the place out. When I opened the patched up door, a couple of miners I'd never seen before came in and ordered beer. I filled the mugs with a sore hand and thus began my first day as a businessman in Jarbidge, Nevada.

Chapter Seven

Owning and operating a saloon was considerable more work than I'd bargained for. I didn't open the place until lunch was over, and tried to close around midnight, but generally it went well past that time.

The most daunting task in this remote place was keeping a stock of supplies on hand. 'Most every single item for human consumption had to be freighted in from Idaho over that dangerous road from Rogerson.

The steepest and most perilous part of this passage was the section just north of Jarbidge called Crippen Grade. There were multitudes of stories about freight wagons, stagecoaches, and automobiles that had crashed into the depths of that cañon.

When the brakes failed on either a wagon or an automobile, the prudent driver bailed out toward the high ground and let gravity take its course without them being present for the event. Since most freight wagons were large, ungainly affairs, pulled by six or eight horses, and usually heavily loaded at the time, the resulting catastrophe was of epic proportions. These occasional losses of freight added to the cost of everything in Jarbidge. The rate for shipping from the town of Rogerson, the nearest source of any goods, was five cents per pound.

I quickly found my biggest selling item was draft beer. Also, this was the heaviest to freight in. Whiskey and wine were in some demand, but nothing like beer. The freight on a single oak keg from Rogerson was fifteen dollars. The things weighed 300 pounds apiece.

One morning, Jackson Lyman came by after breakfast and asked me if I'd like to take a ride to the Pavlak mine with him. The mine was owned by Wheelbarrow Willie's mother, Eppie Pavlak. Jackson had taken a lease on it and had the Bruckner brothers working there. As he promised to have me back in Jarbidge in time to open my saloon, I agreed to go.

Pavlak was actually a small town two miles up the cañon. The only mine there was the Pavlak, but the excitement created by its discovery had led to a few homes being built and a tiny post office established in a rude log cabin by the Jarbidge River.

On our slow ride there in Jackson's creaking freight wagon, he filled me in on a bit of history.

"Mike Pavlak was one of the first to come on the heels of Dave Bourne's finding gold. He found a rich strike and shipped out several thousand dollars' worth of high-grade ore before the pocket petered out on him. I'm presently driving the tunnel deeper in the hopes of hitting another one of those pockets.

"When Mike Pavlak found gold, he built a small home and brought out his wife and son from Kansas City. Willie's their only child. When he was just a baby, he was taken by a fever that left him retarded."

Jackson cut off a big hunk of chewing tobacco and offered me some, which I gladly refused. Twin lines of amber juice ran down his white beard to drip on his pant legs. Most folks spit tobacco; he never did. What didn't overflow out of his mouth, he swallowed. "It keeps a body from coming down with a sickness," was the explanation when I inquired about his habit.

"Pavlak just got his family moved out here when he up and died," Jackson continued, after stuffing the huge chew into his maw. "Pneumonia took him. That kills lots of folks in the high country who don't take care of themselves. Iffen he'd swallered some t'backy juice, he'd still be around."

He commenced to frown at me like I'd committed some mortal sin for refusing to stuff my mouth full of Brown Mule. To get his mind off the subject of the dubious merits of chewing tobacco, I asked: "How long has Willie and his mom lived here?"

Jackson looked puzzled for a moment. "Reckon five years. That's a tolerable long time to be nearly starvin'."

"I thought the Pavlaks owned the mine. Didn't you say he'd taken a lot of money out of it before he cashed in?"

Jackson sighed. "Ole Mike sunk nearly every dime he'd made off that first rich pocket lookin' for another. Then his wife came down sick with consumption. What money he didn't throw back in the mine went to doctor bills. They're poor as Job's turkey."

"How is she doing?"

"Dyin'," Jackson said flatly as we pulled to a stop in front of a pallid frame house at the Pavlak mine.

"How old is Willie?" I asked.

"I don't rightly know, but he must be near thirty. I'd like to hire him . . . he's strong as an ox . . . but all he can do is push that wheelbarrow. That wouldn't be so bad, but once he gets goin' he doesn't know when to turn around and come back. He can only manage to go from here to the general store in Twin Falls and not get in trouble. As long as he stays on the road, he'll be all right. I shudder to think what would happen iffen he ever got off it. I reckon he'd keep right on pushin' that wheelbarrow until he came to an ocean."

Then the door to the house swung open, and out stepped Eppie Pavlak, with Willie close behind her. I was taken aback by her gaunt appearance. The old woman couldn't have weighed ninety pounds. She had pale skin, sunken cheeks, and long, straggly, gray hair. A patched and faded print flour-sack dress hung loosely on her skinny body like a shroud.

"Howdy Mister Milo," Willie said happily, brushing past his mother. "Thanks for fixin' my barrow, it's all better now."

Eppie shuffled her feet, then slowly approached Jackson. She kept her eyes to the ground and started to say something when a wracking dry cough shook her whole body like a leaf in the wind. When she recovered enough to speak, she asked in a raspy voice: "I hate to impose on you, Mister Lyman, but do you think we could have a loan of a few dollars?"

Jackson swallowed enough tobacco juice in one gulp to keep him healthy for years. His face took on a countenance of pain — paying out money always made him look like that. He fidgeted through the pockets of his overalls, finally coming up with four quarters. He handed them to her and said: "We'll be in high grade any day now, ma'am, then things will be fine for you folks."

Eppie cast an eye toward Willie. "Thanks, Mister Lyman, but I don't think things will ever be fine for us."

Just then I got a glimmer of an idea. "Willie, could I hire you and that wheelbarrow of yours to haul kegs of beer back from Twin Falls?"

"He'll have to pick them up at Evan's General Store, that's the only place he knows," Eppie said quickly.

"That won't be a problem," I said. "I'll send instructions out on today's stage. By the day after tomorrow, Willie can make his first trip."

"And may I ask what you intend to pay him, Mister . . . ?" Eppie inquired in a surprisingly strong voice.

I told her who I was and that I owned the Miners' Exchange Saloon.

"You any relation to that bastard, Dave Bourne?" she spat out. "He's the one who got my husband, God rest his soul, to come to this god-forsaken place."

"No, ma'am. If Willie wants the job, I'll pay him eight dollars for every keg he brings me."

Eppie squinted her eyes. "That's a long trip for the boy, ten dollars sounds a lot more fair," she said firmly.

I looked at Willie and said: "Ten dollars it is, then."

He stuck his hands into his pockets and gave me an open-mouthed grin just as we were interrupted by the Bruckner brothers coming out of the mine tunnel.

I nearly had a stroke when Jackson uncovered two wood boxes of dynamite that were in the back of the wagon bed. He had heard the story about what happened to my family and quickly said: "Don't worry, Milo, this is fresh powder . . . it won't blow up until we're ready for it to."

The Bruckners gave me a friendly nod. They were old-country Germans who seldom spoke. Which was good because, when they did, their English was so bad hardly anyone could understand them. Each picked up a case of dynamite as naturally as a lawyer grabs his briefcase and headed back into the depths of the tunnel. I breathed a sigh of relief once those boxes of powder were gone, and climbed back on the wagon seat alongside Jackson.

Eppie Pavlak came close, looked me in the eye, and said: "I'm not an ungrateful person, Mister Goodman. But I expect you to keep an eye on Willie. He's all I've got left in this world. I'll hold you personally responsible if something happens to my boy."

"We'll make sure he stays on the road, ma'am, that's all anyone can do," Lyman told her gruffly as he flicked the reins and started the wagon moving.

When we were out of earshot, Jackson told me: "I paid her a hundred dollars lease money last month, so don't go thinking I'm trying to starve out a poor widow woman."

"She does seem to have her convictions."

"Yep, that she does," Jackson agreed, biting off a fresh chew. "The reason that mine sat unworked for a long spell was folks were afraid to do business with her. I've heard it said the only reason her husband croaked was because he took dying as being preferable to living with that woman."

"I hope I didn't do wrong when I hired Willie."

"Shucks, boy," Jackson retorted. "That woman will send him to Twin Falls to save a nickel on a sack of beans. She's tight as paint on a whore's face. The eight dollars you offered would've been aplenty."

"I guess Willie can use the money."

"You ain't paying Willie, you're paying Eppie Pavlak. He wouldn't know what to do with a dollar if you handed it to him."

"I reckon I've got some learning to do about women."

Jackson let out with a laugh that sprayed tobacco juice on the horses' behinds. "If you ever figger out females, let the *rest* of us men in on it, will you?"

When we got back to Jarbidge, I went to the bank and made the necessary financial arrangements to have some kegs of beer left at the Evan's store for my account. One of the things I learned early on about the liquor business — everything was strictly "cash up front." The only person in Jarbidge who did business on a trust me basis was Dumb Dora, and what she sold didn't cost anything to restock.

I took the necessary correspondence and bank draft to the post office. It was near to noon when I got there, just in time for the stage to take my letter to Twin Falls. Sylvia was getting well along in her cups by then and had difficulty stamping the envelopes, finally putting them on upside down.

Sylvia Searcy always had a cup of coffee in her presence from morning until night. The amount of whiskey she surreptitiously added to it during the day steadily increased until by closing time she was barely able to navigate her way home. Anyone having business at the post office always made it a point to do it in the mornings.

Willie and his wheelbarrow worked out well. He had more stamina and strength than a draft horse. When I hired him for the job, I had no idea his mom wouldn't let him stop to rest until he got home.

When Willie came to my saloon with one of those heavy oak kegs, he'd pick it up like it weighed nothing and put the thing wherever I asked him to. Every time I paid him, he'd give me a big grin and say: "I did good. Ma will be proud of me."

One morning, Willie stopped by before heading off for Twin Falls to have me grease his wheel. He was always proud of the fact that I'd "fixed" his wheelbarrow for him when we first met. I noticed he had one eye swollen nearly closed. Red lines criss-crossed that whole side of his face.

"What in the world happened to you, Willie?" I asked him. "From the looks of things, you must have tangled with a bear, and the bear didn't lose by much."

He gave me his usual open-mouthed grin and said: "I done a bad thing an' split a bag of beans. Ma got mighty mad and whipped me so's I would pay attention an' not do it ag'in."

I smeared some antiseptic on his cuts that caused him to grimace but he didn't complain. I suppose he figured that, if I could fix his wheelbarrow, I was also capable of mending him. After I sent Willie on his way, I spent the better part of the day contemplating on how a mother could get so mean as to do such a thing to her retarded son.

Billy McGraw and Reece Morgan came in the bar one evening to have a beer. They acted like old friends when I inquired about Kitty. They told me she couldn't be with them. She was required to stay at the ranch because of the lawsuit. Her lawyer said that, if the place was left unattended, her ranch could be claimed as abandoned by C. C. Logan.

"How do you like being a bar owner?" Reece asked me.

"Did you hear a bunch of toughs led by that bastard Ben Kuhl actually tried to hang me just for buying the place?" I asked.

Billy shot me a look that would clabber

milk, chugged his beer, and stormed out.

"What did I say to upset him?" I asked.

"Oh, he's on his way up to the Stray Dog to drink with Ben Kuhl. Billy and he are cousins, you know."

"You mean those two are blood kin? If I had known they were related, I'd have kept my trap shut."

"Pretty hard to go wrong when you're talking the truth. Billy knows Kuhl's bad news waiting to be broadcast. I won't let him stop by Kitty's any more. He's always too mean drunk for fit company. Where he gets the money to drink on is what I'd like to know. He ain't done a lick of work since the town quit paying him."

"Well, as long as he leaves me alone, we won't have any more trouble."

Reece smiled and said: "I heard about you and Fred Searcy taking turns coldcocking him. I don't think you can train Kuhl none by hitting him on the head."

Just then a half dozen miners working for the Bluster Company came in followed by Jackson Lyman and the Bruckner brothers. I got so busy working that I didn't see Billy McGraw until he was seated on a stool alongside Reece. He asked me for a beer in a pleasant way. When I brought it to him, he motioned me closer.

"Milo," he said seriously, "Ben Kuhl's my cousin, but when he gets drunk, he gets mean. What I'm telling you is, watch your backside and tell Fred Searcy to do the same."

"Oh, we'll be all right," I answered. "I suspect it's mostly whiskey talk."

"That may be, but the reason we came out here in the first place was because Ben got in a fight. A guy beat him up bad."

"Getting beat up caused him to leave town?"

Billy looked me straight in the eye. "No, we had to leave because a couple of days later, Ben took a shotgun and blew the guy that did it into the next world."

Reece Morgan gave out a sigh and put his hand on Billy's shoulder. "Let's go back to camp, boy. We've got a lot of work to do."

Both of them hesitated when they got to the door. Billy turned around, bit on his lower lip, then said: "Take care of yourself, Milo."

"You two do the same," I told them as they left into the night. I poured myself a beer with a shaking hand, hoping to untie the knot of fear that had formed in my guts.

Chapter Eight

Just keeping the Miners' Exchange running gave me plenty to concern myself with. Having someone wanting to hang me or shoot me was an added worry I didn't need. After giving the matter considerable thought, I realized I'd lost sight of what I came to Jarbidge for in the first place — to find the Lost Sheepherder's Mine.

The first thing I needed to do before I could leave on my quest was to hire a trustworthy bartender. I was racking my brain trying to decide who I could leave in charge that wouldn't steal me blind, when Inman Searcy walked in. I didn't give him time to think it over. I just told him he was hired.

He was concerned about having to wash the beer mugs and how the soapy water might soften his hands, making him unsuitable for real work later on. Once I told him he could just wipe them out with a towel like I did, he took the job.

When Inman agreed to tend bar for me, I tied an apron around his waist and lit out before he could change his mind.

With my first problem solved, I moved on to the second. I now needed to buy a pair of good mules, one to ride and the other to pack my camp gear.

Matt Whort ran a blacksmith shop and livery stable only a couple of blocks from the Miners' Exchange. I'd met Matt for the first time when he'd come along with Ben Kuhl to welcome me to Jarbidge. There was nothing to be gained by holding a grudge. Besides, there was no other place to buy mules this side of Twin Falls.

Matt was without a doubt the fattest man in town. Every movement he made seemed to work up a sweat. When I came in the livery to see him, he was poring over a ledger book at his desk. He added a few extra beads of sweat to his forehead when he saw me standing behind him. I probably saved him from a heart attack when I quickly told him I was there to buy a couple of good mules.

After he settled down, Matt began to treat me like a long-lost relation. I knew nothing about mules, but tried not to let that fact show. Matt selected a pair of white ones for me. He said white mules were the best behaved and are called "gamblers' ghosts" by freighters. I looked them over as carefully as I knew how. Both mules had four legs and were standing up unaided, so I bought them.

Matt happily agreed to board the mules for what seemed to be the reasonable price of ten dollars per month, plus feed. I left a happy and relieved Matt Whort to return to sweating over his books, and went to the general store.

Frank Adams and his wife Minnie ran this business from one of the few two-story buildings in Jarbidge. They had a sign over the front door proudly stating: **If we don't have it, you don't need it.** While this may have been somewhat true, *finding* what you needed from the jumble and hodge-podge that greeted you inside the store was a miracle of Biblical proportions. Merchandise of every description sloped from floor to ceiling, leaving only narrow walkways through the chaos. Then one had to watch his head, for everything from cast-iron skillets to bear traps dangled from beams like Christmas tree ornaments.

When a customer would inquire as to whether or not they had a particular item in stock, Frank's expression would go blank. After giving the matter deep thought, he would begin pawing through various piles of merchandise, tossing items hither and yon. When he came up empty, as he often did, Frank would happily tell them he'd be glad to order it out of Twin Falls.

The Adamses had one of the few telephones in town and were inordinately proud of it. Their day was made when they could call up a supply house in Idaho and order something.

As I assumed it could take me as long as a week to find the Lost Sheepherder's Mine, I felt one of the things I had to have was a decent waterproof tent. Every time it rained here in the high country it was like falling icicles.

Frank went through his usual show of pretending to look for one. I waited until intermission, then beat him to the draw by telling him to order me one using that telephone of his.

"It'll be a couple of days, Milo," he told me, after hanging up. I had been in Jarbidge long enough to know that this meant anywhere from two days to two weeks.

Before going back to my bar for the evening, I decided to celebrate having time off work by eating a steak dinner first. I'd grown desperately tired of my own cooking.

Fong's Oyster and Chop House was reputed to be the best restaurant in town. It was situated next to the Jarbidge Hotel and run by a half-tamed Chinaman named Charlie Fong. The skinny restaurant owner had a gray pigtail that reached to his rear-end. He wore a neatly trimmed white beard and could have been anywhere from fifty to five hundred years old.

The "oysters" he proudly advertised were a great source of amusement to the locals. When some newcomer ordered a plate, everyone there waited in great anticipation for the meal to arrive. When the customer eyed what he was expected to eat, the results were usually quite interesting.

The closest any of Fong's oysters ever came to the ocean was when he washed them in salt water. The variety he sold were Rocky Mountain oysters or steer's testicles, breaded and fried. They really weren't bad if you knew what you were ordering and a real surprise to those who didn't.

Charlie spoke fairly good English until he became excited or provoked. Then he would break into a string of unintelligible banter that would do a lawyer proud. This generally only occurred when some tenderfoot complained about his oysters, adding greatly to the entertainment.

I splurged and invested in one of his

famous butter-fried steaks. Anyone who could afford the seventy-five cents they cost received a steak fit for a king.

After a splendid meal, I went back to while away the evening in the Miners' Exchange. When I got there, the normal crowd was in evidence. Jackson Lyman was drinking beer at his usual table with the Bruckner brothers. A few miners who I only knew by their first names, or nicknames like Butt-Block or Frenchie, were at the bar. Inman looked right at home, wearing that white apron, so I sat down with Jackson. He seemed glad to see me; I suppose he was happy to have anyone to talk to. This was something he couldn't do with the Bruckners. The brothers were unwilling to learn English, and Jackson refused to attempt even a word of German. They had devised an intricate sign language that would have confused the hell out of an Indian but seemed to work for them.

Jackson was in a particularly good mood. "Things are looking up at the Pavlak . . . we just cross-cut a fault and have a quartz seam showing," he proudly told me.

I didn't know whether to tell Jackson I was sorry his seam was showing or not. To keep from advertising my ignorance, I changed the subject by saying: "Now that

I've got Inman tending bar, I think I'll take a few days off and go hunting. A little fresh venison would be nice."

"It's a little late in the year to go looking for the Lost Sheepherder's Mine," Jackson said with a sly grin.

The Bruckners perked up, stared knowingly at me, and grunted in unison: "*Ja, das* Sheepherder Mine." They didn't know but three English words and two of them were about my "secret" lost gold mine.

"I might do a *little* looking for it," I said.

Inman brought me a mug of beer. After I took a swallow, I asked Jackson: "Do you reckon there's a soul within a hundred miles of here who *doesn't* know about the Lost Sheepherder's Mine?"

He picked at his beard. "No, I don't suppose you'd find anyone that close. I'd suspect you might find a few in Salt Lake City. Mormons are mostly into raising crops and kids." Jackson continued: "It's big country up there . . . rugged as hell. Everyone's got their own idea as to where that gold's located. Most have it placed near the headwaters of the Jarbidge River."

I breathed a sigh of relief. Jackson cocked his head and said: "Now *I'd* reckon it to be on this side of God's Pocket Peak. Some guy hunting lions found a pretty piece of rich ore up there last year. He showed it all over town. He got lots of free drinks from that piece of gold, yep, yep."

I chugged half of my beer and, nonchalantly as I could manage, asked: "This lion hunter . . . do you remember his name by any chance?"

Jackson squinted toward the ceiling, lost in thought. "No, I can't rightly say that I do, but his dog was called Nugget. A strange name for a lion dog, for sure."

"Ole Nugget won't be making any more appearances in Jarbidge," I said. "But if you ever see that guy who found that gold again, let me know so I can finish biting off his ear."

While Jackson was pondering on why I would want to chew on some lion hunter's ear, two men came into the saloon. One was a clean-shaven stranger dressed so nattily and unlike the usual Jarbidge retinue, he stuck out like a diamond in a goat's rectum. The other man sporting a pencil-thin mustache and wearing khakis I knew to be Tully Moxness, an employee of Elkoro Mines. I had heard plenty of stories about Tully and his abnormal appetite, but had never seen him perform. I left the table and went to the end of the counter to watch the show.

The pair ordered glasses of beer. Inman

quickly set up the beer and gave me a wink when he passed. I listened intently as small talk passed between the duo for a while. The well-dressed man was called Ray Cameron. He said he was from Denver and working for a Colorado mining man. The Elkoro Mine's manager, David C. Knight, had given Tully the job of getting Cameron settled in at the hotel and showing him about town.

After a few rounds, Tully felt his victim was sufficiently lubricated. "You know," he said, spinning his glass and staring intently at it, "if I was to get ten dollars for the job, I'd eat this beer glass."

Ray Cameron looked aghast. "Why, man, you would cut your insides to shreds."

"So, you're betting I can't do it," Tully said blandly.

"No one could do that and live," Ray retorted.

"Oh, I can eat it all right, but it's going to cost you a sawbuck to see it done," Tully said with a grin. "And don't worry about me getting hurt. Why, if you paid me enough, I'd eat this whole bar . . . everything that ain't rubber anyway . . . I can't abide the taste of the stuff."

"I reckon I'd take a dollar of that," the big miner called Butt-Block blurted out. "And

I'm not worrying about Tully. If he croaks, he croaks."

"Beer glasses cost a quarter," I told them.

Tully chuckled as he slid a quarter down the bar toward me. "I'm glad they didn't hang you . . . a bartender who ain't greedy's a precious commodity."

Ray Cameron paled when he looked at me. "People were going to *hang* you?"

"Yep," I answered calmly. "There's not a lot to do for entertainment in a small town. I'll take ten that Tully can eat that glass. Are you on?"

"Let me see, that comes to twenty-one dollars I have to pay if Tully here consumes the entire glass," Ray Cameron said. "And should you fail in this attempt, or leave any portion of the glass uneaten, then I shall receive the money?"

"You talk prettier than a five-dollar whore," Tully said.

"If you're feeling sporty, you can add me in for four dollars, that'll make it twenty-five! Even money's easier to keep track of," Lyman bellowed. Arithmetic wasn't one of Jackson's stronger points.

"You, sir, are on," Ray answered loudly.

I collected up the money. When Cameron had assured himself I had the entire amount, he turned to Tully. "Now, my dear sir, if you would be so kind as to consume that glass, I shall be obliged to spend some of my winnings on flowers for your grave."

Tully Moxness spun toward Cameron and gave him an evil smile. "First we drink the good part," he said as he chugged his beer, then he stuck his face to within a foot of Cameron's. He put the rim of the glass into his mouth and proceeded to bite off a piece that he immediately gulped down. He continued to break fragments of the shattered glass off with his teeth and swallowed them until he got to the heavy base. Carefully Tully rapped it on the edge of the wooden bar until it broke in pieces. He plopped the fragments into his mouth one at a time and devoured them with obvious relish.

I noticed Ray Cameron was about two shades paler than a corpse. "I have never seen a man intentionally kill himself before," he finally managed to say.

Tully grinned at him and said: "Well, I'm not dead yet. Let's have a round for everyone while I'm around to enjoy it."

No one was surprised when Cameron started making excuses to leave. Finally he simply turned and beat a rapid retreat.

Cameron wasn't the only one to learn a lesson that night. I was educated to the fact no one should ever offer Tully all of the beer he could drink for free. The man was skinny enough to hide behind a fence post. This belied the fact he was a walking hole that could consume endless quantities of anything.

Finally Inman got tired of filling up Tully's glass, took off his apron, and went home. Everyone else had long since left. Jackson and all of the miners had work to do the next day. This left me alone to keep one beer glass full. Tully was so drunk he kept his head propped up with both hands to keep it from plopping down on the bar.

"You know, there's something fishy going on with that Elkoro outfit," he said as I refilled his mug for the umpteenth time.

"What do you mean 'fishy'," I asked casually.

"Oh, I don't know for sure, just a feeling that things ain't exactly what they seem. They've got more money than God. Buying up everything in sight."

"I heard they bought the Success Mine," I told him.

"It's what you *don't* hear that's interesting. LeVey, the assayer, was telling me that Bourne's mine's lousy with gold. 'Most every sample he ran from there was good."

He had my full attention now. "But his

mill never got any gold."

Tully laughed. "Of course not. Bourne's mill wasn't set up to recover gold from the word go."

"But he hired an engineer."

"Nyal Bennett." Tully spat. "That bastard wouldn't be honest if it paid more."

"I suppose now Elkoro will be buying up all of Bourne's stock," I ventured.

"Nah, they'll steal it. This Ray Cameron fellow we had the fun with tonight is here to buy up all he can. I heard him and Knight talking. Then he'll sell it to Elkoro." Tully continued: "Ya know the guy who runs Elkoro, David Knight? Excuse me, that's David C. Knight. He's real proud of that middle initial . . . I think it stands for Crap. One day when David C. Knight went to lunch, I got me a look at the stock ledger. Guess what? Nyal Bennett owns a bunch of stock in Elkoro Mines."

"This was after he finished working for Bourne?"

Tully laughed and blew foam from his beer onto the counter. "Hell, no, he was a stockholder long before he ever went to work for Bourne. Does that speak to you, pilgrim?"

"So, Dave Bourne was set up?"

"Yep. Bourne was shystered by the best of

'em. Also, David Crap Knight keeps a little passing-around money . . . for greasing wheels, if you get my drift. You know one guy who's been spending a passel of it . . . Ben Kuhl."

One more beer later, Tully Moxness passed out on the counter and began snoring loudly. I dragged him outside and propped him up against the building. I locked up the bar and went back to my cabin to try to grab a few hours sleep. Tomorrow was going to be a busy day.

Chapter Nine

It seemed I had just gotten to sleep when the rising sun began shooting its rays into my eyes. I'd forgotten to pull down the shade last night.

I stuck a few sticks of dried aspen wood into the firebox of the cook stove, dashed on a little kerosene, and had a roaring hot fire in minutes. Coffee is something that is necessary to get my brain to engage. The sooner I have my morning cup, the better.

Then I remembered about Tully. I'd left him propped up against the front of the saloon last night. After swallowing all of that glass, I couldn't be sure he hadn't up and died. I threw on my clothes and ran over to check. Having a dead body lying in front of the place would be bad for business.

I was relieved to find he'd either crawled off under his own power or Slabs had already gotten him. All that undertaker had done lately was complain about how healthy everyone was. I wouldn't have been the least bit surprised if he'd begun to circle the town like a buzzard every morning, looking for work.

The coffee had just begun to perk when I got back to my cabin. I poured a hot cup and lit a cigarette. As I sipped on the scalding hot brew, I tried to decide what to do about the situation. All of this skullduggery was new to me. I had yet to learn the depths to which greed can cause people to sink. I doubted Tully Moxness would even remember what he told me, or, if he did, he'd keep quiet about it to save his job.

David C. Knight, the manager of Elkoro Mines, being capable of murdering someone just to pick up stock cheap came as a shock. I'd set eyes on him before at Fong's restaurant. He and his wife were in a booth not far from my table. Knight was a withered, silver-haired older man, maybe fifty, and had the general appearance of a skeleton with a little meat still attached. His wife, in contrast, was at least three times his size. She wore her hair drawn back into a gray bun, giving her face a pained, pinched look. I would have paid them scant attention except for the fact that when Fong served their dinner, they made an obvious and long-winded prayer over their food.

Knight and his wife Iona were the leaders of getting a church built in Jarbidge. Everyone had been so busy with taking care of the necessities of life, like building saloons and whorehouses, that detail hadn't been accomplished yet. Their efforts hadn't been going well. Before I made my appearance in town, they had imported a Baptist preacher from Twin Falls.

The parson came in on the afternoon stage and, in preparing to battle with the devil, dropped into the Stray Dog Saloon to get to know him better. The rest of the details are sketchy, but the fact is he wound up getting his skull cracked down in Cherry Flats by a girl named Irish Rose later that night. The next morning, the Evangelist was freighted out of town with his head wrapped in bandages, while Irish Rose lit out on horseback in the opposite direction. Neither had been seen since. Most of the miners sadly bemoaned the loss; by all accounts the whore had been a real looker.

When Dave Bourne left town, he'd given me no idea as to where he might be headed. Now that I knew he'd been conspired against, it was only fair that he found out about it before he sold all of his stock for next to nothing.

The big question was how to find him;

then I remembered that metal box he'd left behind in the closet. I dragged it out and put it on the kitchen table. When a dog gets kicked, the first place it heads for is home. I assumed Dave had done the same thing. What I had to do was find out where it was he called home. Finally I struck pay dirt. One of the letters was from his mother, Wilma Bourne.

While this letter was nearly seven years old, I felt the chance was fairly good his mother might still be living at the same place in Boise, Idaho. I brought out a tablet and began to write her a letter, setting out the facts as I knew them, then a cold chill ran down my backbone. If David C. Knight had any inkling that I was onto his scheme, my life wouldn't be worth a plugged nickel. Ben Kuhl would likely shoot me without being paid for the job the way it was. A little urging in the form of greenbacks and my days on this earth would be over. If a man wants to kill you bad enough, he'll get the job done eventually. It's impossible for a person to stay on their guard constantly. Many of the famous gunfighters of the old West, like Wild Bill Hickok, found this fact to be all too true. And I sure wasn't any Wild Bill.

There was no way for me to know who

was working for Knight. Should anyone see a letter from me to someone named Bourne, their suspicions would certainly be aroused. Ed Beck had the job of sweeping out the post office. Billy McGraw could get a look at it when the stage made its lay-over at Kitty's Hot Hole.

The more thought I gave the matter, the more determined I grew to find Dave Bourne. I packed my grip with a few days' worth of traveling clothes, then went to buy a ticket on the afternoon stage for Twin Falls.

Winifred Jameson, the express company agent, didn't bat an eye when I came in.

I made a point of telling him the same story I had told Inman and everyone else; I had to go back to Buhl and take care of settling up my family's estate. When you concoct a lie, the first thing you have to do is be consistent when you tell it.

Fred Searcy seemed to be glad to have company on the trip. I sat beside him on the driver's seat as the stagecoach swayed and rattled its way along that narrow dirt road.

Once we got to the top of Crippen Grade, Fred relaxed and started talking. "I want to thank you for giving Inman the job of bartending."

"He needed the work."

"Oh, it's not that. The part about you leaving town and having my brother pouring beer is what I'm thanking you for."

At the time, I was sorely tempted to tell him what I knew. But if I did, that would place him in danger. I couldn't do this to Fred, so we spent the rest of the trip making small talk.

Kitty ran to me and gave me a rib-busting bear hug when we made our stopover there. "Reece and Billy are out rounding up horses," she said happily. "We'll have a good year . . . the grass is high and those mustangs are so fat they won't even put up a decent struggle."

Fred picked up a small bundle of outgoing mail and tossed it in the stage. All of the ranchers for miles around dropped their mail off at Kitty's. She could have put in to the government for a post office appointment and been paid for the job, but she never did. When I mentioned it to her once, she just smiled and said: "The government pays too many people for doing nothing the way it is. One of these days, if things don't straighten out, it'll cost a whole three cents just to mail a letter."

That was Kitty Wilkins, generous to a fault.

Normally Fred only took time to drink a

fast cup of coffee before helping change the horses and continue on his way. Today, Kitty slowed things down a mite when she announced she had a fresh apple cobbler just out of the oven. It was general knowledge that when fresh fruit was available, she made the best cobbler in Nevada. This turned out to be no exaggeration. The pan she had baked it in was six inches deep and laced with cinnamon, apples, and covered with a sugary crust. Kitty ladled out two heaping plates full and set them, still steaming, on the table in front of us.

While we were waiting for the mountainous portions of cobbler to cool down to eating temperature, I had one of my usually brilliant ideas.

"Kitty," I said, "I'm heading for Buhl to settle out my folks' estate and I may need a lawyer. Do you know of a good one?"

She laughed so hard her whole body jiggled. "Milo, you can't use the words 'good' and 'lawyer' together, it goes against the laws of nature. You want a lawyer with the morals of Judas, and I've got one of those. He's so untrustworthy, he has to hire someone to call his dog for him. Milo, you want Theodore Spurgeon. He's meaner than a grizzly bear with hemorrhoids."

One thing I always admired about Kitty

was her directness. "Could you give me his address? He sounds like what I call a *good* lawyer. I like his name anyway, it's the same as my middle one. My folks were taken by Teddy Roosevelt and the way he charged up that hill in Cuba."

She gave me a grin and started fishing around in the front pockets of her overalls finally coming out with a business card. "I liked ole Teddy myself," she replied. "My favorite President was William Taft. He was so fat, he once got stuck in the bathtub at the White House. I'm beholding to anyone who makes me feel slim."

It was well after midnight when we finally reached Twin Falls. There was no way to tell what time it was; the moon wasn't out and the night was darker than a well digger's behind, so I couldn't see my watch.

I walked the dark few blocks to the train station and had to poke the stationmaster in his ribs to wake him up. He groggily told me the next train to Boise didn't leave until seven in the morning. I irritated him by buying a ticket, anyway. Then I stretched out on a vacant wooden bench. I used my grip as a pillow to keep someone from stealing it and slept like a baby until morning.

Train travel was something I loved. They beat a swaying stagecoach six ways from Sunday.

I had breakfast in the dining car — flapjacks buried under a mountain of the best chili I'd eaten in a long time. Most generally folks look at me a little odd when I order this.

I had never been west of Buhl. My guess was the country going toward Boise would be green and tree-covered. I couldn't have been more wrong. Once we left the valley of the Snake River, we traveled through some of the most worthless real estate I'd ever seen.

Miles and miles of rolling dead-looking sagebrush were only broken by the appearance of an occasional skinny, half-starved antelope that looked like they would have gladly jumped in front of the train to end their miserable existence. I don't think a rabbit could cross that barren country without packing a lunch.

Boise was a pleasant change. There were actually a few trees poking up here and there. Some fairly prosperous-looking farms dotted the area. What few cows I saw grazing gave the appearance of being healthy enough to live through the night.

The train steamed into the station in mid-afternoon. That 130 miles had simply flown by in a few short, comfortable hours. I took a taxi to Wilma Bourne's house that turned out to be in one of the nicer sections of town.

Mrs. Bourne, if indeed she was still living at this house, must have had a comfortable retirement. Her home was a massive three-story Victorian, sitting on at least a half acre of manicured lawn. Rows of colorful petunias and pansies lined the cement walkway. Marble columns topped with stone lions, sitting on their haunches, greeted visitors at the entranceway.

I rattled the wrought-iron gate a few times to make sure some man-eating mutt wasn't waiting for his dinner, then cautiously made my way to the front door and politely rapped on it. After a short spell, I heard footsteps approaching. If I'd been wearing false teeth, I'd have swallowed them when the door swung open.

Chapter Ten

I don't know who was the most surprised, me or Dave Bourne. All of the color left his face like he'd been bleached. I was shocked as a Democrat in heaven when I saw how much weight he'd lost. Dave had dropped at least seventy pounds if he'd shed an ounce.

"Milo, how in the world did you find me?" he asked nervously.

"I went through that box of letters you left in the closet."

"Why?" Dave stammered.

"I'm not here to cause you problems, Dave. There's not a soul in Jarbidge that doesn't think I'm in Buhl settling up some family business."

He looked past me to assure himself there wasn't a mob with a hanging rope following me. "I'm sorry, Milo," he said apologetically. "Come on in and meet my mother, only please don't say anything that might upset her."

"That's why I looked you up. When this is over, I think *your* troubles will be over."

"Davy Boy, who is there?" A sweet, strong voice came from inside the house.

"A . . . friend from Nevada, Mama," Dave said loudly. "He's the one who sold me the Model T. His name is Milo Goodman."

"Well, bring him in, for Pete's sake, the flies will be all over," Wilma scolded.

Dave Bourne's mother gave a striking appearance. She was fitted out as prim and proper as an undertaker's wife in a billowy black lace dress. I wouldn't describe her as large, but she was in no danger of getting blown away by a high wind. What I remember most about her was the beehive of purple hair she had sitting on top of her head.

"You boys, sit at the table, and I'll fetch you something to snack on," she said, causing me instantly to like her.

After a few minutes of banging around in the kitchen, Wilma made her appearance, carrying two huge plates of angel food cake surrounded by heaping mounds of peach ice cream.

"I'm going to the library room and read for a while, you young men have a nice visit," she said, then looked at me sternly. "That was a perfectly awful automobile you sold my Davy."

"Yes, ma'am," I agreed. "I'm here to make amends." With that she turned and stalked out of the room.

Dave Bourne slid his serving in front of me. He pushed away from the table, putting his thumbs under his belt, and stared at me. "Now, what's all this news you brought me?"

When I finished telling him what I'd learned from Tully Moxness, Dave wore the open-mouthed expression of a preacher caught leaving a whorehouse.

"Are you saying Elkoro Mines paid Nyal Bennett to make sure the mill didn't work, then gave Ben Kuhl money to hang me so they could buy up the stock for next to nothing?" he asked.

"I think you've got the gist of it."

"Oh, my God, what a fool I've been. I thought Bennett was simply incompetent. I never thought about him stabbing me in the back."

"You can't tell a friendly dog from a mean one until you stick your hand out."

Dave got that bleached look back again. "Milo, I just had a letter from my lawyer in Twin Falls. Bourne Mining Corporation stock is being bought up for fifteen cents a share. I wrote him a letter with a power of attorney and mailed it just this morning. Damn it, Milo, I told him to sell my stock, all one hundred twenty-five thousand shares of it."

When I added up in my head how much money Dave's shares would bring him, I wondered why he was so concerned. At the time, it was a fortune to me. "Why, it sounds like you're getting a passel of money," I told him.

"Milo, you don't understand. My block of stock is controlling interest in Bourne Mining. Whoever owns it can vote to sell the entire company for whatever figure they can get out of it. Since my mine is the key to Elkoro making a go of it, they might do a stock swap. The last quote I got, Elkoro Mines was bringing eight dollars a share."

If I hadn't already been sitting down, I reckon I might have swooned like a fat woman with the vapors. I just saw my hundred-and-fifty-dollar certificate shoot up to eight thousand. I never had even *seen* figures like Dave's stock would add up to. I gulped and eventually said: "Dave, you've already sold your stock?"

"No, but my lawyer will just as soon as he opens that letter. I'm a little behind on paying him, so I wouldn't reckon on him being slow to act."

"You say he's in Twin Falls?"

"Yeah, he's a good lawyer, if you can use the words 'good' and 'lawyer' together. He's meaner than a pile of day-old cat shit."

That was the second time I'd heard about a lawyer in Twin Falls matching that description. "Your lawyer, would he be Theodore Spurgeon?"

Dave blinked. "Why, yes, how did you hear of him?"

"Kitty Wilkins said she was using him. I got his card from her."

"We've got to beat that letter to Twin Falls," Dave said excitedly.

"Why don't you just call him on the phone?"

"And tell Spurgeon not to sell my stock, so he can collect what I owe him? No, Milo, that stock's as good as sold. He has a power of attorney, and there's not a thing I can do about it." He paused to think. "It's just four in the afternoon, if we leave now, we'll have plenty of time. He can't possibly have that letter before tomorrow morning."

"We could take the train," I answered hopefully.

"Why? We'll take that high-priced Model T I bought from you."

I had been afraid he would come up with something like that. It was getting mighty

115

chilly at night and that busted up truck only had a windshield to keep out the cold. There was no arguing with him, though. After saying a fast farewell to his bewildered mom, we threw some heavy coats and blankets, along with Dave's suitcase and my grip, into the Model T, cranked the motor to life, and headed off to Twin Falls as fast as that Ford would run.

The road to Twin Falls was, of course, nothing but a dirt trail where the sagebrush had been cut away. We hadn't traveled much past the city limits before that Model T started plowing through several inches of high desert powder dust.

Dave Bourne seemed more than happy to let me do the driving. He wrapped up in a blanket and tied a handkerchief over his face to filter out the dust. With all of this gray powder flying around, it was difficult to see anything. I never saw that scrawny antelope until it crashed through the new windshield I'd put on that Model T. The antelope wound up in the bed of the truck after also plowing through the back window. I was driving fast, trying to make time; we were probably going thirty miles an hour when the collision occurred. The big problem occurred when, through the dust and confusion, I figured out that antelope had taken Dave Bourne along with it on its trip through the cab.

I slammed on the brake pedal and skidded to a halt. Just as soon as the air cleared enough for me to see the ruins lying in the back, I figured I needed the services of an undertaker and a butcher. Then Dave started cussing his way from underneath the antelope. That heavy felt blanket he had wrapped around him had kept any major damage from occurring. Except for having the wind knocked out of him, Dave Bourne was in fine shape, which was more than could be said for that stupid antelope; it was as dead as a politician's promise after election day.

"Milo," he coughed, after rolling to a sitting position, "the Sandwich Islands are where I'm going, if I live through this. No dust, no antelope flying through the air . . . just green pretty country with an ocean around it. Most of all, I won't have folks trying to hang me, or kill me with bad driving."

"Well, I didn't see the blame' thing," I told him.

"I *know* you didn't run it down on purpose," Dave said with a little more wind in him. "No offense, but, if we're not stranded, I'll drive us to Twin Falls."

Up until then, I'd been more concerned with finding out who had lived or died, instead of worrying about how badly the truck was damaged. I jumped out and helped Dave toss the antelope out to make a feast for the buzzards.

Then we began looking over the Model T. Luckily the radiator was still intact. One headlight and, of course, both the front and back glass were busted out. I tore the broken two-by-fours holding the tin roof loose and threw the whole mess in the general direction of the antelope. Dave took a tire iron and broke out what glass remained. I gave the engine a crank, and it fired right up. No matter what happened to the rest of the truck, that little motor always ran good.

Dave slid behind the wheel and wrapped back up in his blanket that was now covered with hair and antelope blood. He gave me a look like he was mad about something. It was getting dusk by now, so Dave turned on our one headlight and wordlessly started driving slowly toward the east.

The orange rays of the morning sun were shooting over the horizon when we finally chugged into Twin Falls. We were frozen stiff, dirty, and tired. Dave wouldn't drive faster than ten miles an hour, generally slower. Every time he'd glimpse any sage-brush or a tumbleweed, he would think it was another antelope and slam on the brakes.

Theodore Spurgeon didn't seem the least bit surprised to find us sitting on the bench in front of his office when he came to work. He gave the remains of that battered Model T a close look, shook his head, unlocked the door, and invited us inside.

I supposed from all I'd heard about the lawyer, he'd be sporting horns and have a tail folded up inside his pants. He turned out to be a slender, pleasant man, clean-shaven with a touch of gray at his temples. Dressed in a flannel shirt and work pants, he appeared likable enough.

Dave and I took our seats. When the lawyer looked at me, he gave the chilling effect of being able to see inside my head.

Spurgeon listened intently as we both took turns filling him in on the skullduggery going on in Jarbidge. "Gentlemen," he finally announced, "this could be a highly profitable situation for all concerned. It will take some detective work on my part, *expensive* work, I might add. When we determine who the driving force behind Elkoro Mines is, then we can negotiate or sue. Personally I think, under the circumstances, they would want to avoid the publicity of a trial."

"I don't have any money," Dave said forlornly.

"But you *do* have stock," the lawyer replied, with a grin. "I'll take twenty-five thousand shares for my fee. When you sell your remaining stock, you can pay me the ten thousand dollars you presently owe."

"Ten thousand dollars," I blurted out. All of these big figures were clouding my judgment.

"Incorporation fees are not cheap, Mister Goodman," Theodore Spurgeon said firmly. "I have yet to be paid for many of my services."

I decided to keep my trap shut and listen to what the lawyer had to say. His advice was so expensive it seemed a shame to waste any of it.

"No one should know of this," Spurgeon continued, while his eyes burned into me. "Mister Bourne will go to a place of my choosing while I set the wheels in motion. You, Milo, will return home to Jarbidge on the next stage. Should anyone connected with Elkoro Mines learn of your involvement, I doubt you'll be around to see how things turn out. When large amounts of money are involved, human life is often viewed as a cheap commodity."

With that cheery note, the lawyer went over to his wall phone and called for a taxi to take me to the hotel.

While we were waiting for the cab, I listened again while the lawyer explained how dead I'd be if I didn't keep stone quiet until his plan, whatever it was, came together.

When my head hit the pillow, I slept like Spurgeon said I would if the Elkoro people caught on to me. That overnight trip had worn me out. I guess seeing Dave Bourne booted out of his seat by an antelope had gotten me so excited it took a while to settle down.

I caught the stage at one in the morning. I climbed up and took my place alongside Searcy.

Fred said: "I hope you have everything taken care of."

"No, I've hired a lawyer."

"God have mercy on your soul. I hope he's better than the one Kitty has. That guy's not worth the powder to blow him to hell."

I was glad I'd carried my coat along. Suddenly I felt a chill.

Chapter Eleven

We met Wheelbarrow Willie pushing his way toward Twin Falls on the mesa before dropping off into Kitty's Hot Hole. He kept his head down and raised one hand long enough for a quick wave.

When the stagecoach slowly wound its way down Crippen Grade and Jarbidge came into view, it felt, for the first time, like I was coming home.

The stark nakedness of the aspen trees was a surprise. When I left, they had been wrapped in brilliant hues of orange and yellow. Now, only a few faded leaves still clung to gnarled branches. The weather was getting noticeably and progressively colder.

When the sun came up this morning, it failed to feel warm. White fog blew from the horses' nostrils and the cold wind reddened Fred's cheeks. Pewter-gray clouds were floating dark and listlessly above the high peaks west of town. I told myself this was just a cold snap that would pass. I had yet to be introduced to winter in the high mountains. They can begin anytime and last until the next one starts.

The pungent smell of wood smoke hung in the chill air as the stage creaked to a stop at the express office. When we drove past Cherry Flats, I noticed smoke coming from one of those little cabins that hadn't been occupied when I left.

Inman met me when I climbed off the stage, and together we went to the Miners' Exchange, built up the fire, and checked over the books. I'd actually made a profit, even after paying for a bartender.

The contents of the porcelain coffee pot were the consistency of roofing tar so I added some water. While waiting for it to heat, Inman said: "By the way, Milo, that Cameron guy came by looking for you."

I wasn't surprised, but knew I had to act like I was. "I didn't know if he'd ever set foot in a saloon again, considering the outcome last time."

Inman laughed. "Yeah, Tully sure cleaned his clock. You've made a good customer there . . . Tully's been in every night. He says he won't eat glass anywhere but in your bar from here on."

"Glad to hear he's still alive. After what I

123

saw him do, I wouldn't have been surprised if Slabs hadn't finally gotten some business."

"Nah, Tully's fine and the undertaker's still bitching. There's only two big news flashes you missed out on."

"All of the exciting stuff always happens when I'm out of town."

"Ain't it true. The first is, Lyman's struck gold in the Pavlak. He says it's not a big thing yet, but he and the Bruckners are sacking ore."

"That ought to make Eppie happy," I said.

"Nothing could put a smile on that witch's face. Jackson told me the first words out of her mouth, when she found out they'd found ore, was that she was going to hire a lawyer to break his lease."

"Jackson told me he had an attorney draw up the papers."

"Having lawyers arguing back and forth is how they make their money," Inman grumbled. "They ought to put a bounty on lawyers like they do on coyotes. Thin their ranks a little and life would be a lot more pleasant for everyone."

"It sure seems to me gold mines attract more than their share of lawyers. I wonder why?"

"For the same reason Jesse James robbed banks . . . that's where the money is, although I hate to sully the memory of a decent crook by comparing him to a lawyer."

The coffee had finally heated up enough to try and swallow some. After I took one sip of that vile brew, there was no doubt I would personally stop Slabs's losing streak if I drank any more. So to Inman's delight, I poured us a beer.

"What's the other big news?" I asked.

"Oh, that Ray Cameron fellow's turned out to be nuttier than a peach orchard boar. He's running around paying cash money for Bourne stock. Most folks only paid ten cents a share for it. This fool's laying out fifteen cents. Everyone in town that owned any has sold to him."

"I reckon Dave Bourne's in no danger of getting hung any longer."

"Hell's bells, didn't you notice the noose is gone? If Dave showed up now, he'd likely get elected mayor."

It pained me to find my friends had sold out their stock. To change the subject I said: "When we came through Cherry Flats, I saw smoke coming from three of those little cabins. Who's the new girl?"

Inman's mouth flew open. "Blast if I

know, she must've come in on horseback last night." He pulled out his watch and grinned. "That brother of mine won't beat me there this time. It'll take him another hour at the express office. Pay me, Milo, I've got important business to attend to."

He chugged his beer while I counted out the money he'd earned. He scooped it up, thanked me, then hightailed it out the door.

After Inman left on his fact-finding expedition, I went to my house. The first thing I did was dig my stock certificate out of a drawer where I had carelessly left it. I folded that certificate and placed it in the metal box with Dave Bourne's letters, and hid it back in the closet.

After I finally got the place warm, I fried up some eggs and bacon. Once I ate, it struck me just how blamed tired I was. I tossed a big piece of mahogany in the stove, stretched out on the bed, and had the most delightful dream about that cute little redhead down in Cherry Flats.

It seemed dark outside when I woke up, but there was still enough light for me to make out the hands on that big regulator clock on the wall; it showed only five p.m. I wiped the sleep from my eyes and looked out the window. Those gray clouds that were in the distance earlier had moved in.

The weather hadn't gotten any warmer, so I poked the fire to life and added more wood.

I brought up a few buckets of water from the river and heated enough to fill a washtub so I could take a bath. Once I'd scrubbed my skin red with lye soap and a hog bristle brush, I gave myself a careful shave. I climbed into a new pair of denims and put on a red flannel shirt that had been ironed. A generous splash of cologne and I was prepared to do something I had thought about often. Tonight I was going to visit Cherry Flats.

The trees might be droopy outside, but my sap had been on the rise ever since I'd first set eyes on the Red Fox.

From living on a farm for a while, I had all of the mechanics figured out fairly well. My mind was made up; tonight I was going to dip my wick.

First off, I needed to get fortified for the task ahead. I went to Fong's restaurant and ordered a heaping plate of oysters. From everything I'd heard, they were essential ingredients to a good performance. The things were chewy and I didn't like the taste at all, but I didn't leave a morsel. If I'd had any idea at the time that those weren't the kind of oysters you were supposed to eat, I would have gladly skipped that part.

The other thing a man needs before a momentous occasion in his life is plenty of beer. When I left the restaurant, it had grown dark enough that Ed Kinneson was out starting fires in those gasoline street lights that lined the business district. Ed was a consumptive old miner, too infirm to hold a job requiring any stamina; he held the position of street custodian.

"Going down to check out the new whore, are we?" he wheezed with a sly grin as I passed him. I just nodded and beat a hasty, red-faced retreat to the Miners' Exchange. I hung my coat on the rack and took a seat at the bar.

"Hey, Milo, I see you're heading to visit the new whore," Lyman boomed from his table. He held his mug of beer high and smiled.

The Bruckners did the same. "*Ja,* new whore," they grunted in English.

Keeping a secret in Jarbidge was like trying to sneak meat past a starving hound.

"Call her Featherlegs Fern," Inman said with a wink. "She got her nickname because, when she hears the clink of a silver dollar hitting the night stand, her legs just naturally float toward the roof."

"There was a whore in Tonopah who went

by that name," Tully Moxness said from down the bar. "A right cute little brunette . . . she gave everyone who saw her a dose of the clap."

"Nah," Butt-Block muttered, "this one's a blonde, a natural blonde. That's a true fact."

"How would you know?" Tully answered. "You ain't had a silver dollar to pay for getting your ashes hauled since Roosevelt was President."

"I been savin'," Butt-Block retorted, then added with a touch of hope in his voice, "and she's not got the clap, either."

After three beers the conversation hadn't improved noticeably, so I threw on my coat and headed out the door to the tune of hand clapping and catcalls. A few light flakes of snow hit my cheeks, but I paid them no mind. My feet felt like they were made of lead as I made the short walk to Cherry Flats.

Dead aspen leaves crunched underfoot as I stopped and nervously faced those little log cabins on the line. A solitary red lantern flickered in the night. Surprisingly Featherlegs was the only girl not engaged at the moment. A red-globed kerosene lantern hanging outside the door meant the girl was ready for business. When the lady of the night was engaged, she took the lantern inside.

This turn of events was distressing. I really wasn't interested in the new girl; my pump was primed for the willowy redhead. I stuck my hands inside my coat pockets to keep warm and stood there in the snow, wondering why she hadn't been saving herself for me. After a short while, I began debating the possible merits of a blonde. Then the door to Red Fox's cabin burst open. A man with his pants down around his ankles stumbled outside, cursing under his breath. I swallowed hard. Red was as naked as the night. Standing there in that twinkling lantern light, she looked like a goddess.

"Don't ever ask for your money back when you can't get it up," she shouted scathingly at the man who was having an obviously hard time just hoisting his pants. "If you'd drink less, your little soldier might stand at attention once in a while."

I'd begun to think folks getting thrown out of whorehouses was a regular occurrence, then Red saw me standing there.

"Hello, lover," she cooed, her voice now sweet as maple syrup. "I'm glad you could come play with the Red Fox."

When I forced myself to come out of that grove of aspen trees, I got close enough to get a look at the man who was too drunk even to pull up his pants. My mouth and everything else dropped. It was Ben Kuhl! He rolled those dark cruel eyes of his toward me, took a step forward, tripped, and crashed head first to the ground. Kuhl managed to get back into a sitting position, then he puked all over himself, let out a groan, laid back down, and began snoring fitfully.

I was standing there dumbstruck, watching Ben Kuhl blow snot bubbles out of his nose when Red brushed by me. She was wearing a heady perfume that smelled like spring lilacs. Somehow, she'd found time to wrap herself in a frilly robe. Red draped a coat over the prostrate Kuhl, then unrolled a heavy felt blanket and covered him with it.

"He's got too much anti-freeze in him for the cold to do any damage," Red said with firmness. "Don't let it be said I don't take care of my customers."

At the time, I had no more interest going inside that cabin with her than running for Congress. Then Red caught me off guard — women are experts at doing that — when she opened that robe of hers, snuggled up close to me, and swept me into that cabin of hers faster than a politician can tell a lie.

It was cozy warm inside. The aroma of

Red's wonderful perfume hung in the air like a promise. She brought out two glasses and poured a healthy shot of whiskey into each one. "Darling, you don't have to be afraid of little ole me," Red purred, pecking a little kiss on my cheek. "All I want to do is make you feel good."

I slugged down that whiskey mighty fast and Red did the same, then, with a flash of movement, she stripped off that sexy robe she was wearing. After that I simply didn't have any more chance of leaving there with that silver dollar I'd brought than a snowball does in hell.

Later, when I stepped out into the cold, my mind was completely occupied with adding up how many dollar visits I could afford every week. I'd totally forgotten about Ben Kuhl until I tripped over him. The snowstorm had increased to where you couldn't see five feet ahead of you. He let out with a curse and sat up, shaking snow from himself like a wet dog. "You son-of-a-bitch would let a man freeze to death," he grumbled.

"Why, hello, Milo," a cheerful voice said over my shoulder. "I wondered how long it would be before you made it to Cherry Flats."

"Howdy yourself," I said to Fred Searcy

while watching Kuhl finally manage to get his pants hitched up.

I breathed a sigh of relief when I saw he didn't have a gun. He was still so drunk he probably couldn't have hit anything in the state of Nevada, but I didn't want to find out first-hand I might be mistaken. "You been checking out that new girl?"

"Nah, I hear she's got the clap. I just paid Dumb Dora what I owed her. She's good for a long spell now. What's Ben doing out here with his pants down, playin' with himself?"

"I'm goin' to get you two bastards," Kuhl hissed at us while stumbling around trying to get into his coat. He shot us a mean look, then lumbered off toward The Stray Dog.

Red came outside and hung her red lantern from a nail. "You boys should get to town, it looks like we're in for a bad snowstorm."

Fred and I walked back to the Miners' Exchange together. We took our sweet time so as not to catch up with Ben Kuhl.

The snow was nearly a foot deep, and a strong wind had begun whipping it around when we got to the saloon. We warmed our hands over the big potbelly stove while Inman poured us a beer. Everyone in the place was wearing an expression like their dog had just died. I found out what the concern was when Inman spoke up.

"This damn' storm is turning into a full-fledged blizzard. Wheelbarrow Willie's out there. If he gets off the road, he'll get lost and freeze to death."

Chapter Twelve

"Oh, shit!" I blurted out to no one in particular. "We should have turned Willie around when we met him back of Kitty's."

"There was no way to know this storm was going to turn into a frickin' blizzard," Fred grumbled.

I shot a glance through the front window. It was snowing so hard I could barely make out the glow of the street light in front of the bar. Never before in my life had I felt so guilty about anything. It had been my idea to have Willie haul beer kegs from Idaho to save me a few dollars.

"What in the heck do people do when it snows like this?" I asked loudly.

"Anyone with good sense would hole up," Jackson Lyman said with concern. "But we're talking about Willie."

We spent a long time in that saloon, listening to the wind howl its mournful tune and watching snow being whipped into deep drifts. Around midnight, everyone went home, agreeing to meet at daybreak and mount a search effort for Willie.

If I hadn't known where my cabin was, I couldn't have found it, the snow was so intense. Somehow, I managed to get a little sleep, but when I woke up at six a.m., I felt more tired than when I'd gone to bed.

The first thing I did was run to a window. It was still dark outside, but I could see the street lights plain as day. The snow had stopped. After wrapping up in my thick, knee-length overcoat, I started slogging my way to Fong's.

There was a sled hitched to a pair of horses standing ready in front of the restaurant. Through an opening in that iron-gray sky I noticed a building glow to the east. The sun would be making its appearance soon.

Inside the restaurant, probably thirty men, many of whom I didn't know, were drinking coffee or eating breakfast, waiting for enough light to head out.

I took a table with Inman, Fred, and Jackson. None of them looked like they'd slept a wink. They were somber as a preacher at a funeral. Fong set a cup of coffee in front of me. "Hey, Willie, him like horse, him be OK," the Chinaman said.

"You'd better eat something, Milo, this could be a long day," Fred Searcy advised.

"We might have a bunch of shoveling to do to get up that grade," Inman added. "Right near the top is where that road always drifts shut. I've seen it pile up twelve feet deep."

Even though I wasn't hungry, I had Charlie cook me up a stack of pancakes and bury them under a mountain of chili. When no one made any wisecracks about my breakfast, I knew just how worried they were.

A gallon of hot coffee later, the sun began peeking through a broken sky. Fred Searcy took the driver's seat on the sleigh with Inman by his side. Jackson and I took the rumble seat, and Fred cracked the reins starting us on our way, breaking a trail for others to follow.

The air was crisp and still. When we drove past the little cabins on Cherry Flats, I noticed smoke from their chimneys rose straight up. Until then, I had no idea how much Willie was liked. Looking back down the road behind, a long line of men carrying shovels were struggling through the snow, Ed Beck and Ben Kuhl among them.

We began shoveling at the first switch-back. The men on foot caught up with us easily, making me wonder why the sled had been hitched up. Then it finally dawned on me this was the only way to bring a frozen body back to town.

It was midday and a cold bright sun was hanging in a cloudless blue sky when we finally fought our way to the rim of the mesa. A huge drift stretched across at least a hundred feet of it, piled higher than a man's head.

After an hour of hard work, we finally shoveled our way to where the road broke onto the flatness of the mesa. I was the first one to see Willie. He stood behind that wheelbarrow with a keg of beer on it, stuck in a snowdrift. I thought he'd frozen to death, standing up. He'd been in that one spot so long, snow had piled up on one side of him. When I struggled closer, the stiff body I had expected to find began moving around and shaking snow from itself.

"Howdy, Mister Milo," Willie said as cheerfully as if we'd met on the street in town. "I got stuck an' the wind blew my hat away. I liked my hat."

"I'll buy you a new one," I told him.

"If you'll get the snow out of my road, I'll go home. Ma's prob'ly mad, an' I'm powerful hungry," Willie said.

Fred and a dozen other men slogged

through the drift to come to Willie's aid. He seemed little worse for wear and even gave us an argument about riding back to town. Finally he relented, picked up his wheelbarrow, beer keg and all, and placed it in the back of the sleigh. He piled into the seat alongside me. With Willie grinning like a man who just struck gold, we headed back to Jarbidge.

Charlie Fong wound up cooking Willie three huge breakfasts. The big galoot loved the attention he was getting. While Willie was stuffing down another dozen eggs, I walked to Adams's General Store and bought him a hat. They didn't have a small bowler like the one he'd lost, so I opted for the biggest fur cap with earflaps they had.

As I was leaving, Frank hollered after me: "By the way, Milo, your tent came in yesterday!"

I took one look at the thick blanket of snow outside, shook my head, thanked him, and told him I'd pick it up later. The Lost Sheepherder's Mine would have to stay lost for a while longer.

Willie pulled that cap over his head the moment he saw it. The thing was a few sizes too small, but it seemed not to matter to him. The earflaps stuck straight out like bird's wings. I told Willie to go home and stay there until the snow was all gone. He didn't think that was a bad idea.

I have no idea how Willie Pavlak survived that night stuck in a snowdrift with an arctic blizzard whipping snow around him. He had long hair that may have kept his ears from getting frostbite. I was totally taken aback when I found out Ben Kuhl had paid for Willie's food. Even a mean dog can have a day when they don't bite someone.

With Willie safe and sound, things slipped into a routine. I made a deal with Emil Larson, Slabs's cousin who owned a freight wagon, to bring in my beer for me. After seeing what that road was like in the winter time, fifteen dollars a keg seemed reasonable.

I kept Inman tending bar and began fixing up my cabin. This was mostly "make work" on my part; I was awaiting what Dave Bourne and the lawyer would do.

Ray Cameron came by the saloon every night and tried to buy my stock. After a week, he raised his offer to thirty cents a share. This put Fred Searcy and others into a stew since they'd sold at fifteen cents.

A week after we'd dug Willie out of that snowdrift, I had to run the bar for a while to allow Inman some time off. He'd gone to the bathroom and livened up everyone's evening by screaming with pain. Featherlegs Fern had given him a present that required a visit to a doctor in Twin Falls. Butt-Block and a half dozen other groaning miners filled the stagecoach when it left the next afternoon.

Featherlegs must have gone through this before and knew to be on her way to another town before her condition became known. She had saddled up her roan and ridden off a day before the storm struck.

Three more slow weeks dragged by before I got a letter from Theodore Spurgeon. Inman was back working the bar for me, at least every other day. I'd grown fidgety and needed something to do, so I had begun tending bar on alternate days with him.

Spurgeon's letter came on my day off, so I stuck it inside my coat and waded through the snow back to my cabin. His message was brief and ominous. It said simply:

Arriving in Jarbidge October 30th at 1 p.m. We are negotiating with appropriate party. Company presidents will accompany me.

T. Spurgeon

A quick glance at the calendar showed another week of waiting. The part about "company presidents" mystified me. As far as I knew, Dave Bourne was the only president for Bourne Mining.

I had learned a good method to handle waiting. After going to the saloon and fishing a shiny silver dollar out of the cash drawer, I headed off to see the Red Fox. Later that evening, I went back to the Miners' Exchange to visit. Fred Searcy was there, bellied up to the bar, grinning like a cat looking at a canary.

"Well, Fred, having a day off seems to agree with you," I said, taking a stool beside him.

"That's not the reason he's happier than a rabbit in a carrot patch," Jackson informed me loudly. "The man has a plan to get himself hitched."

"Dumb Dora quit letting him run a tab, that's his problem," Tully Moxness added.

"Do you mean hitched . . . like in getting married?" I asked, taken aback. "You aren't marrying Du . . . Dora, are you?" I asked, stammering over the "Dumb" part to save my pearly whites should that be the case.

"Nope," Fred answered. "I'm going to pay Dumb Dora the ten dollars I owe her, then I'm going to walk the straight and narrow until my bride shows up."

"What's this girl's name? Where's she from, and how did you ever meet her?" I asked, dumbfounded.

"He don't know her name. He's buying a pig in the poke," Butt-Block interjected.

"He's ordering one in from Saint Louis, Missouri," Tully Moxness said with a grin. "It's like shopping from that Sears and Roebuck outfit, only Fred's not getting any money back guarantee."

"Is this true, Fred? You've sent for a mail-order bride?" I asked.

"There ain't nothing wrong with that," Fred replied firmly. "They only cost twenty-five dollars, plus freight."

"I hope you get a skinny one," Jackson Lyman advised. "Those freight rates from Saint Louie would be awful if you have to pay for a fat one."

"The bigger ones have a better disposition," Tully said. "The lean ones have a mean streak in 'em."

"That's a true statement," Jackson Lyman said. "I didn't factor in having to live with 'em. A big 'un would be good on a cold night, though . . . they put out tolerable more heat than a little one will."

"This bride of yours, when is she coming?" I asked to Fred's obvious relief.

"I'm not real sure. The order form said it

143

might take a couple of months," Fred replied. Then, looking at Jackson, he asked: "How are things with Eppie and the mine, anyway?"

"She's been too broke to hire that lawyer. We've got ten tons of good ore at the mill now. I reckon it'll yield at least a hundred ounces of gold. That woman gets ten percent. Once she's paid, I'm sure her lawyer will get all her share just to cause me problems."

Tully started to say something, then he looked toward the door and his expression turned grim. I spun around on my barstool and saw Ray Cameron and Ben Kuhl coming inside. They hung up their coats and took a seat at an empty table.

"A bottle of your best whiskey and two glasses for us," Cameron said pleasantly to Inman. "And a round for everyone in the place, especially Mister Goodman."

"I reckon I can buy my own," I said in a firm voice.

"Now, my good sir, we are only trying to be friendly," Ray Cameron said with a sickly sweet voice. "Please let us enjoy the privilege of your company at our table."

When I slid back a chair to join them, I noticed Ben Kuhl was wearing a pistol stuck under his belt.

"My dear sir," Cameron continued, "I

have, in the past, attempted to purchase your stock in the Bourne Company from you at a fair price. I would like to make another offer."

"Go ahead and make it," I told him.

Ben Kuhl took a shot of whiskey, then let his hand rest on the butt of his gun.

"Fifty cents a share, cash on the barrel head," Cameron said loudly, causing Fred Searcy to choke on his beer.

"I reckon not. I'm thinking of having it framed."

Ray Cameron's face flushed red. "I think it would be wise of you to reconsider."

"Nope, not interested," I said simply, noticing Kuhl's hand begin to wrap around the butt of his pistol.

It turned out I wasn't the only one keeping an eye on his gun hand.

"Hey, Kuhl!" Fred Searcy yelled out loudly. "It's too bad that gun you're petting is the only hard thing you've had in your pants lately, ain't it?"

Ben Kuhl gave out a snarl. Cameron sprang from his seat and put a restraining hand on Kuhl's gun arm. "Settle down," Cameron told him. "There is a time and place for everything. Right now, we are going to leave."

"You might consider staying gone longer next time," I said.

"Mister Goodman," Cameron said curtly, "you have made a very unfortunate choice."

I said: "Now what was that part about your leaving?"

Kuhl gave me a cruel look as he slowly slid his hand from his gun and joined Ray Cameron. I breathed a sigh of relief when they put on their coats and left.

"You must be nuts," Fred said to me. "That was five hundred dollars."

"Take the money," Jackson advised. "You could plumb tucker out that redhead in Cherry Flats and have enough left over for a steak dinner."

Tully Moxness was lost in thought for a while, then he looked at me. "It might be a bunch healthier for you to do like Jackson says. Just remember, it's hard to spend money when you're pushing up daisies."

Inman and Fred saw me to my cabin that night. Fred carried a shotgun loaded with buckshot in the crook of his arm. I felt it was foolishness and told them so, but they insisted. I didn't think that Elkoro bunch would try anything so soon, and I was right.

It was the next morning when I headed to Fong's for breakfast that Ben Kuhl stepped from the shadows of an evergreen tree and stuck the barrel of his pistol into my ribs.

Chapter Thirteen

"There's some folks who want to talk to you," Kuhl hissed, his breath white from the cold.

I managed a nod. He jabbed me hard with the barrel of his pistol and motioned with his head. "Up the street . . . we're going to take a nice, friendly walk."

The frozen snow crunched under our feet in the still air. A few people were milling about, but none of them paid us any mind. Kuhl's gun was inside his coat so no one could see it. I wasn't the least surprised when we crossed the river and walked up a small hill to the big office building of Elkoro Mines Company.

David C. Knight looked gaunt and hawkish from across the expanse of the sprawling oak desk he sat behind. Ray Cameron was standing beside it, dressed as nattily as ever.

"You have become a considerable inconvenience, Mister Goodman," Knight said. "I would have preferred you simply selling us your stock. Now I'm afraid you will simply have to give it to me."

"Go to hell," I told him.

"Mister Goodman," Knight yelled, "I will not allow the use of foul language here! It is a sin condemned by the Scriptures."

"And stealing a man's property isn't?" I added, causing his face to flush red.

"*Reason* with him, Mister Kuhl."

That was the last thing I heard Knight say before a two-by-four came out of nowhere and smashed into my gut, knocking me to the floor. I slowly managed to sit up, trying to get my breath, while the room spun about.

"You should have taken my offer last night," Ray Cameron said. "It would have been much more pleasant."

"I see your point," I finally managed to cough out.

"Would you care to deliver your stock to me now, or should I have Mister Kuhl continue to *reason* with you," Knight stated.

My mind was racing wildly as my heart was beating. "I'll let you have the stock," I rasped.

"An excellent choice. Mister Kuhl will accompany you to get the certificate."

"I don't have it," I lied.

"What do you mean you don't have it?" Ray Cameron yelled.

"I left it with my lawyer when I was in Twin Falls."

Kuhl spoke up. "He was there on business a while back."

David C. Knight walked from around his desk and looked down at me. "I trust you'll tell me this lawyer's name."

"Theodore Spurgeon," I answered.

"Ah, yes, the great mining lawyer who is selling Bourne's stock to me. I'll get him on the phone, and you can tell him to bring along your certificate, also," Knight said happily. "Then Elkoro Mines will have complete control of the Jarbidge mining district."

I finally got enough wind to stand. Knight went to the wall telephone and started calling Spurgeon. Whether my head was spinning from Kuhl's blow or what the Elkoro manager had said, I didn't have a clue. The very thought that Spurgeon was selling out Dave Bourne was more than I wanted to believe.

From listening to half of the conversation, once Knight got Spurgeon on the phone, I decided they were bosom buddies. After a lot of small talk, I was motioned to come and talk to the lawyer. Ray Cameron listened in on another phone.

"Well, Mister Goodman, you are in good health I trust?" Spurgeon said.

"My stomach's acting up," I answered.

"Are we able to talk privately?"

"Yes, sir," I forced myself to say, staring at Cameron.

"You agree to give me power of attorney on your behalf when I arrive in Jarbidge on the Thirtieth of October?"

"Yes, sir," I said, nodding.

"I will need your signature on the document, then. In the meantime, I hope your stomach improves."

"I'm feeling better already," I said bitterly.

"You are a stubborn man," Knight snarled, "and a stubborn man can have any number of accidents happen to him. When you sign over your stock to me, you will also execute a deed to your bar, then immediately leave town. I'll pay you five hundred dollars for it, so you can't say I wasn't fair. Then I will close down that den of iniquity and turn it into a house of the Lord. It will be Jarbidge, Nevada's first church."

I wish I could say I handled the situation like a hero in some Western novel, but I didn't. My breath was coming in short, painful gasps and I'm sure there were tears in my eyes as I slowly stumbled back to my cabin.

The first thing I did was swallow four aspirin tablets. When I pulled off my shirt, I saw my whole abdomen was becoming an angry purple bruise. For the next three days, I stayed in my cabin, peeing blood. I told Inman I had the flu. He told me I looked like death warmed over, which made me feel a lot better.

The fourth day after Kuhl's beating, I began to get around some. My gut still looked like one big bruise and was sore as a boil. I began going through the few things I owned, trying to decide what I could take with me when I left Jarbidge. Since I'd have to take the stagecoach, my baggage would be small.

Then I walked to the post office. I hadn't picked up my mail for days. Sylvia Searcy met me, carrying her usual cup of coffee. She told me how glad she was to see I was feeling better, then handed over my only letter. It was a bill from Matt Whort, at the livery stable. When I saw those two mules had already eaten a $100 worth of hay and oats, I felt like someone had hit me with a club again.

This was *not* going to be a good week I decided. I wrote a check and paid Whort on my way home. Since I already owned the mules, I decided to use them to leave town with. At least then I could take a few more things with me than I could carry on the stagecoach.

It would be three more days before I had to sign my stock and bar over to Knight. I didn't want to go out any more than necessary, so I dropped by Adams's store to buy some groceries. I wrote another check there for fifty-two dollars to pay for the tent I hadn't picked up yet. Then I hightailed it for home. I couldn't afford to do any more visiting.

My back was against the wall with no way out except to do as the Elkoro manager ordered. Although the soreness was still in my chest and gut, I discovered I was too nervous to stay inside. I fished a silver dollar from a stash I kept in the kitchen cabinet. I then headed for Cherry Flats. It was far cheaper to go there than town.

When the Red Fox saw how bruised my gut was, she let out a sob. "Who did this to you?" she cried.

"Oh, it was Ben Kuhl showing how tough he is."

"That bastard would drown a puppy, he's so mean."

"I just wanted to tell you good bye," I told her, plunking a dollar down on her night stand. "It looks like I'm going to have to leave town."

"What do you mean, Milo?" she asked with concern.

I'd been aching to tell someone of my troubles. I stretched out on that soft feather mattress of hers and began talking. I told Red everything that had happened; how I was going to have to sign over my stock and the bar just to stay alive. All the while, she was running velvet fingers through my hair.

After I was talked out, she went and blew the flame out on her lantern. "You'll be staying the night," she said softly as she took off her lacy robe and carefully laid her soft body next to mine.

Theodore Spurgeon had said he would arrive in Jarbidge at one o'clock. I'd been outside the saloon, pacing back and forth in the snow for nearly an hour, before a huge black car pulled up and stopped. This was the first limousine I had ever seen. It was a new Cadillac V-8. The thing was as long as a politician's speech. Chains on the back wheels rattled against the frozen snow.

A muscular chauffeur dressed in a neat blue suit and matching cap climbed out of the cab and opened the back door of the limousine with a bow. I swallowed hard and, feeling like a lamb being led to the slaughter, walked over and peered inside. The huge automobile had two seats facing each other. In the back seat were Dave Bourne and Theodore Spurgeon dressed in suits and smiling broadly. Facing rearward was a pinch-faced little man, tightly clutching a brown leather briefcase to his lap. He wore an expensive suit of clothes as easily as a politician does a smile.

"Well, get in, Milo, you're letting the heat out," Dave Bourne said with a grin.

I sure didn't know what he had to be happy about, but I wanted to get this over with, so I climbed in and sat beside the little man with the briefcase. The chauffeur shut the door after me. I noticed there was a glass window separating the driver from us. My mouth felt dry as that huge car started slowly to where I knew we were headed: the office of Elkoro Mines.

"I hope your stomach is feeling better," Spurgeon said.

"Yeah, not having it whacked with a club for a few days has done wonders," I answered.

"I'm sorry for what you had to endure," the lawyer said.

The little man next to me nervously puckered his lips and finally took a cigarette from a gold case. Silently he offered me one. I gladly accepted. Dave Bourne produced a lighter and lit our cigarettes.

All too quickly we were parked at the Elkoro office. As we climbed out into the crisp air, Spurgeon gave me a playful tap on the shoulder. "Hey, this is going to be fun, I love times like these."

Lawyers have a strange sense of humor, I thought. The little man melted into the shadow of his huge chauffeur as we walked the few feet to the office door. The Elkoro building was a high-ceiling affair totally paneled with beautiful cherry wood wainscoting. Behind the huge manager's desk were two huge windows overlooking the town of Jarbidge. A crackling fire was burning in a rock fireplace along one wall.

David C. Knight stood in front of it, warming his hands. Ray Cameron was sitting in a chair underneath a huge chandelier, thumbing through some papers. Ben Kuhl stood alone, the two-by-four that he'd used to hit me with leaned against the wall next to his feet.

"Mister Spurgeon," Knight said firmly. "How very good to see you and your company. I trust you've brought the stock certificates."

"I think you will find my work has been thorough," the lawyer replied.

"Excellent, I will also want you to execute a deed from Mister Goodman to me for that saloon he owns. I wish to make it into a house of the Lord for the town of Jarbidge," Knight said cheerfully.

"I'll be glad to do that, if he wants to sell it to you," Spurgeon said, sweeping his arm toward me. "First, I think you should have a little talk with this gentleman." He stepped aside to let the man I'd sat beside step forward. The chauffeur, I noticed, had his hand on a lump under his jacket and kept an unblinking eye on Ben Kuhl.

Knight sneered at the little man. "And just who might you be, sir?"

"I am the director of this company, Daniel Guggenheim. I have had it brought to my attention there have been some . . . irregularities in your conduct." The man's voice was soft, but the effect he had on Knight was like a bullet striking. In those days everyone knew of the wealthy Guggenheim family.

The cocky manager for Elkoro Mines turned ghostly white and began to shake. "I . . . I can explain," Knight sputtered.

"The record speaks for you," Guggenheim said firmly. "When I was informed of your misconduct, I ordered Pinkerton's to do some detective work. I'm sorry to say the reports I received show Mister Spurgeon's allegations to be true. You are hereby fired, sir! Clean out your desk and be gone from these premises before nightfall."

Ben Kuhl just stood with his mouth open while the chauffeur grabbed his gun from him. The big driver frowned down at the startled Kuhl, and simply said: "Beat it."

Ben ran out so fast I'd say he was halfway to the Stray Dog before another word was said.

I really didn't have a good handle on what was going on, but I liked it. David C. Knight shook like an aspen leaf while Daniel Guggenheim continued.

"I apologize," he said, looking at me, "for any inconvenience or pain you may have suffered at my *former* employee's bidding. Elkoro Mines is a subsidiary of American Smelting and Refining, the largest mining company in the world. We do not do business in the manner Mister Knight attempted. Our geologists confirm a large ore body in Jarbidge. We do want the Bourne property, but are willing to pay a fair price for it. Your attorney, Mister Spurgeon, has

157

negotiated the sum of ten dollars per share for the remaining stock. If that price is acceptable to you, Mister Goodman, we can put this unfortunate incident behind us."

"Take it, son," Ray Cameron said. "You've got the last Bourne Mining Company stock there is out, aside from Dave's that is."

I couldn't understand why Cameron wasn't as frightened as Knight. He'd been there when Kuhl had whacked me. I looked him in the face and said: "You've been pestering me to sell my shares for weeks, why should I start trusting you now?"

"That was business. The way the game is played," Cameron replied. "Mister Guggenheim sent me here to buy up stock. That's my job. Some people make a little money on a buy out. A very few, like yourself, will make a lot. It's all a matter of timing. I have been in contact with the home office several times about Mister Knight's underhanded attempts to achieve his ends. When I was present at your 'incident' with Kuhl, I was under strict orders to make certain you weren't severely hurt."

"I imagine getting whacked in the gut with a club isn't very severe if you're not the whackee," I grumbled.

"Mister Goodman," Daniel Guggenheim

interjected, "I'm a very busy man. I need to get back to New York. Will you or will you not take my offer?"

"What about my bar?" I questioned naïvely.

"Son, that was an empty threat made by a man who will be leaving town shortly," Guggenheim said, then his cold gaze fixed on David C. Knight. "When I am finished blacklisting that man, he won't even be able to get a job sweeping out a fine establishment like yours."

"Then I don't have to leave town?" I asked unbelievingly.

Dave Bourne put his hand on my shoulder. "Milo, it's all right now. Theodore only said he would deliver my stock as a way to delay things until Mister Guggenheim could arrive. If you had been forced to sell, we would have voided the transaction. No one is going to cause you to give up your bar. Knight has more pressing concerns now than closing the Miners' Exchange."

"Are you selling your stock?" I asked Dave.

"I already have. I'm taking Mom, and we're moving to the Sandwich Islands, like I told you earlier when you tried to kill me with that antelope."

Daniel Guggenheim started to say something, then thought it over and just shook his head. Things were going so fast and unexpected, it took a while for it to soak in just how much money I would get by selling out. When it finally did, I turned to Theodore Spurgeon and asked: "How do I get my money?"

The lawyer laughed. "Take the certificate to Ben Jorgason at the Jarbidge Bank. He's been authorized to pay ten dollars a share and credit it to your account."

"So, Mister Goodman, you *are* willing to dispose of your holdings?" Daniel Guggenheim asked.

"Oh, yes," I replied quickly, getting excited about my unexpected reversal of fortune.

"Wonderful," Guggenheim said, clasping his hands. "Now I need a new and hopefully more trustworthy manager. Have you anyone in mind, Mister Cameron?"

"There's the foreman, Tully Moxness. He has a rather odd habit of eating glass, but, aside from that, he's honest and capable," Cameron replied.

"I'll never understand Westerners," Daniel Guggenheim said, shrugging his shoulders. "See to it, then."

My first thought was what 10,000 silver

dollars would look like stacked neatly into piles. When we left to climb into that huge Cadillac, Knight was still white as a sheet and shaking uncontrollably. At the time, I thought he looked like a corpse. I had no idea how prophetic my observation would be.

I was a very happy man when the chauffeur opened the door for me in front of my bar. "Thank you," I said to everyone inside.

"No need to thank me," Theodore Spurgeon said happily. "Mister Guggenheim and Dave Bourne have already seen to that."

Daniel Guggenheim winced and pursed his lips at the lawyer's words.

When Dave Bourne looked at me, I noticed a tear was streaking down his cheek. "*You* are the one who needs thanking," Dave said, his voice cracking. "If it hadn't been for you. . . ."

Dave Bourne shoved an envelope into my hands. The driver shut the door, and I stood there in the cold air like a statue as I watched that black car head out of Jarbidge. After a short while, I opened the envelope. Inside was another of those beautiful stock certificates for Bourne Mining. This one looked even more appealing; it was issued in my name for 5,000 shares.

I never laid eyes on Dave Bourne or heard from him after that day. I can only hope he made it to those tropical islands he loved so much and never caught another antelope in his bread basket again.

When I cashed in my stock, Jorgason's mouth fell open. I felt like the richest man in the world. $60,000 was a huge fortune in those days. A man with that kind of money could even afford to own a pair of mules.

It was growing dark outside. Ed Kinneson was lighting the street light in front of the bar when Slabs came in and ordered a beer.

"Did you hear about Knight, the Elkoro manager?" he asked.

"He got himself fired," I answered.

"No, that's not it," the undertaker replied solemnly. "I just nailed him into a coffin. He hung himself with a telephone cord from a big chandelier in the office up there. From the looks of things, he should have put some rocks in his pockets. I think it took him a long time before he finally strangled. That's a hard way to die."

"My God," Tully blurted. "I expected him to just leave town, not kill himself."

"He's leaving town tomorrow," Slabs said. "His wife's taking him back East somewhere. There's a mean one. She even chiseled me down five dollars on the price of a box to ship him in."

I was stunned by the news. The man who had worked so hard at getting me hung wound up meeting that fate himself. Even after all the skinny Bible-thumper had tried to do to me, I felt sad.

The day had been a long one and I was desperately tired. I left the bar, went to Fong's, and ate one of his delicious butter-fried steaks. For some reason, I had been under the mistaken impression things would be roses from here on. When I walked out of the restaurant and saw Ben Kuhl standing under a street light, sipping on a bottle of whiskey, I knew my troubles were far from over.

Chapter Fourteen

While I had healed considerably, I was in no condition for a fight. Neither was I in a mood to turn tail. Feeling angrier by the foot, I started past Kuhl. I gave him some room, allowing for the slim chance he might behave himself. One thing about that man — he was predictable. When he saw me coming, he corked his quart of whiskey and headed toward me.

"You owe me, man," Kuhl growled as he stopped and looked me over with bloodshot eyes.

"Well, that's strange," I told him. "I don't remember borrowing anything from you."

"That man took my gun, today, and kept it."

When you're dealing with people like Kuhl, it's best not to use any big words that might confuse them. "Go screw yourself."

I braced for the charge I knew was coming. Kuhl hunkered down like a snake getting ready to strike, then he froze like his mainspring had broke.

Charlie Fong stepped alongside me. He held a huge meat cleaver menacingly over his shoulder. "Heem a customer!" Fong yelled at Kuhl. "You go or I make chop-chop on you."

Ben Kuhl took a quick glance at the Chinaman holding that cleaver at the ready, turned pale, and quickly started backing up. "There's no problem here."

"You make go *now*," Fong said, stepping toward him.

Kuhl was so shaken by the unexpected turn of events, he spun to run away from the Chinaman, slipped on the ice, and sprawled out flat. He quickly came to his hands and knees and started scooting away as fast as he could. Finally, when he reached what he felt was a safe distance from the meat cleaver, Kuhl came to his feet. "Goodman, you're a dead man," he said firmly.

"Kuhl," I said to him, "I'm going to buy a gun, but, if you think you're going to see any part of it except the hole in the end of the barrel, you're dumber than you look, and that's mighty dumb."

My anger had reached the boiling point. I started to plunge ahead to get this fight over with. Fong's surprisingly strong hand

165

gripped my coat collar.

"No good," the Chinaman said. "Heem be enemy of ownself."

Ben Kuhl shivered like a wet dog, then spun around and lumbered up the snow-covered street in the direction of the Stray Dog Saloon, melting into the shadows.

Looking back on the situation, there's no doubt in my mind that Fong saved my life that evening. If Kuhl had pounded on my gut, which I knew he was planning to do, he would probably have ruptured something I vitally needed.

I slept late the next morning. Around ten, I went to Fong's and ate breakfast. The little Chinaman never mentioned the events of last evening. After a huge plate of his wonderful sourdough pancakes, I headed off to see Frank Adams.

The first thing he did was hit me up to take that tent I'd bought. I was still far too sore to carry the heavy thing, but I didn't want anyone to know. I made the excuse I had other errands to run, then asked him to show me the guns he had for sale. I wrote a check for sixteen dollars that paid for a small .38 pistol and a hundred cartridges. Shoving my purchase into my pocket, I headed for the Miners' Exchange.

Over the next several days Ben Kuhl was notable by his absence. I carried that little pistol with me whenever I left the bar or cabin, but I never once set eyes on him. In a small town you know what's going on, though. From the accounts I heard, Kuhl had become the town drunk. Ed Beck had become about the only person in Jarbidge who would have anything to do with him. They made a good pair. If both their brains were dynamite, they couldn't have blown their noses.

Tully Moxness took to running Elkoro Mines like a duck to water. He hired over thirty men and began construction on a huge ore mill at the base of the mountain, across the river from my bar. A portly German mining engineer named Adolph Huptman was brought in to oversee the task.

Huptman watched over the building of that mill like a mother hen looks after her brood of chicks. He kept a monstrous crooked stem pipe hanging out of his mouth from morning until night. Every evening the engineer would come into the Miners' Exchange and consume unbelievable quantities of beer. He would take a table with the Bruckners, and they'd jabber for hours in German.

A contract was let the middle of November to build a power line to Jarbidge from a generating plant in Idaho. The cost of the seventy-three mile line was over a quarter of a million dollars. Elkoro was bringing in the electricity to power their huge mill. Most of the business owners, including myself, were looking forward to having electric lights.

"I need those new lights more than you do," Tully said.

"Why's that?" I asked.

"When Davey Crap Knight hung himself from that big kerosene lamp chandelier in the office, he bent half of the burners so bad I can't use 'em. The light's so blasted dim, my peepers have to strain themselves to do paperwork."

Fred Searcy generally had a stagecoach full of wide-eyed hopefuls every time he hit town. I didn't realize the last great gold rush ever to occur was going on about me. Most of us were simply too busy to notice what others were doing. Probably the most single-minded man at the time was Fred, preparing for his mail-order bride.

Fred decorated his bedroom in the hotel with some bright yellow wallpaper with little red roses splattered around on it. Framed pictures were hard to come by, so he cut some pages out of magazines and tacked them up. On one trip, he brought back a Graphophone and records. The clerk who sold it to him had convinced him all women liked Italian operas, so Fred bought a stack of them.

One evening Fred packed that player over to the bar to demonstrate just how cultured he was becoming. We all waited patiently while he cranked it up. Then he put on one of those opera recordings and let it rip. A woman began screaming out of the Graphophone horn, doing a splendid imitation of a cat with its tail caught in a door. Then to my relief, Fred put everyone out of their misery by lifting the needle.

Jackson Lyman shook his head. "That's my ex-wife, as sure as God made little green apples. Every time I came home with beer on my breath that's just how she sounded."

"You galoots wouldn't know culture if it ran over you driving a truck," Fred said.

"Maybe not," Butt-Block said. "But if you fire that thing up again, we're going to kill you."

"It takes a while to appreciate good music," Fred grumbled.

"He got a letter from his future bride today," Inman said, wiping the bar with a towel. "If you guys ask real nice, he might show you her picture."

Fred Searcy had his usual grin back when he reached into a pocket and produced a letter. "It's even got perfume on it," he remarked.

When I sniffed that envelope, I noticed it was the same lilac aroma the Red Fox used so liberally, but good sense kept me from mentioning the fact. The young girl in the picture was without a doubt one of the loveliest women a man ever set eyes on. A cascade of curly dark hair framed her smiling face. I could make out a scattering of freckles running from her nose and across her cheeks. Inviting full lips completed the image of a goddess.

"Her name is Marybeth Sears," Fred proudly told us. "She's twenty-one years old and will be here about the middle of December. Her hair's auburn in color. Saint Louie, Missouri is her home."

"I'd freight one in myself if I thought for a minute I'd get one that pretty," Tully said.

No one could believe it was that easy to get a pretty wife delivered to Jarbidge.

"There's got to be a catch somewhere," Butt-Block commented after assuring himself Fred was gone. "All we saw was her face. I'd guess she's as big as a circus elephant."

"Nope, fat women have jowls," Inman quipped. "I'll bet you ten bucks there's not an ounce of fat on her."

"You're on," Butt-Block retorted.

"I'll take ten of that myself," Frenchie said from down the bar.

When the betting was over, Inman found himself having to cover $100 that Marybeth Sears wasn't fat.

Jackson Lyman had been unusually quiet for a long time. "You know, boys," he finally said, "her name being Sears, maybe she *does* come with one of those money-back guarantees."

All through the next day, I moped around thinking about how nice it would be to have a wife. Women smelled nice and they had the delightful attribute of being able to cook. I wasn't too sure of Italian opera, however. Then I remembered my mother had been a woman. All the time I was growing up, I'd never had to listen to anything that sounded as awful as opera, except maybe church singing.

I'd had an idea festering for quite a while about how I might beat Fred to getting married and wind up with a plumb cute one to boot. Once I'd made my mind up, all I had time to do was go to Adams's store and buy a bottle of lilac perfume, then haul that damned tent home through the snow before having to tend bar.

The next afternoon I scrubbed myself nearly raw with that hog-bristle brush while sitting in a washtub full of hot water. Then I put on some fresh washed clothes that I had hanging over the kitchen stove to dry.

Feeling as spry as a speckled pup, with that bottle of perfume in one pocket of my coat and some silver dollars in the other, I headed for Cherry Flats.

"Why, Milo, honey, how good to see you," the Red Fox purred.

She was wearing that frilly robe of hers that always seemed to fall open at just the right moment. I drank in her beauty, then handed her that bottle of lilac perfume, dumped a handful of silver dollars on her night stand, and took off my coat.

Red looked at the pile of money and laughed. "Sweetie, I don't know what kind of party you have in mind, but whatever you want, the Fox is ready."

When I didn't get undressed, she looked puzzled. I sat down on that featherbed and patted my hand for her to join me. "Hon," I told her, "I've come into some money, and, if you'll marry me, I'll take good care of you."

Red let out a sob and bolted from that bed. She stood there with her robe open as one wave of crying after another racked her small body. "I'm a whore, Milo," she said after gaining some composure. "Good boys like you can't marry a whore. It's a thing you can't leave behind."

"I'll sell the bar, and we'll move to somewhere no one will know," I said hopefully.

"Milo, I've had sweaty men pounding away on me since I was fourteen. I'll be twenty my next birthday. Women get judged different than a man. No matter where I go, I'm just going to be thought of as a whore."

"Please, Red, at least tell me you'll think about it," I said, with my own eyes getting leaky. It dawned on me I didn't even know her real name.

"Put on your coat and get out of here," she said with a sudden harshness.

I did as she told me, feeling numb and foolish.

Red stuffed the silver dollars back into my pocket. "Don't come back to see me. Find yourself a nice girl."

When I left her little crib, I hung that flickering red lantern back on the porch. After I'd walked some distance, I turned around and noticed it could be seen from a long ways away.

★ ★ ★

Since the incident with the dynamite that had killed my family, I'd been forced to do a lot of growing up. In spite of all that had happened to me, I was still just a seventeen-year-old boy with a broken heart. I'm sure I would have quickly gotten over the Red Fox. Or, at least, I would have if things hadn't taken a turn for the bad.

Living in Jarbidge in those days was like being a blind man in a den of rattlesnakes — you couldn't make a move without getting bit.

I had just opened the bar the next afternoon. Old Ed Kinneson was my only customer. Ed's lungs were so rocked up, he couldn't walk to the bathroom without causing himself a coughing fit.

I always gave him a beer. There was a jar full of dimes kept under the bar to keep him and a few other old-timers in beer. Most of the miners, when they had any extra money, would add to the jar. Mining is a tough occupation; everyone who gave money knew that they could be on the receiving end some day.

Ed was coughing so loudly I didn't notice Wheelbarrow Willie had come in. He just stood in the middle of the floor with his hands stuffed in his pockets, staring at me.

"Mister Milo," he finally asked, "could you come fix my ma like you done my barrow? She's been sleepin' for two days, an' I can't get her to wake up."

Chapter Fifteen

I sat Willie down at a table and gave him a cup of coffee. Ed caught onto the situation right away. He walked over, put a comforting hand on Willie's shoulder, and wheezed to me: "I'll stay with him. You'd best go rustle up Slabs."

The first place I ran to was the Jarbidge Hotel. Inman was attempting to hang some wallpaper for Fred and not making a success of it.

"You're a tad late. That redhead left on the stage just a bit ago," he said, grinning.

"It's not that," I told him. The urgency in my voice wiped his smile away. "Willie's at the bar . . . he says his ma won't wake up."

"Hell's bells!" Inman shouted. "I'll go see Tully at the mill. They've generally got a sled or wagon hitched up. You fetch Slabs and tell him he's likely got a customer. We'll meet at your place just as soon as we can."

When I rushed past Fong's restaurant, I

saw Slabs inside having a late lunch. After I told him the situation, he grabbed up his sandwich and wolfed it down on the way to the saloon.

I wished at the time there had been a doctor available. Elkoro Mines had one on order but, like Fred's wife, he hadn't showed up yet. Deep down, I doubted the best sawbones in the world would do any good. Eppie Pavlak had had one foot in the grave and the other on a banana peel for years.

Folks in a small town move mighty quick when there's an emergency. In short order, Tully appeared with a freight wagon.

I left Ed Kinneson to keep the bar open and piled onto the wagon, along with Inman and Slabs. Willie climbed into the back, wearing his usual grin. Inman flicked the reins and with a groan that big freight wagon headed up the cañon, wheels creaking in the cold, still air.

Snow was coming down heavily from a pewter sky by the time we pulled to a stop at Eppie's shack. Jackson Lyman was in the dry house next to the tunnel. He trudged the short distance over to see what was going on.

"Howdy, boys, what brings you out on such a nice day?" he asked cheerfully. "I was just making up some primers."

I jumped when I saw some sticks of dynamite in his coat pockets. To this day, those red cartridges scare me worse than a tax collector.

"Mister Milo's come to fix Ma," Willie said calmly from the back of the wagon. "She won't wake up."

"He says she's been sleeping for two days," Inman said.

Jackson's body sagged like a balloon with a hole in it. "Willie, I've been here every day. Why didn't you come and tell me?"

"You don't fix things," Willie replied simply.

With a building dread, I followed the big man into the one-room shack. It felt colder inside Pavlak's cabin than it was out. The fire had obviously been burned out a long while.

Eppie lay sprawled on top of an iron frame bed, open eyes staring dully at the ceiling. Her arms reached out as if she'd been trying to claw her way to heaven; however, I doubted that was the direction she had taken. Willie's mother was dead as a doornail and frozen stiff as a flagpole.

"Will you fix her now?" Wheelbarrow Willie asked.

I swallowed hard. Everyone in that little cabin was looking straight at me.

"Willie," I said gently, "sometimes, when things are broken real bad, no one can fix them."

"I had a wheel come off my other barrow once," Willie said. "No one could fix it, either. Is my ma gonna stay busted like my pa did?"

"I'm sorry, Willie," I told him, "but I'm afraid there's nothing anyone can do."

A look of dull acceptance washed over the big man's face. His smile fled. "Ma always tol' me what to do, an' when to eat or build a fire." Willie's voice showed building fear. "She tried to learn me to be smart like ever'one else, but I don't learn good. Who'll tell me what to do now?"

"We're all your friends," Jackson said soothingly. "Folks will watch after you."

Slabs took a crumpled, dirty sheet from the foot of the bed and covered Eppie's frozen body with it. "We should be getting her to town," he said.

"Is Ma gonna have to be put in the ground like they done my pa when he got broke?" Willie asked flatly.

"Yeah, Willie," Slabs answered, "we have to bury people when they can't be fixed."

"OK," Willie said agreeably. "Can I go to town with Ma? I'm powerful cold an' hungry."

It struck me hard that Willie had been in this freezing cabin with his dead mother for over two days.

"Sure, Willie," Inman spoke up. "I'll take you to Fong's and you can eat all you want. We have an extra room in the hotel. You can stay there."

I helped Slabs carry Eppie and put her in the freight wagon. She was skinny and not much of a burden, but we had to angle her out the door because of her arms being stretched out and rigid like they were.

"She'll have to thaw some before I can fit her into a box," the undertaker commented.

When we climbed on the wagon to leave, Willie yelled for us to wait, ran to where a snowdrift had piled up alongside the cabin, and began pawing his way into it. We watched as the snow flew. After a few minutes, he had that wheelbarrow of his dug out. He brushed the bed clean with his gloveless hands and carried it to the wagon.

"I wanna bring my barrow," he said.

"Sure, Willie," Slabs said with compassion as he reached over to take it from him.

"No!" Willie screamed, yanking his wheelbarrow back. "I want to take Ma in my barrow."

All of us looked at him, wondering what to do.

"Let's put her in it," Jackson said, walking to stand beside Willie. "I don't reckon Eppie'll mind, and it's too cold to argue."

"Well, at least tie her on so she don't fall off," Slabs ordered.

I climbed down from the wagon and helped get Willie's mother lined up in that wheelbarrow. Jackson went looking for some rope, but couldn't find any, so we tied her on with dynamite fuse.

"I'll be down early tonight," Jackson Lyman said before we left. "You boys take good care of Willie."

Slabs's parlor was in a frame wood building alongside his log cabin. A hand-painted sign over double doors announced **R. Larson, Undertaker** in bright red letters. Willie headed straight to the place.

"Here's where my pa went when he got broke," Willie said as we came to take Eppie's body off his wheelbarrow.

The undertaker's lack of recent business hadn't dimmed his optimism. Inside, the parlor was piled full of coffins. I noticed a few of them were tiny. I'd never thought of having to bury a baby before.

We put Eppie on a long wooden table next to the wall. Slabs went to the stove and began tossing in wood. "You fellows had best get Willie fed. There ain't no hurry to plant her. I'll have to hire a miner to blast a grave . . . the ground's frozen too hard to dig one."

While Inman went with Willie to eat, I took the wagon back to Tully at the mill. When I told about Eppie's being dead, he shook his head. "Willie's going to need a keeper. Either that or the sheriff'll have to take him to the booby hatch."

"Someone will look after him," I said, then walked to my bar.

A couple of hours later, Inman came over. The snow had stopped falling, but the sky had grown dark and Ed had just left to fire up the streetlights.

"I got Willie fed and into the hotel," Inman said. "He ate four steaks. My guess is the guy hasn't had a bite to eat or slept for days. When his head hit the pillow, he began snoring up a storm."

"Tell Fong I'll pay for what Willie ate," I said.

"Already done that," Inman replied with a smile.

Jackson Lyman came in later wearing a concerned look. "Milo," he said, "could we talk by ourselves?"

I tossed Inman my apron and took a seat

with Jackson at the back table.

Jackson flicked his eyes about the room and pulled some envelopes out of his coat. "I was closing up Eppie's place after you guys left," he said. "These papers were there on top of the table. Eppie had a deed to the mine laying there. I reckon she knew her time was short because she'd made out a deed to Willie, giving him the mine, but hadn't gotten it recorded yet."

"Then Willie owns the Pavlak mine," I said.

"Yep, but, if he can't eat it or push it, I reckon Willie wouldn't have much of a clue what to do with it."

"You're right, Jackson. What do you think ought to be done?"

"Milo, we just hit a big strike," he said in a hushed tone. "That gold vein is now as wide as Dumb Dora's bottom."

"Then Willie's got money?"

"The lease calls for the Pavlaks to get ten percent of the mill receipts. I've got a check for just over two hundred dollars with me for their part of that first ore run."

"No one needs to know any more than the fact he owns the mine. It's going to cost money to watch after him. If you made out a check, do you suppose Willie could sign his name?"

"When pigs start flying, maybe," Jackson said hopelessly through his tobacco-stained beard.

"Maybe we could get the law to set up a guardian?" I ventured.

Jackson glared at me like I'd just thrown up on the table. "Milo, they'd just stuff poor Willie in the nut house and take the mine for their troubles. If Jesse James were alive today, he'd be a working for the gov'ment."

I knew he had a point. "Just make out the check to Willie, and I'll witness his mark. We can do that at the bank. I don't think Jorgason will give us any problem. Then we'll set up a checking account for him. You can deposit his money into it."

"That's a good idea, but who's gonna see after him?" Jackson asked. "The Searcys don't have the time to make sure he don't head off some place, pushing that wheelbarrow."

"He can stay here in the saloon. Inman or I will keep a watch on him. We'll let Willie chop wood and keep the place swept out."

Jackson looked relieved when he tucked those envelopes away. At the time, I didn't realize what I'd done to myself. I was mighty good at letting my mouth overload my hinder in those days.

Slabs came over the next afternoon and told me Eppie had finally thawed out enough for him to nail her into a box. Then he looked at me and said: "I heard you took Willie to the bank and opened him an account."

"And I reckon the ink hasn't dried," I answered testily.

"Well, I was wondering," the undertaker asked, "do you think maybe Willie could pay me? It's been a long spell since I've had a customer. I've hired Turkey Curley to blast out a grave. He'll want to be paid when he's done with it."

I said: "Sure, Slabs, how much?"

"Fifty dollars is all, unless you want a stone with her name chiseled on it."

"I think we can do without the rock," I said, taking a check from the cash register.

Ed Kinneson had sat Willie down at a table, trying to teach him to play dominoes. They both seemed to be enjoying themselves.

I went over and had Willie make his mark, then I filled out Slabs check. By taking over watching after his money, it was becoming apparent to me, I'd also inherited Willie himself.

"What about a funeral when we bury

her?" Slabs asked, as he grabbed his money. "Most folks think it's only right to say some words over 'em. Maybe you could read a little from the Good Book?"

"That would be a right nice thing for you to do, Milo," Ed Kinneson wheezed in agreement.

"I'll cover the bar while you're gone," Inman said cheerfully.

I've always been amazed at the number of pickles I could get into by just standing in one spot, trying to mind my own business.

"If we gotta put Ma in the ground, I'd like you to be there," Willie proclaimed, sealing my fate.

I was to get little sleep that night. Before Slabs left, we had agreed to bury Eppie at two o'clock the next afternoon. Jackson Lyman told me the Bruckners and he would take off work to attend. Then Tully said he'd show up. There were probably five hundred people living in Jarbidge. Before the night was over, it seemed half of them were going to make an appearance at Eppie's funeral. And every dad-blasted one of them was expecting me to say the words.

When I got back to my cabin, I lit a couple of kerosene lamps and began poring through stacks of books. I wished I'd had a Bible, but the one Mom had always carried to church had gotten blown up and I'd never replaced it.

The Ten Commandments were all I remembered. How that could help, I didn't know. The one about love your neighbor wouldn't do for Eppie Pavlak. If God had thought of her when he wrote it, Bible-bangers would have to make do with only nine rules.

Then I thought of that metal box of Dave Bourne's still buried in the closet. I'd planned to give it to him, but, with everything going on, I forgot. When I dug through it before to try and find where he had gone, I saw the eulogy for his wife, Hattie, inside.

When I read it by flickering yellow lantern light, I felt like I might not make such a fool of myself in front of everyone tomorrow.

The Jarbidge Cemetery lies on a treeless and wind-blown piece of flat land on the west side of the river about a mile north of town. The iron gate had been opened to admit Slabs's black and polished silver hearse pulled by an old dapple horse.

Fred Searcy and I walked together behind the undertaker's coach, followed by what seemed to be most of the people in town. Until that time, I had not realized how many women were living here. I counted over thirty, dressed in black and wrapped in heavy coats as we trudged through the snow in our deliberate pace to the cemetery.

Willie Pavlak followed behind Fred and me, pushing that wheelbarrow of his. We had tried with no success to talk him into leaving it behind.

The weather was fitting for a funeral. A pewter sky blotted out the sun. Gusts of frigid wind bit at reddened cheeks as it blew flakes of snow down that steep cañon.

Dark dirt from the freshly dug grave stood out forebodingly against the white blanket of snow. Slabs and Turkey Curley carried the pine box to the open, final resting place of Eppie Pavlak and lowered it into the depths by ropes.

I took the eulogy I'd worked so hard on from my coat pocket with gloved hands. I swallowed hard and, remembering to speak loud against the wind, I read.

"First I must say to all of you assembled here to bid farewell to Eppie Pavlak that I'm no minister. I'm only a fellow human being on this planet, struggling as we all are upon the mystery of death. Only days ago, Eppie was as we are now, a living being with hopes and aspirations, trials and tribulations. Now, she has crossed that great chasm that must forever separate us.

"As Eppie Pavlak is now, so shall we be. I do not know what awaits us in death, nor does anyone. We can only live in hope of a better tomorrow on the other side of this veil of tears. The most mortals can do is say good bye from the depths of our hearts and as long as we, the living, remember them, the dead are not truly so."

Dave Bourne must have had a good minister, for, when I folded that piece of paper and put it away, I could hear any number of sobs through the wind. When I saw a tear leak out of Fred Searcy's eye, I knew I'd done a decent job.

When we began our walk back to town, I was relieved as could be that it was over. I was looking forward to forgetting all about funerals. Little did I know just how shortly it would be before I would be called on to perform this sad task again.

Chapter Sixteen

After we got Eppie planted that bleak and cold November afternoon, the urge struck me to get out of town for a couple of days. Moving around always perks me up when I get down in the dumps. I bought a ticket on the stage and rode on top alongside Fred. All he could talk about was Marybeth and how much he was looking forward to being married.

"You know, I even bought her one of those new Mississippi washing machines," he proudly told me as we drove through lightly falling snow. "All you do is dump your dirty clothes in. Then you add some soap and a few gallons of hot water. There's a handle on the side. You grab that and shake the thing for a quarter of an hour or so, and you're ready to hang 'em up to dry. Life's a bunch easier on a woman when you buy her work-saving things like that."

I cocked my head toward him. "You might

think on getting some new records for that Graphophone. Italian opera sounds an awful lot like having a weasel in your chicken coop."

"Nope," he replied firmly. "All women with class like that stuff. Opera ain't so bad once you get used to it."

"Folks say the same thing about having a carbuncle."

"You done a right nice job of laying Eppie away yesterday," Fred said to change the subject. "I reckon you'll do until we get a preacher."

"Have you heard anything about one venturing to Jarbidge?"

"Nope, but, with the place booming like it is, we're bound to get one sooner or later. Marybeth and I are gonna need a sky pilot to say the words when we get hitched. If we don't have one by then, you'll have to do the job."

"Fred Searcy," I said tersely, "just watch the dad-blasted road, will you?"

Kitty Wilkins ran over and gave me one of her rib-cracking bear hugs when we made our stopover there. "Some freighters said you made a decent stump preacher when they laid Eppie away."

"Reckon that's why we thought you might

be a damn' lawyer the first time we seen you," Reece Morgan said with a grin. "Preachers and lawyers both have a way with fancy words. Lawyers charge more for theirs, however."

"Milo's got too much good sense to be either a preacher or a lawyer," Fred Searcy interjected, "but he can talk prettier than a ten-dollar whore. He's gonna marry me and my bride iffen we don't have a *real* parson by the time she gets here."

"That's good to know," Kitty said to Fred while I was standing there with my mouth open. "Reece popped the question to me just the other day. We'd be real beholding if Milo here could do a wedding for us, too."

My head began spinning from how fast a man can get hornswoggled into one thing after another while he just stood in one spot and kept his mouth shut.

"I'm happy for you," I managed to say, "but you need a real preacher. Don't you have to have paperwork filled out?"

"Damn it, Milo," Reece boomed. "My folks were married for forty years, and they didn't fill out no blasted papers. If Kitty wants you to say the words, you'll do it."

Reece swatted Kitty playfully on her ample bottom, eliciting a schoolgirl yelp as she spun to go into the kitchen.

★ ★ ★

The rest of that cold and rattling trip, I was lost in deep thought, planning dark and devious methods to get even with Fred Searcy. Being made into a preacher was grounds for fighting. Finally I decided there was nothing I could do to him that would be any worse than what he'd already done to himself when he bought that Graphophone and a stack of screaming Italian opera recordings.

I checked into the hotel, took a long, hot bath, and slept until nearly noon. After stopping by a restaurant for the best plate of chicken and dumplings I'd ever eaten, I was off to reward myself for my good fortune. So far this year, I'd nearly been blown up, hanged, shot, and almost killed by a two-by-four. The fact I was still around was cause for celebrating.

There was absolutely no doubt in my mind what I wanted: a shiny new Packard twelve-cylinder automobile. It was every young man's dream in those days to own a car like that. I had been unsuccessful in love and the Lost Sheepherder's Mine was still as lost as ever, but, thanks to Dave Bourne's generosity, I *could* buy that new car.

The Packard dealer tried to give me the bum's rush. A fat, hog-jowled, cigar-chomping salesman sized me up as just a skinny kid and wouldn't even show me a picture of what I wanted. I was getting into a huff when Theodore Spurgeon walked out of the owner's office.

"Well, hello, Mister Goodman," the lawyer said cheerfully, "how is your business in Jarbidge doing?"

"Mighty fine," I answered. "So good, in fact, I think I may take the train to Boise and buy my new car there."

At that statement, a slender, gray-haired man popped out of the office, pushed his way past Spurgeon, and offered his hand. "My name is Russ Alexander. I own this business. You'll save money by buying that car right here."

"Mister Goodman was one of the owners of Bourne Mining Company when we sold to the Guggenheims," the lawyer said loudly, obviously enjoying himself.

I nodded toward the fat salesman. "This fellow doesn't seem to want to do business with me."

"Why don't you buy the dealership, then you can fire him," Spurgeon said. "I think owning a Packard franchise would be a good investment."

The pig-faced salesman's mouth fell open. That stub of a cigar he was chewing on dropped and landed in his pants cuff. When the fat man burned his fingers, trying to fish it out, I decided lawyers aren't all bad.

"Nelson," Russ Alexander said icily to his employee, "we'll have a little talk about your attitude later."

Spurgeon and I couldn't help but chuckle when the pudgy salesman beat a red-faced retreat, sucking on two fingers.

"By the way," the lawyer finally managed to say, "that Model T of yours is out back of my office."

"That's Dave's truck," I said. "He bought it from me."

"And he gave it right back," Spurgeon affirmed. "Dave left a bill of sale to you."

Russ Alexander took great pains to make sure my new Packard was ordered exactly the way I wanted. "A car this nice is far too expensive for me to keep in stock," he said apologetically. "But I will have one for you in a month or so. We'll personally deliver it to you in Jarbidge."

I wrote a check for the full amount and handed it to the grinning dealer with a flourish. When I left with Spurgeon to go to his office, the fat salesman looked questioningly from a window at me. I couldn't help sticking my tongue out at him.

"How's Kitty's lawsuit going against that Logan character?" I asked the lawyer as we walked the few blocks to his office.

"Not good, I'm afraid. Logan has a strong legal position. If Kitty had just filled out some simple paperwork earlier, this whole matter could have been avoided."

"She's not real big on signing papers."

"People like her and Reece made this country," Theodore Spurgeon said with a touch of feeling in his voice. "Governments create nothing . . . they exist by taking from those who do. C. C. Logan has the support of the letter of the law. Kitty has the spirit of the law . . . and me . . . on her side. We'll go to court next spring most likely."

"As long as she can run that little way station and sell some wild horses, I reckon she'll be happy." Then, as an afterthought, I blurted out: "She and Reece want to get married, and they want me to do the preaching."

The lawyer stopped dead in his tracks. "Milo Goodman, how in the world do you get involved in the things you do?"

"I seem to have a talent."

Theodore Spurgeon sighed and resumed walking. "Those two have been living together so long, it's common law already. If it makes them happy, go ahead and say some words."

This wasn't what I wanted to hear, but quickly decided Fred Searcy wouldn't consult a lawyer on the matter.

The Model T looked worse than I remembered. That antelope had completely taken out the front windshield. It would be a cold and windy drive home.

While I was waiting for the engine to warm up, Spurgeon walked over. "Milo, you should leave some of that money you made with me."

"Why's that?" I asked.

"If I've ever met anyone who's likely to need a lawyer in the future, it's you."

A bright sun that gave off as much warmth as a banker's heart was hanging in a cloudless blue sky when I headed home the next morning, driving that battered Model T.

Snow began laying across the road in scattered patches. Before I hit that precipitous drop-off into Kitty's Hot Hole, I stopped and put chains on the two wheels that had brakes. About halfway down, I rounded a sharp curve and nearly ran into Willie, pushing his wheelbarrow up the middle of the road. I jammed my foot down hard on what brakes there were and slid on the snow, finally coming to a stop only inches from Willie.

He looked at me and grinned. "Howdy, Mister Milo. I got to worryin' about you an' come lookin'."

My heart was doing flip-flops. "Willie, you can't go running around the country with that wheelbarrow," I sputtered. "You'll get yourself killed."

Willie shot a glance at the narrow space separating his wheelbarrow from my front bumper. "There's lots of room."

Reece Morgan came riding up on horseback. A look a relief washed across his leathery face when he saw Willie hadn't been flattened. "Kitty saw him when he came through. It took me a few minutes to get saddled up."

"I was comin' to help Mister Milo," Willie spoke. "I like to help."

"We know you do, Willie," I said, calming down. "If you'd put your wheelbarrow in the bed and ride back to town with me, I need your help at the bar."

"OK," Willie said agreeably.

I was glad to have Willie along when it came time to tackle that icy grade back of Kitty's. The chained drive wheels didn't have enough weight over them to get traction. We threw a few hundred pounds of rocks in the bed, and, with Willie pushing away, we finally got that Model T backed up to the top of the mesa.

The rest of the trip, Willie sat beside me, grinning at everything he saw. When a large herd of wild horses ran by us across the snowy flatland, however, he got so excited he stood up and nearly fell out.

A new crib in Cherry Flat's had been finished during my absence. Smoke coming from the chimney told me it was stocked and ready. I thought I might check it out, as long as the newcomer wasn't a blonde. After that disaster with Featherlegs, I was still skittish about the species.

My biggest concern at the moment was Willie. The fact he'd slipped past everyone in town with that wheelbarrow and headed off, looking for me, was disturbing.

When we came into the saloon, Inman expressed dismay over the fact Willie had ever left, thinking he was in the hotel. There was no doubt in my mind that in a short period of time, I'd become both a preacher and the guardian for Willie Pavlak.

The next few weeks passed routinely. As long as I stayed in town, Willie seemed content. His restaurant bill at Fong's was staggering. One evening alone, he ate six steaks. Jackson Lyman was taking out plenty of ore, so money wasn't of much concern. My biggest problem was keeping him busy. Finally Matt Whort became my lifetime friend by letting him help out at the stable. Willie loved feeding and grooming the mules and horses. When I paid those god-awful feed bills for those two mules of mine, who did nothing but stand in one place and eat, I felt like I was getting something in return. With Willie occupied, I now had time to do a few things I wanted to do.

The new girl in town turned out to be a plump blonde called Lumpy Linda. From Inman's reports, her lumps were all in the right places, however. Since she had the same hair color as the gal who gave half of Jarbidge the clap, I decided to see who had taken over Red Fox's old place.

It seemed like all it did was snow that winter. When I walked to Cherry Flats, the stuff was coming down so heavy I could barely see two feet. That was no problem because the trail was well beaten. The only crib with a red lantern out was the one Red used to occupy. A couple of miners were standing around, nervously blowing on their hands to keep them warm. I'd heard nothing about this new girl, so I walked up and knocked.

A wispy-thin, young girl with a ghostly white pallor and deep sunken eyes opened the door. She wore a thin nightgown and heavy make-up in a sad attempt to look appealing. When the cold air struck her lungs, the girl began coughing uncontrollably, a sure sign of consumption. Finally she was able to compose herself. "I'm Tina, please come in, it's awful cold out there."

"Uh, no, thanks," I stuttered. My inclination and everything else had softened when I set eyes on this pathetic creature.

"Please, mister," she sobbed, "no one will go with me. I've not had anything to eat for two days."

I tossed the silver dollar I'd been clutching onto her bed. Then I turned away. I heard more coughing echoing in the chill quiet air, then the sound of the door slamming.

One of the men brushed snow from his long coat as I walked past. "Now you know why we're waitin'. At least she'll be gone soon, then maybe we'll get a healthy one."

I shoved my hands into my pockets and, without saying a word, walked back to the bar in the snow.

The storm increased in its intensity that night. With the light of morning, drifts could be seen blown even with the roofs of some houses. During the day, the snow and wind continued unabated.

By mid-afternoon, the wind quit as suddenly as it had begun. A few flakes of snow drifted lazily from a dark sky when the road crew finished their task and returned to Jarbidge.

Inman was tending bar to a packed house. Most of the mines were snowed in; even the Elkoro mill construction was halted due to the heavy snow. Huptman and the Bruckners had Willie at a table, playing dominoes. To my amazement, Willie had not only mastered the game, few could beat him. I noticed Inman kept nervously looking at that big regulator clock.

"What's the matter?" I finally asked. "You have a hot date with Lumpy Linda?"

"The stage isn't in yet," he replied in a worried tone.

Tully shot a glance outside. "It'll be dark pretty soon. If we're gonna go looking to see if he's slid off Crippen Grade, we'll have to do it right soon."

Inman said: "Fred was concerned about making this trip. He's carrying over three thousand dollars in cash money."

Chapter Seventeen

"I'll run up to the Stray Dog and round up some more men," Butt-Block said quickly.

The place grew quiet and a few men began murmuring among themselves, then left to get guns. I wasn't the only one concerned that Fred may have run into more problems than the weather.

Only a few minutes after Butt-Block left, he returned accompanied by over a dozen men. If I'd been wearing Roebucker teeth, I'd have swallowed them when I saw Ben Kuhl leading the pack.

"They were getting ready to head out when I got there," Butt-Block said, shaking snow from his boots. "Kuhl had already pointed out how late the stage was and was getting folks together to go looking for it."

I didn't believe Ben Kuhl could organize a decent dog fight, but there he was, barking out orders and urging men to hurry.

Then I saw Billy McGraw standing by the

stove, warming his hands. I walked over and put my hand on his shoulder. He bolted like a green colt, his blue eyes wide with fear.

"Leave me be," Billy growled. "I didn't do nothing."

"No one said you did," I replied in surprise.

"Nothing to say," he mumbled, pulling his hat down hard. "Nothing at all." With that, he spun and walked away, leaving an odor of whiskey lingering in the air.

"Let's get moving, boys!" Ben Kuhl's voice boomed. "It's gonna be dark soon."

I felt something strange was going on here, but I couldn't put my finger on it. I pulled on my heavy felt topcoat and followed behind Kuhl as we headed out into the cold and gloomy twilight. The snow came up to our knees, making for hard going. As we trudged slowly past Cherry Flats, heading toward Crippen Grade, many of the older men fell behind. I was surprised to see Billy McGraw among them. At the time, I couldn't understand why he was hanging back.

Ben Kuhl kept a fast pace, his breath leaving white clouds hanging in the still air as he pushed onward. Inman and I were hard on his heels. Then, in a grove of leafless aspen trees, we saw the stagecoach.

The six horses pulling it had wandered off the road. Faced with a precipitous rock cliff ahead, they were unable to go any farther, or back up. Fred Searcy was sitting high in the driver's seat in his usual place on the right hand side by the brake.

"Hey, Fred, we've come to help!" I yelled.

"He's so cold, he can't move," Inman said.

I pulled myself up to that seat alongside Fred where I'd spent so many hours. "We'll get you into town and warmed up."

Fred sat there staring straight into the rock cliff. I had a feeling of dread as I reached over and shook his shoulder. Then his hat fell off and I could see his brains from where a bullet had blown away the back of his head.

"Oh, my God!" I shouted, nausea sweeping my guts.

"They've robbed the stage and killed the driver," Ben Kuhl snarled.

Fred always carried the first-class and registered mail in heavy, canvas bags stowed in a compartment under his seat. Now they were alongside his body and covered with blood and bits of flesh. White envelopes with crimson smears made by the killer's hands littered the top of the stagecoach.

"Let's get a posse together, boys. We'll go after the bastards!" Ben Kuhl yelled out.

Tully Moxness was standing in the road where the stage had left it. "There's no new tracks heading up the pass," he announced. "Whoever did this went to town after they finished."

"You don't know any such thing," Kuhl growled.

"Tully's right," Jackson Lyman said firmly. "Fred was the last one down the hill. The stage tracks cover the rest. You can even see where the robbers waited, trampling the snow down. There's some cigarette butts that tell me they was here a spell."

Butt-Block held his arms wide to keep men away. "There's footprints from two robbers. One set's bigger than the other."

"Sure as hell, ain't no one left over the pass!" Inman bellowed loudly. "The murdering sons-of-bitches that did this are still in Jarbidge!"

"I tell you, we've got to get after them," Ben Kuhl repeated. "They're getting away while you men are yammering."

"Show me some tracks leaving town after that stage came down, and maybe I'll believe you," Tully Moxness said. "It seems to me you're mighty anxious to lead everyone off on a wild-goose chase."

"Hey, me, Ed, and Billy were at the Success when this happened. You can ask anyone!" Ben Kuhl shouted angrily.

"They made a mighty big point of letting us know they were there, too!" a miner yelled. "Kuhl bought a round for the bar and made sure to tell us what time it was when he did it."

While this arguing was going on, I kept my eyes on Billy McGraw. He had walked away from the crowd to the stagecoach. For a while he stood beside it with his head lowered, then he climbed up and looked at Fred Searcy's body. I heard him starting to gag. Then he jumped down, ran a few feet, and began throwing up.

I trudged through the deep snow to stand behind him. "What is it, Billy?"

"Leave me alone, Milo," he snapped.

"They're going to find out what happened here."

Billy McGraw's voice shook as he cried: "I didn't know they were gonna do this. I don't want to hang!"

"Who did it, Billy?"

"They didn't tell me nothing until it was over."

"Who did this, Billy?" I repeated.

"He just told me he wanted to borrow my gun. Ben Kuhl and Ed Beck . . . they had my

207

pistol." Billy's lanky body began quivering like an aspen tree in the wind. He fell to his knees and sobbed: "I don't want to hang. I don't want to hang."

I went back to the road where everyone was still arguing. When I told them what Billy had confessed, anyone who had a gun pointed it at Ben Kuhl or Ed Beck.

"Tie 'em up and don't be gentle about it," Inman Searcy growled when he brought a rope back from the stagecoach.

Kuhl and Beck began cursing and fighting, but it did them no good. In short order they were wrestled to the ground and hog-tied. Billy meekly stuck his hands out to be bound, tears streaming down his pale cheeks.

Leaving a few men to bring in the stage-coach and Fred's body, the rest of us marched the robbers to the Jarbidge jail. It was a small, one-room concrete and log building with a single iron-bound door. Since I'd been in town, the only use it had gotten was to sober up an occasional drunk.

Inman grabbed Ben Kuhl and threw him into the cell so hard he smashed his nose on the wall and it began bleeding.

"I'll get you bastards," Kuhl snarled through the dripping blood. Then his cold gaze fixed on me. "You did this to me,

Goodman. I had a job, then you went and ruined me. It may take the rest of my life, but I *will* kill you."

"I don't think Milo's the one who oughta be worried," Tully Moxness said as he herded Ed Beck and Billy into the tiny little cell and slammed the door closed. "If you boys don't get lynched before the sheriff takes you to get hung, you should count your blessings."

Ed Beck and Kuhl shared a one-room cabin no bigger than a crib below the Elkoro mine office next to the river. When we searched their rat's nest, we found an overcoat Kuhl wore occasionally, hanging on a nail. Dried and crusty patches of blood covered the front of it. I found a .44 pistol in a drawer with one spent cartridge under the firing pin. Nearly 200 silver dollars were crammed under a mattress.

"I thought you said Fred was carrying over three thousand dollars," Jackson Lyman asked Inman.

"He was bringing in three thousand in gold for the bank and two hundred in silver for Adams's store."

"They didn't have to kill him," Inman said flatly, as if he'd been drained of all emotion.

"That's something Kuhl just wanted to do," I replied.

Tully said: "I'll get hold of the law in Elko."

"Let's hang the bastards," Inman said coldly.

Tully looked him in the face through a flickering light. "The law's what separates us from the likes of Ben Kuhl. I reckon you'll see him hang, but let's do it legal."

Inman pursed his lips. "I've got to go tell Ma before she finds out from someone else. After losing Pa and now Fred, I think this'll kill her."

Once Inman left on his sad task, Tully, Jackson, and I went to the Elkoro office. When the lights were turned on, the huge amount of blood that drenched Kuhl's overcoat glared at us. The pistol had Billy's initials carved deeply into the wood grip. The groves were filled with blood.

Tully made his call, and announced the sheriff and deputies were leaving as quickly as they could.

"What do you think they did with the gold?" Jackson queried.

"I'm betting Ben Kuhl's the only one who knows," I said. "Billy wasn't there, and Ed Beck isn't smart enough to hide an Easter egg."

Tully looked at me. "Let's go to your place. I need a beer."

That night of December 5th was a long one. The bar was packed with men, some angry and others quietly sitting alone, lost in thought.

Jackson came back from checking out the jail around midnight. "There's two guards with shotguns watching over 'em," he said. "Kuhl and Beck are snoring up a storm. They went to sleep like nothing happened . . . all but that McGraw kid, he's humped up in the corner, crying."

Willie had been sitting at the end of the bar for a long time, listening to everyone's talk. He was wearing that fur cap I'd bought him with the earflaps that stuck straight out. He looked at us and asked: "Why do folks have to die?"

Two days later, Sheriff Joe Harris, from Elko, came into town, driving a prison wagon with steel-barred windows. The thing was so heavy it was pulled by a team of ten horses. The sheriff was accompanied by a United States marshal and a postal detective. Since the robbery included tampering with the U.S. Mail, it became a federal as well as state crime.

Sheriff Harris took the bloody overcoat,

Billy's gun, and the cut mail sacks and letters that had been smeared with blood into evidence.

After securing notarized statements from witnesses, including me, the tired lawmen took the three robbers into custody. When they led them from the little jail to the waiting coach, I walked down to watch. Huge, heavy chains fastened to their wrists and ankles rattled in the still air when they walked. When Ben Kuhl saw me, he stopped.

"Goodman," he spat, "you're a dead man."

The marshal had something black and leathery in his hand. He swatted it hard against one of Ben's big ears, knocking him to the snow-covered ground.

"No talking," he growled at the chained Kuhl.

Ben Kuhl slowly straightened up and tried to reach his bloody ear, but the handcuffs attached to the leg irons prevented this. Before he climbed into the iron-covered coach, he received one more blow from the officer when he looked at me colder than the icy air and growled: "Believe it."

I was gratified to see Ben Kuhl in the company of such fine, upstanding law officers.

Sylvia Searcy took it hard. Inman said all she would do was sit in her rocking chair, crying and drinking. He quit his job tending bar to run the post office. Under the circumstances, I couldn't blame him. Sylvia had had a hard time sorting mail even before all this happened.

Fred Searcy's burial service took place on a sunny Friday afternoon, the 8th of December. The town had dug itself out from that heavy storm and work on the Elkoro mill resumed. Every single business and mine in the vicinity shut down at lunchtime that day. Some men snow-shoed in for miles from remote mines high in the mountains to attend Fred's funeral.

At one o'clock, Slabs slowly drove his somber hearse down the main street of Jarbidge. The coach's polished silver ornaments sparkled brightly in the sun. By the time he reached the Miners' Exchange, people walking behind were stretched out so far up the cañon, I couldn't see the end of them.

I took my place behind the hearse. Inman followed, driving a freight wagon he'd borrowed from Tully. His mother, Ed Kinneson, and a few folks too old or stove up to walk were bundled up in the back.

Turkey Curley was too drunk to help

213

Slabs handle the coffin so I assisted with the task. The undertaker had done a nice job of fixing Fred up. There was a glass window in the casket through which you could see him. No one could tell, when they looked, that the back of his head was gone.

It took a long time for everyone to file past the coffin and pay their last respects. Dumb Dora and the girls from Cherry Flats were there; even Tina, the skinny sick one from Red's old place coughed her way past. Everyone was surprised when each laid a fresh flower on Fred's casket. To this day, I have no clue how they came up with them.

Slabs and I lowered the coffin, then I read the same eulogy I'd used for Eppie, only I added some words about how good a man he was and would be deeply missed. Except for Tina's coughing and the occasional sob, not a sound could be heard in the cold, still air but my voice. The Bruckner brothers walked to the head of that open grave and began shoveling dirt. I was taken aback when they began singing loudly in German. They might not have known English, but they sure knew how to sing. Their wonderfully clear and strong voices reverberated from the snowy cliffs like a silver bell. No one except Adolph

Huptman understood a word, but, when they were finished, everyone's eyes were leaky, including mine.

My friend, Fred M. Searcy, innocent victim of the last stagecoach robbery ever to occur in the United States, was in the ground.

Over the next several days, things returned to what passed for normalcy in Jarbidge, Nevada. I was kept busy running the bar. All I knew of what was going on was from what folks told me. This was no problem because in a small town, you get the news at a bar before God does.

With the stagecoach robbers locked up in Elko jail, talk turned to what happened to the missing $3,000 in gold.

So many had searched the route from where the stage was held up to Kuhl and Beck's cabin, the snow was beaten flat as a Democrat's thinking. That shack of theirs was pried apart, board by board, and holes dug everywhere. A couple of desperate and not so bright searchers even shoveled out the bottom of their outhouse.

"They found a lot of interesting shit, but no gold," Jackson Lyman quipped.

Ed Kinneson came by early one afternoon just as I was opening up.

"I'm taking the stage out today," Ed

wheezed. "Wickenburg, Arizona's where I'm heading. The doc sez my breather will work better at low altitude." His gray eyes flashed about the room. "Take this an' add it to that jar you keep under the bar. It's hell to be old and sick." He dropped two twenty-dollar gold pieces in my hand. "You might oughta keep this between us."

As I took the money, I remembered the storm that day of the robbery had ripped out some mantles on those gas street lights. Ed had taken a ladder to replace them that afternoon. From a high vantage point, it was possible to see all the way to Cherry Flats. He could easily have seen Beck and Kuhl as they walked back to town — and underneath that bridge would have made a wonderful hiding place. . . .

"I'll take care of it," I told him.

I hope old Ed Kinneson got to enjoy Arizona for a long while.

Christmas was drawing near, and Jarbidge began taking on a festive air. A few spruce trees along Main Street were draped with tinsel. Charlie Fong had a tree cut and placed in a front window of his restaurant. Willie was fascinated by it, especially the gaily-wrapped boxes underneath.

"I never got a Christmas present," he said.

"Ma always tol' me it was a waste of money."

The next morning I kept Willie from his job at Whort's. Together, we walked up the hillside back of town and cut a Christmas tree. We put it next to the front window in the bar and wrapped the tree with strings of popcorn. After putting a bright gold star on top, I brought out two presents for Willie and set them underneath. He giggled like a little kid.

"Now, you can't open them until Christmas morning," I told him sternly.

"OK, Mister Milo," he said obediently as he scooted up a chair to sit in while staring longingly at his presents. Earlier, I'd ordered a fur cap for him from Frank Adams that would be big enough to fit his large head. The other box contained his own set of dominoes.

I had just finished swamping out some brass cuspidors that some customers had made an effort to hit when I answered a soft knock at the door. My heart went to somewhere near the bottom of my gut and began doing flip-flops when I opened that door.

The most beautiful girl I'd ever set eyes on stood there with a worried look on her freckled face. I knew in a heartbeat who she was.

"They told me at the express office to come see you," she said meekly. "I'm looking for Fred Searcy. My name is Marybeth Sears."

Chapter Eighteen

Before I could get a word out, Willie blurted: "Mister Searcy got himself kilt by outlaws. They had t' bury 'im like they done my ma."

I watched in helpless shock as the color drained from Marybeth's freckled face. She let out a soft sigh like someone had let the air out of her, then swooned limp into my arms.

Willie grew so frightened when he saw her faint, he jumped up, sending his chair flying. "I didn't mean to break her, honest, I di'n't."

"She'll be fine, Willie," I said. "The lady's just fainted. She's not broken."

The sweet familiar scent of lilacs hung in the air when I carried her inside. I had taught Willie always to make sure the front door stayed closed. This time the poor guy was so rattled, he stood on the wrong side when he shut it and locked himself out.

I didn't have much of a clue what to do. Smelling salts were something I'd heard were necessary in situations like this. The only problem was, I didn't have any.

Willie's face pressed against the front window, staring in like a cow looking at a strange calf.

"Run to the store and bring back some smelling salts, and hurry!" I yelled. He nodded and ran off.

Marybeth's blue eyes flickered open as a sob escaped her lips. "I'm fine now . . . please put me down," she said softly.

There was no hurry on my part to let her go. "You've had a terrible shock. I'm sorry about Willie. He's a little simple."

For such a frail-looking girl, she was surprisingly strong. Marybeth elbowed her way from my arms, stomped her feet to the floor, and backed away. "Thank you, Mister . . . ?"

I told her my name and asked her politely to take a chair at a table, which she did. "Would you like some brandy or coffee?"

"A cup of coffee would be nice," she said, dabbing at her eyes with a hankie. "Then would you please tell me what happened to Fred Searcy?"

I told her I would, then decided to wash out the cups before filling them. While doing this, I couldn't help but stare at her.

The picture I'd seen earlier didn't begin to do her justice. Locks of long, curly auburn hair cascaded down her shoulders, framing the cutest face a girl could own. I also approved of her choice in perfume.

After setting down the two cups of coffee, I scooted back a chair when a loud banging on the door forced me to go let Willie in.

"I'm powerful glad she ain't broke," he said happily, shoving a box into my hands.

I didn't know what use I would have for a sack of salt and some tins of sardines.

"Them smelly little fishies are good eatin'. Do they help fix folks, too?" Willie asked.

After I got Willie settled down at the bar with a root beer, crackers, and a can opener for the sardines, I sat down with Marybeth. She looked at me with sad acceptance as I told her how Fred Searcy had been murdered by Ben Kuhl and Ed Beck for the money he was carrying on the stagecoach.

"I don't know what to do," she sighed. "All I knew of Fred was from the letters he sent me. He seemed like such a wonderful man."

"He was. Fred was a good friend of mine. He was one of the first people I met when I came to town," I said, carefully leaving out just *where* I'd made his acquaintance.

Marybeth pursed her lips and looked so sad and helpless I felt like crying myself.

"I can't go back to Missouri," she said despairingly. "When I told my grandmother I was going out West to get married, she sold her home and moved into a boarding house."

There were at least 200 men in Jarbidge who would have gladly come to her rescue. A beautiful single girl like Marybeth would have miners tripping over their tongues, running just to get a look at her. Under these trying circumstances, I felt it was my responsibility to make sure she was spared this fate.

"Please," I said softly, "let me see to a room for you at the hotel."

She looked at me with sad doe eyes. "I'm afraid I have no money. Fred sent me just enough to get here. I never expected that I might have to leave."

"Don't you worry about a thing," I said in the most comforting tone I could muster, then went to the cash register, took out a handful of money, and handed it to her. "This is the least I can do. I'll walk you to the hotel. When you've rested, maybe you can join me for dinner at Fong's restaurant, this evening."

She looked at the stack of bills with fresh tears welling. "I can't accept this. You don't even know me."

That was something I desperately wanted to change. "Of course, I do. You're name is Marybeth Sears, and I think you could use a friend right about now."

I felt better when she tucked the money into a small purse, then took my arm when I escorted her to the hotel.

Once I had her settled into the room next to Willie's, I began racking my brain, trying to come up with someone who could tend bar while I took Marybeth to dinner. I decided Jackson Lyman would do it; friends are totally worthless if you can't use them for something once in a while.

The saying — "When it rains, it pours." — was born in Jarbidge. I was tending bar by rote that afternoon, thinking of nothing else but having dinner with a beautiful, sweet-smelling girl. A few miners, mostly those who worked nights, were soaking up suds when suddenly one of them shot a glance out the window and shouted: "Oh, my God, look at that, will you!"

I spun around to see what the attraction was. The sharpest-looking, jet-black Packard twelve-cylinder automobile in the state had just parked in front of the bar.

Russ Alexander climbed out and stood looking impatiently down the street. Shortly the fat salesman, who had nearly set himself on fire, pulled to a stop behind the Packard. He was driving a white Buick with a canvas top. His face was red from the cold and his teeth were clenched tightly around the stub of a cigar.

"Tarnation," one miner said longingly, staring at the shiny Packard, "that thing's purtier than a twenty-dollar whore."

I felt the buttons strain on my shirt. "Boys," I said proudly, "you're looking at my new car."

A miner held his glass of beer in front of his face and spun it. "I've gotta quit lookin' for gold," he commented dourly. "Owning a bar's where the money is."

I grinned and went to meet Russ and his hired man as they came in the front door, stomping snow from their boots.

"Your car should have been here over a week ago," Russ Alexander apologized as he handed me the keys. "That storm delayed its arrival. Please feel free to drop by my dealership any time for the next two years, and we'll wash it for free."

It's nice being the center of attention when you're not at a hanging. The miners at the bar left their drinks to gape and paw

224

over my new Packard. I couldn't have felt more proud if I'd been elected to Congress, only then I'd be headed for perdition. You can own a fancy car and keep your soul.

My mind was on picking up Marybeth and driving her the few hundred feet from the hotel to Fong's. I knew she'd be impressed. Then I was given something else to think about.

"Well, Mister Nelson, I hope you enjoy living in Jarbidge," Russ Alexander said. "I've got to be going back to Twin Falls."

The fat salesman rolled the cigar in his mouth and looked at me. I noticed he didn't have a fire in the thing, so, if he dropped it this time, he wouldn't burn his pants up.

"I got fired," he said simply. "I guess selling cars isn't something I'm cut out for."

Russ Alexander nodded his head in agreement. "In three months of working for me, Egbert never sold a single car."

"*Egbert!*" I blurted without thinking. "Now, there's a name that fits. I've never seen anyone built more like an egg."

The ex-car salesman's chubby face took on a crimson glow. "I'll have you all know I was named after the first King of England."

"We're fresh out of kings and the like here in Jarbidge," a miner chuckled. "I reckon we'll just call you Eggs."

"What kind of work have you done in the past?" I asked, hoping to stop a row.

"I'll have you know I've tended bar in the best hotels in San Francisco," the fat man shot back proudly.

Occasionally I've let my mouth overload my hinder. I wanted a bartender more than anything right now.

Putting on my best I'm-sorry-trust-me smile, I turned to Egbert Nelson. "Come to think of it, I've never met anyone named after a king . . . that's quite an honor."

A miner began choking on his beer.

"Why, thank you," Egbert replied cheerfully. "I believe possibly I've misjudged you."

"Enjoy your new Packard," Russ Alexander said, shaking my hand. "Please don't hesitate to contact me should you have any questions or problems."

I said my good byes and watched as he went to the still-running Buick, set out two suitcases, and drove away. The tire chains crunched in the frozen snow when he turned around.

"He'll freeze his ass off," Egbert commented. "That car doesn't have a heater."

Egbert retrieved his luggage and carried it into the bar, puffing from the effort. "Let me buy a beer," he wheezed, dropping a quarter on the counter, "then I'll make the rounds to see if I can find a job."

A few minutes' worth of well-placed bullshit can often accomplish wonders. In twenty minutes, I had Egbert Nelson wrapped in an apron and washing beer glasses. When he took his hat off, the only hair he owned was a brown swath just above his ears. The rest of his head was bald as a rock.

"Grass don't grow on a busy street," he commented jovially about his lack of hair.

With a fresh cigar clenched in his teeth, Eggs watched over customers like a mother hen looking after a brood of chicks. He always carried a towel draped over his forearm to wipe up any spills. All told, he was a real improvement over Inman — or me.

After telling Eggs how he would have to keep an eye on Willie, I went to my cabin to get cleaned up for dinner with Marybeth. I had a new Packard and a bartender hired; I was immensely proud of myself.

That new car purred like a contented kitten when I pulled up to the hotel. I left the motor running to keep the heater on. Marybeth acted duly impressed when I opened the door for her. I would have liked to have driven her around town, but the snow was only shoveled out where the freight wagons went. Getting stuck would cast a shadow on my natural good sense.

When we entered Fong's restaurant, Marybeth took off her coat and hung it on a rack by the door. This caused at least two glasses to spill and twenty eyeballs nearly to pop out of their sockets. She had a body on her that would have caused Adam to eat an apple knowing God would kick his butt for it. Her ample breasts strained against a tight print dress. When she walked, her movements were soft and fluid as if she was moving to music.

I don't recall what I ate for dinner that night, my mind was on other things. Marybeth ordered the oysters. It never occurred to me to warn her what she was getting, but she never complained. I remember her picking at them, saying she was a light eater. Later, over coffee, we talked for hours.

From our conversation I learned Marybeth was twenty-two years old. By the standards of the day, that put her in the "old maid" category and the reason for her answering an ad to become a mail-order bride.

A little white lie is necessary on occasion, so I told her I was twenty-two.

"I simply don't know what to do," she said. "Perhaps I should stay in town for a while. There seems to be more single men here than any place I've ever been."

From all the lecherous looks Marybeth was receiving, I figured her waiting time to find a man could be measured in minutes. Her hand trembled slightly when I grasped it.

"Now, don't you worry your pretty head about a thing," I told her sincerely. "Let me take you back to the hotel. If you'll consent to have breakfast with me in the morning, we can talk some more then."

"I'd like that very much," she cooed.

I took her by the arm and we walked together through a gently falling snow the short distance to the hotel. When we were at the door, I hoped she might give me a peck on the cheek. Instead, Marybeth wrapped her arms around me and squeezed tightly for the longest while. Then she softly kissed me on the lips. With a girlish giggle, she turned and fled into the hotel, leaving me standing there open-mouthed, trying to slow my heartbeat. A fragrance of lilacs hung in the chill mountain air for a moment, then drifted away on the breeze.

Eggs was tending to a packed bar when I went over to drink a beer and calm down. Butt-Block and Willie were playing dominoes at a back table. I was surprised to see

Willie losing for a change. The Bruckner brothers and Huptman were jabbering away in German, so Jackson Lyman seemed glad to see me. I had Eggs get us a couple of beers, and we took an empty table, up front, by the Christmas tree.

"How's the Pavlak mine looking?" I asked.

"Getting richer every time we blast. Willie can eat steaks for a long time on just what ore we have in sight. Maybe I can make enough money out of it, so I can afford to head off to Arizona like ole Kinneson done. God, I'd love to live where it don't snow so damn' much."

I looked past the Christmas tree to the street light and saw the snow was falling heavier than before. "Jackson, if you lived in the desert, you'd still crawl into a hole and work all day. It doesn't snow underground."

"Nope, but shoveling my way to and from that hole gets mighty old after a spell." He took a sip of beer, and his smile fled. "Did anyone tell you about Ben Kuhl and the other robbers?"

"I've been . . . busy."

"They've gone and pled not guilty. The newspaper said Kuhl claims to have shot Fred out of self-defense when he wouldn't divide the loot with 'em and pulled a gun."

I felt a chill in my spine. "Shooting a man

in the back of his head is a strange way to defend yourself."

"Yep, but a sharp lawyer can make the Ten Commandments seem like a bad idea. They claim that the whole thing was Fred's idea, so he could have enough money to get married on."

"That's ridiculous," I sputtered.

"You know that and I know that, but, when a man's facing a firing squad or hanging, he'll do or say anything to live."

"Has Inman heard about this?"

Jackson spun his beer mug. "He's the one who showed me the paper. He was concerned about what this news would do to his mother. I reckon it was as close as I ever come to seeing a man cry."

"The truth will come out when it goes to trial," I ventured.

"That may be true, but a lot of times you can do more damage to a person with a lie than a bullet," Jackson said.

I scooted my chair back, took a drink, and looked at Willie's presents under the tree. Ben Kuhl was without a doubt the most evil person I had ever met. The last words he'd uttered to me were that, if it was the last thing he ever did, he would kill me.

That can work the other way, too, I thought to myself.

Chapter Nineteen

Ever since the Red Fox, I had given a lot of serious thought toward the benefits of having a wife. Being seventeen years old, the most immediate reason was to save a pile of silver dollars. Aside from that I was lonely, plain and simple. All my life there had been family around to talk things over with. That had ended on the 15th day of April, 1916. So much had happened to me since then my head spun when I tried to add it all up.

I laid awake thinking for the longest time that night. Just after midnight a wind began blowing out of the west, hooting and moaning in the eaves of my cabin. I had never paid this any mind before; now, it reminded me of a wailing woman. Marybeth Sears had no one to care for her. That double four-poster brass bed felt empty and cold. Suddenly I recalled something I'd seen before.

With a sense of urgency, I threw on a robe and lit a kerosene lamp. By flickering yellow light, I fished that metal box of Dave Bourne's from its hiding place in the closet and carried it into the kitchen. I tossed some wood on the fire and poured a cup of coffee that was strong enough to kill a lesser man. Then I flipped open the lid and once again went through the contents of Dave's small safe.

Tucked safely away in an envelope, I found a simple gold wedding band. I knew it must have been Hattie Bourne's. Somehow, I felt Dave would approve when I laid that ring on the table and returned his box to the closet.

I finished my coffee without taking my eyes from that band. When I went back to bed, the wind wasn't moaning, it was singing.

Before going to pick up Marybeth for breakfast the next morning, I waded through some snowdrifts to Shaky Sam's barbershop. The sun was just beginning to peek over the mountaintop, but old Sam already had whiskey on his breath. This was the safest time of day to visit him and leave with both ears. I had my hair trimmed, then decided to chance it and told him to give me a shave. God was watching over me, and I escaped with only one nick. Smelling heavily of aftershave, I went to escort Marybeth to breakfast.

Marybeth greeted me with a kiss that caused my toes to curl. Arm in arm, we trudged our way to Fong's restaurant. When we took a table, every miner in the place was looking through me and seeing only Marybeth.

I ordered hotcakes smothered with chili, which caused her to look at me strangely. Marybeth put away a huge plate of bacon, eggs, and fried potatoes. Since she hadn't eaten much last night, I guessed she was nearly starved.

Fong came by and refilled our coffee cups. "Missee, you so pleety, maybe I hire you sit here all day. More business than Charlie ever have when you here."

Marybeth's cheeks flushed crimson. "I've never had so many men just stare at me," she said as Fong left.

"Few ever see beauty such as yours," I said, desperately trying to remember some Sir Walter Scott. "Spending time with you is like walking in a field of lilacs on a spring day."

"Milo, that's the sweetest thing I've ever heard."

I didn't want to explain just why I was

taken by the aroma of lilacs, so I moved on. "You are a woman any man would be proud to grow old with. Will you marry me?"

I fished that gold ring from my pocket and placed it on the table in front of her. Tears welled in Marybeth's blue eyes. She took a handkerchief from her purse and started sobbing.

"What did you do to the little lady?" a burly miner growled, scooting his chair back. He ran over, grabbed my shirt, and pulled me skyward. "If you've hurt her feelings, I'll hit you so hard you won't stop rolling until you get to Idaho."

It's always been a source of amazement to me the number of fixes I can get into with no effort on my part. I started to explain when Marybeth placed her hand on the man's arm.

"It's all right," she said firmly. "Mister Goodman has asked me to marry him."

"Ah, nuts," another miner grumbled.

The big man lowered me back into my chair. "Sometimes women cry when they're happy," I said.

I straightened out my shirt collar, then nervously fidgeted with my coffee cup while Marybeth took one final dab at her eyes.

"I'm sorry about crying," she said. "It's just so sudden."

235

"Sometimes Cupid is fast on the draw," I said sincerely.

"It's just scary, making a commitment so quickly."

I held her hand. "Let's head for Twin Falls tomorrow and rustle up a preacher."

Marybeth slid her hand from mine and picked up the wedding ring, holding it between her fingers. Suddenly she began glowing and squealed: "Could we get married in a Presbyterian church?"

Not only did it tickle me pink that Marybeth would marry me, but I was also glad to find out she wasn't a hard-shell Baptist. Religion was something we hadn't talked about. Baptists are more of a pain in the ass than Democrats. "I'd like that, too. I was raised a Presbyterian."

She gave me a kiss right in front of everyone. It was just a peck on the cheek, but it made me feel like a million dollars. We made plans while Fong's restaurant emptied. When I walked Marybeth to the hotel, I knew I was the luckiest man in Nevada.

As I walked through the snow back to my cabin, the biting cold did little to take my mind from Marybeth and put it back on work.

Turkey Curley was finishing framing an

addition onto the river shack for Eggs to have a bedroom. I wanted my new bartender to be happy and stick around, so I told Curley, if he could get the job done quickly, I'd pay him a twenty-dollar bonus. It took a few moments for him to figure up how many bottles of cheap whiskey that would buy, then he started working faster. I could hear Eggs snoring away in the shed. I wondered why all the hammering and sawing didn't wake him. Eggs, I found out later, could sleep through a war.

When I went to swamp out the bar, I was totally taken aback. The whiskey bottles were wiped clean. All the beer glasses and mugs sparkled in neat rows and even a supply of firewood had been laid in neatly alongside the potbelly stove.

I tossed a couple of logs on the fire with a contented feeling. Not only was I getting the prettiest girl in the world for a wife, I had found a decent bartender to boot. Eggs wasn't worth much as a Packard salesman, but when it came to pouring out booze, he knew his stuff. I was glad now he hadn't burned himself up when he dropped that cigar into his pant's cuff.

I needed to put another beer keg on tap, so I was glad to open the door to Inman's knocking. He had that Graphophone Fred had bought tucked under one arm and the stack of screeching Italian opera records under the other.

"We want you to have this," he said somberly. The smell of whiskey was heavy on his breath. "We've sold the hotel and are leaving town. I know you and Marybeth are gonna tie the knot. Fred would approve. He liked you a lot."

I thanked him while taking the Graphophone. Inman bent over and carefully stacked the records on a shelf under the bar, all the time I was racking my brain trying to come up with some way they could have an "accident" before Marybeth found them.

"When did you sell the place?" I asked.

"We made the deal yesterday. Their name's Lawton. They came here from Utah."

"Where are you moving to?"

"I reckon we'll head to California, so Ma and me can be able to forget some of what happened."

Then I felt a chill trickle down my backbone. "Has anyone mentioned to Marybeth that lie circulating around about Fred and Kuhl working together."

Inman sighed. "She'll hear about it sooner or later."

I set a bottle of whiskey on the bar. "Here, Inman," I said, "stick around and settle your nerves. Eggs will be around soon. Right now, I've got to run."

Before I knocked on Marybeth's door, I could hear her crying. I knew she had heard the cruel rumor about Fred. She felt frail and helpless when she wrapped herself around me.

"Some woman at the store showed me a newspaper," she sobbed. "They're claiming Fred Searcy was in on that stagecoach robbery."

I held her tight. "Those outlaws are saying anything to keep from hanging."

Marybeth looked at me and pursed her lips. "I'm sorry, it's just that things are happening so fast."

"At least you aren't bored."

A smile crossed her freckled face. "From what I've heard about you, *that* won't be a problem." Then she mentioned she wanted to see the Miners' Exchange.

I noticed both Inman and the whiskey bottle were missing. Eggs was wrestling a beer keg, so I pitched in and helped him. Marybeth started poking around. All women have an uncanny ability to find what you don't want them to. The first thing she noticed was that Graphophone and stack of

Italian opera recordings.

I swallowed hard and walked to her side with a feeling of dread as I watched her shuffle through those records.

"Do you actually like opera?" she asked cautiously.

Often it's safer to answer a question with another question. "Do you?"

"I love soft music and good singing. Operas always remind me of listening to a cat fight."

Marybeth looked surprised when I planted a kiss on her lips. The pedestal I'd placed her on grew ten feet higher.

"We'll pick up some new records," I said, relieved as a turkey the day after Thanksgiving.

Eggs came over, and I introduced him to my future wife. Then I broke the news that we were leaving for Twin Falls tomorrow.

"You young folks take all the time you want. Willie and I'll take good care of the place." He flashed a knowing grin. "My third wife and I took a whole week and went to Yellowstone Park for our honeymoon. Old Faithful put on a great performance."

Eggs had let his mouth beat his brain to the draw. He began sputtering so badly, he dropped that cigar into his pant's cuff again. Marybeth watched in sweet innocence as

Eggs began shuffling his feet and didn't have a clue as to what was wrong with my bartender.

"He has these little attacks once in a while," I said.

At eight o'clock sharp the next morning, I picked up Marybeth at the hotel. Thankfully it only took one anvil in a suitcase for her to get married, so I managed to get her luggage into the Packard without calling for help.

Once Marybeth slid close to me, I dropped that Packard into gear and, with tire chains crunching against frozen snow, hit the road to Twin Falls, heady from the smell of lilacs in bloom.

There was a lot of traffic on that road in those days. Crippen Grade was shoveled out and presented no difficulties to a twelve-cylinder automobile. It felt simply wonderful to push down on the accelerator pedal and have the power to go straight up a hill without having to turn around and back up the damned thing.

Marybeth loved the Packard, especially the heater. She turned it on high, and, by the time we reached Kitty's, the inside of the car was so warm she took off her heavy coat. I nearly ran into a snowdrift admiring the enticing way her pert breasts strained against her dress. There was no doubt in my mind I would enjoy unwrapping my Christmas present more than Willie would his.

The first thing we did when we reached Twin Falls was to get a marriage license from the county clerk. I had to bite my tongue to keep from saying something when it cost a dollar.

Preachers are like toilet paper — they're never around when you really need them. The Presbyterian minister was busy at a funeral. It would be the middle of the afternoon before he had time to attend to a wedding, so Marybeth and I decided to have lunch at the hotel.

I excused myself for a moment and went to the front desk. The gray-haired clerk shot me a knowing grin when I rented the honeymoon suite for three nights and ordered a dozen long-stemmed red roses to be set in a vase alongside the bed.

"How about a couple of bottles of champagne iced down in your room, Mister Goodman?" he asked with a wink. "I'll be happy to see to it. Also, we can have breakfast sent up, no matter how late it is."

The man's smile broadened when I slipped him a few dollars and told him to take care of everything.

Marybeth changed into a beautiful dress that was whiter than freshly fallen snow. To this day, I have never set eyes on a more beautiful lady. She was radiant as a rainbow after a spring shower.

"I'll make you a good wife, Milo," she whispered sweetly in my ear. "I love you."

"No more than I love you," I answered, squeezing her hand.

At three o'clock, on a clear, blue afternoon, the 24th day of December, 1916, Marybeth changed her last name to Goodman.

There is nothing on God's green earth that makes a man happier than having a wonderful wife. That little log cabin in Jarbidge would no longer simply be a house, it would be a home. I had a family again, and knew for a fact that I would have to die and go to heaven ever to feel this happy again.

For three days, folks working room service at the Snake River Hotel earned their tips. Marybeth and I never left that suite. We talked and made love the entire time. Once, when she brought up the fact we could save money by going downstairs for dinner, I told her how much I had made from Dave Bourne's stock.

"I never knew there was that much money in the entire world," she said with awe. "You're the richest man I ever met."

"From here on," I answered, giving her a hug, "it's ours to enjoy. The saloon makes a good profit, and, when I find the Lost Sheepherder's Mine, we'll sell out and move to where it's warm."

"We could do that now," Marybeth said dreamily. "I believe together, we can do anything."

"One thing I promise is you won't be bored," I said, lifting my head from the pillow to blow out the flickering coal-oil lamp by our bed.

The problem with having a wonderful dream is eventually you have to wake up. Before we headed back to Jarbidge and reality, Marybeth spent the morning shopping for those little things a woman likes to have in a home. When she bought a stack of Graphophone records and not a single one was a screaming Italian opera, I knew I had good taste when it came to women.

Kitty Wilkins squeezed me so hard she nearly broke my ribs when we stopped to visit. Reece came in and congratulated us.

"You know Kitty and me are gonna get hitched up in June," he said happily. "That new husband of yours is doing the preaching. He's mighty good at using fancy words."

Marybeth choked. "Milo is a *preacher?*"

Kitty put her hand on Reece's shoulders. "Not the big city variety. He does a good job at buryin', so it stands to figger he can do hitchings, too. Ain't been a real preacher set foot in Jarbidge since the last one got himself beaned in a whorehouse."

A look of shock washed across Marybeth's freckled face. "I didn't know there were such places in our town."

"Hell's bells," Reece spouted, "every man's gotta dip his wick once in a while!"

The scathing glare Kitty gave him would have peeled paint. "Reece, mind your manners."

"You folks take care," I sputtered. "My wife and I have to be moving on. Looks like it might snow."

"Is there really a house of ill repute in Jarbidge?" Marybeth asked. When a woman gets her mind set on a subject, they're worse than a snapping turtle. A turtle won't turn loose until it thunders; a woman takes even longer.

"That's what I've heard, but I don't know where they are."

She cocked her head. "You don't know where *they* are?"

The heater in that Packard felt like it was working overtime. "Uh . . . well, a man hears things."

Marybeth slid close and began nibbling at my ear. "I'll bet I can keep you from having to find the path there in the dark. Gramma taught me a few things about men."

After the past three days, I had no doubt Marybeth's grandmother had seen the elephant more than once. My biggest concern at that moment was keeping the car on the road.

It was late afternoon by the time I had Marybeth settled into the cabin. The moment I walked through the door of the saloon, Willie ran to me and gave me a rib crushing.

"I really like my stuff, Mister Milo," he said happily. "I never got no Christmas gifts to open before."

Willie had his set of ivory dominoes spread out on a table and was playing with Jackson Lyman. This surprised me. Jackson seldom came into the bar this early. Even more of a shock was finding Tully there, drinking beer. Willie went back to his dominoes, and I went to see Tully.

"Things have a way of happening when you're gone," Tully said gravely. "I just got back from visiting with Huptman, our engineer. He's at Doc Harlan's. It's a good thing that doctor finally showed up. Last night, a bunch of thugs nearly beat him to death."

I pictured the smiling, old, silver-haired man with a crooked stem pipe stuck in his mouth. "Why on earth would anyone want to hurt him?"

"Because he's German," Tully answered. "We've hired a lot of new men at Elkoro. Some of them have family who's been killed in Europe. I guess they've decided to bring the war here."

"Huptman's a nice old guy . . . he's got nothing to do with the war," I replied.

"Hate's a mighty hard thing to figure out," Tully said.

Jackson Lyman came over. "We need to get hold of that lawyer, Spurgeon," he said seriously. "Some toughs, carrying guns, took over the Pavlak mine two days ago."

I exploded: "Willie's mine! Who'd do a thing like that?"

Jackson spat out bitterly: "His name is C. C. Logan!"

Chapter Twenty

"Well, at least the bar didn't burn down," I said, after hearing about all that had gone wrong.

Tully Moxness chewed on his lip for a moment. "We're all happy for you, Milo. I guess bad things came in like a flock of buzzards. Adolph will be all right. The worst of it was they used a rock to smash his front teeth in. The poor old guy will be eating through a straw for quite a spell."

"Where are the Bruckners?" I asked.

"Holed up in their cabin," Jackson said. "They're afraid the same thugs who beat Huptman will likely thump on them next. We can't work the mine, anyway . . . Logan has two guys at the Pavlak with double-barreled shotguns."

I shook my head. "How in the heck did that happen? I thought we filed that deed to Willie."

"There's the problem," Jackson said with

a worried look. "The assessment work was filed under Eppie's name. Logan's claiming the Pavlak mine was open ground because I used a dead person's name on the paperwork, instead of Willie's."

"Outlaws these days don't have any class," Tully grumbled. "They use fine print and lawyers, instead of a gun, when they hold you up."

"Lawyers don't work cheap," I said. "You'd better plan on spending a passel to get rid of Logan."

Tully spoke up: "They don't accomplish anything *fast,* either. My guess is you can get a court order to keep Logan from working the mine, but I suspect Willie might be in for a dry spell until it's over."

This was a chilling thought. If Willie's money ran out, I would wind up being the one to take care of him.

Eggs took time to visit. He came wearing his usual sly grin and a towel draped over his pudgy arm. He knew I was hearing nothing but bad news. He slid a frosty mug of beer over the counter in front of me. "Well, outside of *that,* Missus Lincoln, did you enjoy the play?"

It felt good to laugh. Even Jackson let out a chuckle once he finally figured out what Eggs was talking about. Then the bartender turned serious. "The new owner of the Jarbidge Hotel came by wanting to talk to you. The guy's name is Claude Lawton."

"Did he say what he wanted?"

"Nope," Eggs replied, "just looked down his snout at me and grumbled about how much he hated coming into a den of iniquity. He kept hugging a Bible, to keep the sin chased away, I guess."

"God save us from Bible-thumpers," Tully said after a swallow of beer. "They're worse than claim-jumpers."

I chugged my beer and slid the empty mug toward Eggs. "Well, boys, the only way to find out what this fellow wants is to go ask him. I'll just do that right now."

Claude Lawton must have weighed over 400 pounds, all of it droopy fat. He was clean-shaven and not too old. His long black hair showed only a hint of gray at the temples. His bulk filled the doorway.

"I'm Milo Goodman," I said, offering up a handshake. "Folks said you wanted to talk to me."

The fat man thrust his hands into the pockets of his overalls. Dark, deep-set eyes glared at me like stale water in a rain barrel.

"Ma an' me don't abide sinners." His voice was harsh and raspy. "A tavern like yours is the devil's playground. All who abide therein are damned to perdition."

"I'd like to think there's more than one way to make it to hell," I replied with a thin smile.

"What I wanted to tell you is Ma and me can't have that half-wit living here any longer. He spends his evenings in your den of iniquity."

Through clenched teeth I answered: "Willie will be out of the hotel tonight." Then, as an afterthought, I said: "Should you ever actually *read* that Bible of yours, instead of pound on it, there's some words in there about loving your neighbor." I never got that last part out before the door slammed hard in my face.

"That didn't take very long," Tully said when I came back in the bar.

When I told of my conversation with Lawton, there wasn't a man in the place who didn't look mad enough to bite nails.

"Reckon the law would get upset if we hung him?" Butt-Block asked hopefully.

"He's so fat, all you'd accomplish is busting a limb off a perfectly good tree," Tully retorted, "but I'd suppose that would get his attention."

Jackson looked lost in thought for a moment, then said: "He's got to be kin of

C. C. Logan. It don't stand to reason there could be two assholes of the same dimensions in such close proximity lessen they're related."

I started to say something when the door opened and Willie came in. A heavy smell of smoke clung to his clothes. I assumed he had been helping Matt with blacksmith work. The place grew so quiet you could have heard a mouse fart. Everyone was wondering what I would tell Willie.

"We're going to move you out of the hotel," I said.

"That's OK," Willie said happily, "the new folks that own it don' like me none. They tol' me I was gonna go to hell. Is that where I'm movin' to?"

Then Eggs spoke up. "Willie, I'd be plenty happy if you'd stay with me. Once Milo finishes building on, you can have your own room."

This was the first I'd heard of my keeping Turkey Curley pounding nails, but there seemed no way out of it now.

"We've got an extra space in the bunkhouse at the mill," Tully said. "I'd be pleased to let Willie stay there until his room's built."

"Or he can bunk at my cabin," Butt-Block said.

Willie spoke up: "I'd sure like to stay with Mister Eggs, iffen that's OK. He plays dominoes an' cooks food that tastes mighty good."

A curtain parted and dark eyes watched as I and a half dozen miners carted Willie's few possessions to Eggs's cabin. There was no doubt in my mind that, when Gabriel blows his horn, I wouldn't want to be wearing Claude Lawton's shoes.

It's a wonderful feeling being married to a good woman. Marybeth had the cabin spruced up in jig time. There's little things that only a female can do to make a place feel like a home.

Most wonderful of all were the nights. I never stayed at the bar any longer than necessary. I would come home and slip into bed beside Marybeth, who was usually reading a book. Then we made love and I would drift off to peaceful sleep lost in a hazy field of lilac blossoms. When the morning sun peeked around a curtain, Marybeth lay curled softly against me. I knew only then I wasn't dreaming.

Jackson Lyman and I made a phone call to Theodore Spurgeon from the Elkoro office. The lawyer said he would get a court order immediately to prevent Logan from mining any ore until the dispute was resolved. We made an appointment to meet with him on January 2nd, after the New Year holiday. Spurgeon told us to bring all copies of the paperwork when we came. I was surprised when the lawyer mentioned that C. C. Logan owned a big hay farm just outside of Twin Falls. With all the money that hay brought in, I didn't think he'd need a gold mine, too. Greedy people never seem to get enough.

New Year's Eve was a real blow-out in the Miners' Exchange. Marybeth came over and helped Eggs tend bar, which doubled our business. Adolph Huptman was out of the hospital and stopped by. He looked like he'd run headlong into a tree while going thirty miles an hour. There was a little opening to one side of his swollen mouth where he could hang his pipe or pour in a little beer, so he began enjoying himself.

I brought out the Graphophone and put on a waltz. Tully came over and asked permission to dance with Marybeth. Of course, I told him it was all right by me. Shortly every miner in Jarbidge wanted to dance with my pretty wife. She seemed to enjoy the attention immensely. I was pleased to see even the more drunken party goers watched their language and treated her like a lady.

Willie had been watching the dancing for quite a while, clapping his big hands in time with the music and grinning up a storm. Then Marybeth asked him to dance with her. When the music started, Willie began imitating the steps he'd watched the other men do. I thought for sure Marybeth could wind up crippled for life but to my — and everyone else's — amazement, Willie moved with a smooth grace, never once making a misstep.

"Willie, you dance better than any man here," she complimented him when the dance was over.

What flesh you could see under that scraggly beard of his flushed crimson.

At midnight, Tully lit a stick of dynamite and tossed it into the street. When the blast went off and the windows quit rattling, we all drank to the New Year of 1917 and gave our hopes for good fortune during the coming year.

"This is one C. C. Logan is not going to win," Theodore Spurgeon announced after poring over the paperwork on the Pavlak mine. "The biggest problem I can see is the owner of the mine will have to testify. I understand Willie Pavlak is not competent to be put on the stand."

"No, sir, he ain't," Jackson replied nervously. "He'll put his boots on the wrong feet, then wonder why they hurt."

"Are you saying he's phlegmatic?" the lawyer asked.

"Well, I don't rightly know what religion he is," Jackson said quickly.

That was the closest I ever saw Spurgeon come to laughing. "No, what I meant was is he mentally defective?"

"He's retarded," I said to save Jackson any more embarrassment. "Willie wouldn't be able to testify as to which direction is up and have it come out right."

"I see," Spurgeon answered. "Then get his mark on a quit-claim deed, giving the mine to someone who *can* testify as to the facts, and act as a fiduciary."

Jackson's mouth dropped open, and he looked blank as a Democrat's idea book.

"It's a position of trust, Mister Lyman," the lawyer explained. "A person who will look after Willie Pavlak's interests."

Jackson looked relieved. "Hell's bells, I've got a lease on the mine. I reckon you can trust me."

Spurgeon lit up a cigarette and leaned back. "That's precisely why you can't act as

256

guardian. You have a vested interest."

"Damn right, I'm interested," Jackson retorted.

"Milo Goodman is not at all involved, is that correct?" Spurgeon questioned.

I had the feeling I'd better speak up. "I have Willie's money from the mine in the bank and pay his bills."

"Excellent. You will be the new owner of the Pavlak mine and act as trustee for Willie," the lawyer said firmly.

I felt a little numb while Theodore Spurgeon made out the deed for Willie to sign. Jackson Lyman undoubtedly felt worse than I did when he wrote the lawyer a check for $1,000.

When Jackson and I piled into the Packard for our trip home, he commented: "How does it feel to own a gold mine?"

"Like a lot of problems just got laid on my shoulders."

"Welcome to the mining business," he chuckled as I put the car in gear and headed off into a snowy day.

Time slid into slow motion for the next several weeks. Marybeth made every day and most especially the nights memorable. I began tending the bar two days a week to give Eggs some time off.

Claude Lawton and his wife operated the Jarbidge Hotel to a dwindling crowd. Charlie Fong, always one to sense business, quickly built a ten-room hotel alongside his restaurant. Anyone asking where to stay for the night was immediately sent to Fong's Gold Bar Inn.

I first set eyes on Claude's wife, Minnie, in front of Adams's store a week after they threw Willie out of the hotel. While he was the fattest man in town, she took the grand prize for fat *and* ugly. If both of them had been on the *Titanic*, there wouldn't have been any question why the boat sunk. Minnie had a figure like a truckload of turnips and the disposition of a grizzly bear with a toothache. She snarled something at me to the effect that I was hell bound, then stomped off down the boardwalk, shaking nails loose as she went.

The Lawtons also introduced cockroaches to Jarbidge. We never had a single one until they showed up. Then the town got overrun by the blasted things.

The trial for ownership of the Pavlak mine was set for September, the month before Kuhl, Beck, and Billy McGraw were to go in front of the jury. All of them now had lawyers and were pleading not guilty.

A twist was, the prosecution planned to

introduce an expert in what the newspaper article termed "fingerprints." They claimed to be able to match the bloody palm and fingerprints left on the mail by the murderers to the hand that touched it. This sounded far-fetched to most of us.

On April 1st, I saw my eighteenth birthday. I was sorely tempted to tell Marybeth how young I really was, but decided against it. I was afraid she might get a tad upset by the fact.

In contrast to the desperately severe winter, spring came early and surprisingly warm to the high country. By the middle of May, only a few snowdrifts lay scattered in areas of shadow. A few hardy flowers, like peonies, began to poke through the freshly thawed soil.

The time had come for me to do what I'd originally planned.

I was going to find the Lost Sheepherder's Mine.

Chapter Twenty-One

I hated to leave Marybeth alone for the entire week I thought it might take to get rich. The glitter and hefty feel of that piece of gold ore Cal McVey had let me hold was a mighty convincing argument, however.

When I told her enough snow had melted for me to go, she kissed my cheek and said: "Be careful, I've heard that's rugged and remote country up there."

She was right about the remote part. I had obtained a government map of the area. God's Pocket Peak showed to be over 10,000 feet high and several miles southeast of Jarbidge.

Early in the morning, on the 18th of May, I went to Whort's livery and picked up those two gray ghost mules that had done nothing all winter but keep their heads in the feed trough. They were sleek and fat as I had expected them to be after paying out nearly $2,000 to keep them from starving.

Willie was there, happily pumping on the forge bellows. "I hope you find that mine, Mister Milo, I surely do!" he shouted out as Matt come to help me saddle the mules.

"I'm just going hunting for some venison," I said quietly.

Matt tossed the pack saddle on one mule. "What you're looking for is most likely on God's Pocket. That's where a lion hunter found some rich high grade."

I started to protest I was only going after a deer when Jackson Lyman came in and handed me an empty tobacco can along with some blank papers.

"You'll have to stake a claim if you find the Sheepherder's Mine," he said. "Fill out a notice and stuff it in the can. Place it in a mound of stones at least four feet high. I reckon you don't want Logan to jump your claim like he done Willie's."

It was easier to find a virgin in Cherry Flats than keep a secret in Jarbidge. "If you get a chance, drop by and check on Marybeth. You never know when a woman's going to get herself in Dutch."

"Ain't that the truth." Jackson chuckled. He flashed his eyes at me. "You weren't in the bar last night when this rounder came in. He was plenty drunk and running off at the mouth. If you believe him, a couple of his buddies was paid to beat up Huptman, and you'd never guess who hired 'em. It was Claude Lawton. He thinks Germans are the Antichrist and wanted to run them out of town."

"We oughta run that bastard out of town on a rail," Matt spat.

"Water seeks its own level," I said. "Jorgason at the bank told me Lawton's way past due on the hotel loan and Adams cut off their credit at the store. I think Lawton's days in town are numbered."

"We'll see," Matt grumbled. "If he's slow leaving, maybe some of us will speed him up some."

I stopped by the cabin and loaded the pack mule with a week's worth of supplies and lashed on that tent I'd bought. After I slid the Winchester into its scabbard on my riding mule, Marybeth came and gave me a toe-curling kiss that nearly delayed my start. I had a little difficulty getting settled into the saddle but, after a moment, grabbed up the jerk line and headed out of town.

I took the trail that followed the Jarbidge River toward its headwaters. When I passed the Pavlak mine, Logan's guards were there, carrying shotguns in the crook of their arms. They took me as no threat and one even gave a feeble wave as I headed into the high country.

Soon the mountains grew even steeper and more rugged. High peaks stood along the cañon walls like castles in a fairy tale. Snowdrifts grew in size and number. Beaten paths through and around them bore mute testimony I was not the first one to make this trek since the weather broke.

Mules are by nature not very ambitious animals. At first, I was proud of the fact mine were gentle and well behaved. I hadn't traveled five miles when it dawned on me they were simply fat and out of shape. By the time I reached Jarbidge Lake at the river's headwaters, both of them were wheezing worse than Ed Kinneson ever had.

My plan was to take the established pack trail up the mountain to the west and follow it until I was on the east fork of the Jarbidge River, opposite God's Pocket Peak.

There were quite a few fresh tracks in evidence. I didn't want some prospector to trip over my vein, so I pulled those mules away from the clear waters of the lake and began urging them up the narrow trail that would drop us over the divide to where I should be able to see God's Pocket.

I had heard much about the natural prowess of mules in the mountains. Some of the freighters who occasionally dropped by the Miners' Exchange told many tales of how pack mules could safely traverse trails steep enough to scare a bighorn sheep into a heart attack. This was reassuring, for the pack trail began edging its way along a steep cliff. The higher I climbed, the narrower and more treacherous that rocky path became.

Then I came to a sharp switchback. The mule I was riding swung around like he was supposed to. That gray ghost attached to my jerk line didn't. She just kept going straight, and plain and simple, walked off into space. The rope burned my fingers as I watched in open-mouthed awe as a $100 mule that had eaten a $1,000 worth of hay fell off the mountain, taking a fifty-dollar tent and all my supplies with her.

Carefully I dismounted and walked back to survey the disaster. My first guess was that pack mule would keep rolling until it smashed into the side of my bar down in Jarbidge. I was surprised to find she'd only traveled 100 feet or so before becoming jammed in an outcropping of rock. From the way the mule's head bent back, looking at her own tail, I knew the stupid thing had broken its neck. All I had to worry about rescuing were some supplies and my tent.

I tied the reins of my remaining mule to a large rock and began trying to edge my way down. That slide rock was too treacherous; I knew I would fall farther than that blasted mule, if I persisted. I worked my way back to the relative safety of the trail and stood there for a while, trying to decide what to do, when a voice boomed behind me.

"Ya know, I've been prospecting fer years and never seen nothing like that before!"

I had thought I was the only human for miles. He scared me so bad, I nearly fell over the edge myself. When I spun to see who was there, I found myself looking into the grinning face of a gray-whiskered old man leading a burro. "My mule went over the cliff," I blurted out.

"Yep, I saw that part," the old man said, coming closer. He offered out his hand. "Dan Dugan's the name." He walked to the edge of the trail, looked down at the dead mule, and shook his head sadly. "Durndest thing I *ever* saw."

"I need to get my tent and supplies."

"Reckon you do at that," the old man muttered. "Did you by chance get that mule off Matt Whort down in Jarbidge?"

"Yes, I bought her last fall. This is the first time I've had her out, though."

The old prospector clucked his tongue.

"Don't reckon you'll get any more use outta that mule from here out. I thought I recognized that animal. A friend of mine used to own her. Ole Dutch was mighty glad to get shed of it. Said she nearly ate him out of house and home. Also, it had a bum eye."

"Matt sold me a blind mule!" I blurted.

"Ya ain't listening, son," Dugan replied. "Only one eye was bad. Iffen you'd been going the other way, none of this would 'a' happened."

"Could you help me get my gear?" I asked testily.

The old man's voice turned kindly. "Sure, son, I was gonna do that. You young 'uns these days have got no patience a-tall."

Dugan produced a thin rope that was barely long enough to allow me to climb down and drag up my tent and foodstuffs. When I got everything worth saving on top, I tied my gear onto the saddle of my remaining mule. From here on, I had to walk. I knew this would slow my mine-finding considerably, but, at least, I had my supplies.

"Thanks for your help," I said.

"Weren't no problem, sonny. Just seeing that mule keep walking on where there weren't no mountain was somethin' to behold. When ya go after lost gold mines, get a burro. They're more dependable."

I felt a chill building in my spine. "You're out here prospecting?"

"Looking for the Lost Sheepherder's Mine. That's the only reason a body would have for coming up here."

I swallowed so hard I nearly lost my tonsils. "Then you're headed for God's Pocket?"

"Yep, Fridley and Dutch are most likely already there by now. Iffen you're going there yourself, we might make camp together. Cooking's a bunch easier when everyone pitches in, and the cabin's big enough you won't need that tent."

I had supposed that I might run across a lone prospector or two up here. Now it was beginning to look like a convention of Lost Sheepherder's Mine seekers was being held on God's Pocket. "You have a *cabin* up there?"

Dugan looked at me like my nose had just fallen off. "Tarnation, son, you are a real greener, ain't you? Of course, we built a cabin. A body needs a stove and a table to play cards on. Finding a lost mine takes time. Do you think a man just walks out and stumbles on a vein of gold?"

Actually that *had* been my plan, but I decided this might not be a good time to say so. "How long have you been prospecting up here?"

"Since the summer of Oh-Seven."

"That's ten years."

"I count the same myself."

"Yet, you think you know where that mine's located?"

The old prospector's eyes narrowed. "Sonny, give me a coin, just a small one. That's all this lesson in gold hunting will cost you."

I pulled out my coin purse and dug through it. "A quarter's the smallest thing I've got," I said.

"Reckon it'll be worth it to you. A piece of gold this size would be a rich strike if it were sticking out of a vein."

Dugan held the quarter between his thumb and forefinger. "Now look over at that the mule you own that's still breathin'."

I did what he said and heard his arm whistle in the air when he threw my quarter over the cliff.

"Why in hell did you do that?" I spat out.

"It's as big as a nugget and you know where it is . . . go find it."

When I looked over the ragged, boulder-strewn mountainside, the prospector's point became clear. I knew within 100 feet of where my quarter had gone, yet it could take weeks to find it.

The gray-bearded prospector grinned like he'd found a whorehouse holding a fire sale. "Ya see, there's more to it than most figger. Grab up that mule of yours and let's head off. God ain't gonna make any more daylight just because you had problems."

The sun had dropped and a chill was building in the air when we finally reached our destination. I tethered my mule that was so worn out it was having a hard time just standing up, unsaddled her, and brought my gear into the welcome warmth of the rude log cabin.

Dan introduced me to Fridley and Dutch who were there like he'd expected. Once they got tired of ribbing me about what happened to my other mule, we threw together a pot of stew.

Later, playing poker by the flickering light of a kerosene lantern, Dugan skinned me out of two dollars. I knew the old man was cheating but, for the life of me, couldn't figure out how. Then talk turned to the Sheepherder Mine. Everyone here had seen ore that supposedly came from the mine, but no one had actually found any gold themselves.

I was dejected as a politician after losing an election when I rolled up in a blanket and laid my head on the tent I'd decided to use for a pillow. The scurrying noise of pack rats running around on the ceiling beams kept me awake.

"Those rats won't be around long," Fridley announced in the darkness. "Ole Stinky'll be here in a few days."

"Yep," Dutch agreed, "when he breaks wind the smell will run 'em out. It does every year."

For the next three days, I wandered around the south slope of God's Pocket carrying a pick hammer and whacking away at rocks. It's amazing how much one rock resembles another. Then, on the third day, I struck a wide streak of brown-colored material that, when broken, sparkled in the sunlight with a wonderful yellow glint.

I quickly built a claim monument and filled out the papers Jackson had given me, then I relaxed. I now legally owned the Lost Sheepherder's Mine.

It was a total mystery to me how all of these so-called experienced prospectors had missed it all these years. The vein was only a short walk from their cabin. I stuffed some gold into my pockets and headed in early.

Dan was already there when I got to the cabin. He had run across a patch of snow mushrooms growing at the base of a receding drift, and had picked a hat full.

"We'll fry these up with some of that elk Fridley shot yesterday and have us a feast," he announced proudly.

"Take a look at this," I said in a hushed tone as I showed him a chunk of gold from my new mine.

The old man twirled the rock in his hand, then tossed it out the open doorway.

"You sure like throwing things away," I seethed. "At least I know where it came from."

"Reckon you do, sonny boy. That vein of fool's gold has been found by every greener that's hit this mountain." I guess I must have made a sorrowful sight because Dugan's face softened as he continued: "Real gold don't glitter none. It's dull and don't come in square cubes like fool's gold."

We were just sitting down to supper when Stinky Palo arrived, leading two burros laden with supplies. He was an amiable fellow, younger than the others, sporting a full black beard and a beer belly that drooped heavily over his belt buckle.

I had been around Kitty Wilkins too much to take any chances around a fat person when it came to food, so I grabbed my steak and mushrooms before he got a plate. My intuition had been correct. Stinky grabbed the biggest piece of meat from the skillet, and left only a single mushroom to go with Dan's thin steak.

Dugan smiled broadly when I scraped most of my snow mushrooms onto his plate. Sometimes it pays to keep quiet.

We just got sacked out for the night when Stinky lived up to his name, nearly blowing the cabin door off its hinges when he cut loose a thunderous fart.

"At least we won't be bothered by rats any more," Fridley announced.

Once I got a whiff of the air, I understood why those poor pack rats left. I decided I would go sleep on the little porch under the stars rather than suffer through another of Stinky's explosions, but it never came.

What sounded like a woman screaming outside the cabin woke me with a start. It took a moment to clear my head enough to realize where I was and the fact there were no women up here.

Dan lit the lantern and was throwing on his clothes. "It's a cougar, boys."

I was sleeping in long johns, so I pulled on my boots and grabbed the Winchester. The screaming increased only to be joined by a second scream, this one from a terrified animal being ripped to shreds by a mountain lion. The light was so poor all I could make out was wild shadowy movements where the pack animals were tied up.

"Durn, I can't see nuthin'!" Dan hollered, rushing to my side carrying an ancient, rusty pistol. "Yur eyes are younger than mine, kin you spot that dad-durned cat?"

"I'm more likely to hit a burro or mule if I shoot."

"Well, fire in the air, dang it!" he yelled.

I did as he said and watched a graceful shadow streak silently away into the dark timber.

"Why didn't you shoot *at* him?" Dan complained.

Fridley and Stinky came out, carrying the lantern.

"Where's Dutch?" I asked.

"He's still sleeping," Dan said. "When his head hits the pillow, he wouldn't wake up for the Second Coming. Let's go see what got killed."

When Fridley held the lantern high over the gray bulk laying still on the bloody grass, I knew my luck with mules was holding. Not a burro could be found with even a scratch on it.

"That's a relief," Dugan said. "A burro'll

kick the snot out of a mountain lion. That mule didn't have spunk enough to do nothing but eat."

Dan put a reassuring hand on my shoulder and clucked his tongue. "Take some advice from an ole-timer, and don't buy another mule. I don't think your luck runs in that direction."

I woke at the crack of dawn. Actually it was Stinky owning up to his name that did it. To this day, I've never known anyone who could chase away rats when he broke wind, but Stinky could.

So far, I had lost both of my mules and staked a claim on a vein of fool's gold. I began to have nagging doubts as to my abilities when it came to finding lost gold mines.

The only things of value I had left were my Winchester, bedroll, saddle, and that damned tent. This was more than I could pack out on my back, so after breakfast I made a rope sling to carry the tent and rifle. I donated the rest of my grub to the camp and told them I was going back to Jarbidge.

"Your saddle and stuff'll be here when you come back," Dan said.

Dutch slowed down on eating the rest of the biscuits and honey long enough to give me some advice. "Now you see why I got rid of that durn' mule. They're all a pain in the rear, just like Democrats. That's why the party uses a blasted mule for their mascot."

Looking back on the time, that was when I decided to vote Republican. I hitched up that tent and told everyone good bye.

"You'll be back, sonny boy!" Dan shouted after me. "Once gold gets in your blood, there's no way to get cured."

Not having a mule to contend with helped with the time it took to get off the mountain. The guards at the Pavlak mine paid me no mind this time. They were both standing in the open, gawking down the cañon.

My heart nearly jumped out my throat when I saw what was holding their attention. A thick column of black smoke was rising in the air from Jarbidge.

From the looks of it, the entire town was on fire.

Chapter Twenty-Two

All I could think of was Marybeth. I chided myself for leaving her alone. As I ran down that dirt road, the rope holding my gear chafed at my shoulder. There was a sharp pain in my side and every breath was a struggle by the time I got close enough to see what was burning.

I relaxed slightly when I found it was only the Jarbidge Hotel that was on fire.

When I reached my saloon, I didn't have the wind to go any farther. I tossed off my pack and stood gasping as I watched the milling crowd. Jarbidge and Elkoro Mines both had water pumpers for fire protection. They were parked side-by-side in the middle of the street. Their gasoline engines roared and heavy streams of water shot into the air.

As I regained my breath, I realized none of the fire-fighting efforts was being directed toward the hotel, which by now was nearly totally destroyed. All water pumped from the river was being shot onto the adjoining buildings, which appeared undamaged.

After a few moments, I made my way down the street. Willie was the first to see me. He was watching the fire with all the glee of a kid at a weenie roast.

"Hi, Mister Milo," he said happily, "we got such a big fire, it ain't even cold out."

I felt Marybeth's arms wrap around me. "Oh, honey, I'm so glad you're home."

Tully and Butt-Block were standing by the Elkoro pumper. They saw me and came over. "You can't ever leave town again," Tully told me firmly. "Every time you do, something f . . . fouls up." His face flashed red when he noticed Marybeth.

"Did anyone actually put water *on* the hotel?" I asked.

Butt-Block was so excited by the goings on, he spouted off without thinking: "I don't reckon anyone in Jarbidge would piss in Claude Lawton's mouth if his teeth were on fire."

Marybeth surprised me by laughing. A red-faced Butt-Block decided the pumper needed tending, and beat a hasty retreat.

"What started the fire?" I asked Tully, remembering Matt Whort's implied threat.

"It was some whiskey peddler from Twin Falls smoking a cigar. He said when he woke up, all he saw was fire."

"Then no one got hurt?" I asked.

Tully watched as the back wall of the hotel collapsed. "The peddler got himself singed a bit around the gills and won't need a haircut for a spell. He's over at Doc's."

I started to ask about the Lawtons, then I saw them standing in the distance.

Willie grinned as he pointed to his fur cap. "It's a good thing I moved in with Mister Eggs, or my new hat might 'a' caught fire an' burned up."

I was exhausted and hadn't had a bath since I'd left, so Marybeth and I went to the cabin. With all the excitement came a real plus; no one asked me why I happened to be short two mules.

Later that evening, Marybeth and I went to the bar. Eggs seemed in good spirits when he brought us a beer.

"Welcome back, Midas," he said loudly.

Since I'd had enough of lost mine talk, I changed the subject. "What are the Lawtons planning to do now that the hotel's burned?"

Tully overheard and said: "They're flat busted. We're collecting money so they can leave town." He motioned toward a jar at the end of the bar. "Folks are anxious to help 'em on their way."

I put ten dollars in the jar.

"Willie offered Lawton his old hat with the earflaps so he wouldn't catch cold," Eggs said. "The fat man just snorted and walked away."

"It's a real pleasure to see some folks going," I mentioned.

"At least the fire didn't spread none," Jackson said, coming to join us. "That was a stroke of luck. We could have lost the whole town."

Then Willie blurted out: "Mister Milo, Matt at the livery stable wants to know where your mules is at."

My explaining how I had managed to kill off two mules in one prospecting trip attracted more attention than the hotel fire.

When Tully finally quit laughing, he said: "Matt's going to be plumb crushed when he finds out about this. He's been living high on the hog stabling that pair of critters."

I put on my best pokerface. "The way I see it, a car beats mules six ways from Sunday."

"Cars ain't worth much for prospecting," Jackson ventured.

Marybeth shot me an evil smile. "Apparently neither is a mule, if Milo happens to own it."

It was a strain, but I finally saw a little humor in the situation and told Eggs to give everyone a drink on the house. After a short while, I grabbed up Marybeth and we went home for the night. I was anxious for her to know just how glad I was to be back.

The next morning, Eggs and Willie took the Model T and headed for Twin Falls. Groceries were cheaper there, but, most of all, I think my bartender wanted a day off. Willie was always happy to go anywhere.

The electric power was finally wired in. Tonight would be the first time light bulbs would illuminate the Miners' Exchange. While I was at it, I had a crank telephone installed. This was not one of my better ideas, but cheaper than buying another mule. Marybeth tried it out by calling her grandmother. It's mind boggling how long a woman can talk over one of those things and not say anything. When I overheard the conversation drifting toward mules, I headed for the post office.

Slabs Larson had taken over as postmaster when Sylvia left. I teased him about folks no longer dying to do business with him. He gave me a dead-pan look and said:

"One thing you've got to remember about an undertaker . . . we're the last one in this world to let you down."

My chuckle was cut short when Slabs plunked a packet from Theodore Spurgeon onto the counter. I snatched it up and went to Fong's to read over what the lawyer had to say. The pungent smell of burned wood hung in the air; a hint of smoke still seeped from the pile of rubble that used to be the Jarbidge Hotel.

The Chinaman seemed glad to see me. "So solly you mules die. Maybe Charlie look for lost mine now. Dammy near have this place burn down around ears. Gold no burnee."

I took a sip of coffee and spread the documents out on the table. From what I could make of the legal gobbledygook, the trial for the Pavlak mine was set to begin September 16th and could run for a week's time. I perked up when I decided to take Marybeth with me. Elko might have a hotel with room service.

Then I read a handwritten note Spurgeon had enclosed. The lawsuit over Kitty Wilkins's ranch had gone against her, the judge awarding it to C. C. Logan. Spurgeon said he had filed an appeal to a higher court, *pro bono,* in her behalf. I knew Kitty had to be crushed by the decision. I sincerely hoped the lawsuit over the Pavlak mine would go better.

Eggs and Willie returned the next afternoon. As soon as their groceries were put away, they came over to visit. Willie was so excited he kept jumping up and down.

"Mister Milo," he shouted, "we stayed in a big hotel an' they had this little room that went straight up in the air an' straight down ag'in and ag'in!"

Eggs poured a beer and grinned. "I gave the elevator operator a dollar to let him keep riding. He'd still be there if he hadn't gotten hungry." Then Eggs said: "We stopped by and visited with Kitty. She said for you to plan the marriage ceremony for June First. Marybeth is to be the matron of honor, and Reece wants Willie to be best man."

Willie looked scared. "I never been a bes' man before. Most folks think I ain't even smart 'nough for a good 'un."

"Most of us think you are," I said, putting my hand on his shoulder.

"Well, I'll be," Willie mumbled.

Eggs shot me a skeptical look. "I never thought I'd be so far from God that folks would have to resort to the likes of you for a preacher."

One good thing about Eggs was, you

couldn't stay in a dark mood long with him around. "I don't do baptisms or pass around a collection plate."

"Like I tell folks," Eggs said, lighting a cigar, "you get what you pay for in this world."

Marybeth was ecstatic over Kitty's impending wedding. The first thing she did was go shopping for a new dress. Of course, nothing in Jarbidge even came close to being good enough. The handle on that crank telephone was too hot to touch when she finally got one ordered from Twin Falls with instructions to put it on the next stage.

Then Marybeth heard about Willie's being the best man. She grabbed him from the livery stable and dragged the poor guy to Adams's store. A new white shirt and black bow tie later, she was satisfied. I thought Willie looked ridiculous as a politician in a parade, but Marybeth was pleased as punch with her efforts.

It was a clear, blue, and warm morning in the mountains when we piled into that Packard for the drive to Kitty's. Not even a hint of clouds hung over the high peaks.

Marybeth had picked a bouquet of pink peonies. She thought they were the prettiest of flowers and had planted a large patch in front of our cabin. Marybeth had stuck one through the lapel of Willie's coat and pinned it from behind so it would stay put.

I hated wearing a tie and had talked Marybeth into letting me keep it in my pocket until we got to the wedding. Willie wasn't so lucky. He'd already had that bow tie wrapped around his neck. He sat in the back seat proudly holding a present for Kitty.

The new road being built down the river looked inviting when we drove past it. By the middle of summer, it would be completed all the way to Kitty's, but, for now, Crippin Grade was the way we had to go.

Just before coming to where the road dropped off into the steep cañon where Kitty's ranch was, Marybeth's eye caught something.

"Stop the car, Milo," she said excitedly. "I see an airplane!"

Sure enough, once the gray cloud of grime we were making cleared, a bright red, two-cockpit biplane was winging low over the sagebrush-studded flat land. We climbed out to watch it. Any airplane in those days was a rare sight.

Willie was amazed. "Look at that, will ya?" he said, pointing. "It's mighty big to stay in the air like that."

"There's people in that thing," Marybeth said to Willie. "What I can't understand is why it's here."

Willie shook his head in wonderment. "Gol durn, I never seen nuthin' like that before."

The plane banked steeply about a half mile away, leveled out, and began heading in our direction. At first, I thought the engine was backfiring. A steady *rat-tat-tat* sound boomed in the still, clear air. A huge cloud of dust began building in front of the biplane.

"That thing's scarin' the horsies!" Willie shouted.

His sharp eyes were the first to see them. A large herd of wild mustangs were running in panic from the airplane. I saw a few horses toward the rear of the running herd fall. Then I could make out the figure of a man in the rear seat of the biplane with a gun.

"They're killing the wild horses!" I yelled.

"Oh, my God," Marybeth sobbed as she saw the mustangs were being driven in wild-eyed panic to the edge of the steep cliff that dropped off into the Bruneau River.

I have played the scene that followed in my mind hundreds of times since then, wondering what I could have done differently, wishing fervently I had done anything but watch.

"The horsies are gonna fall off the cliff!" Willie screamed. He jerked the peony from his lapel, tossed it to Marybeth, and ran wildly through the sagebrush toward the stampeding horses.

The men in the biplane must have seen us because the plane turned sharply away, but their mission was already accomplished. A large piebald stallion was in the lead of the panicked herd. It passed so close I could see the horse's fear-glazed eyes.

Willie ran headlong into the horses' path. When the thundering herd approached him, Willie waved his arms, vainly attempting to warn them away from the cliff. In an instant it was over. When the piebald hit him, Willie wrapped his burly arms around the horse's neck. For a brief second, I thought he might make it to the stallion's back, but his grip failed and he was swept under.

Marybeth screamed and grabbed onto me, burying her eyes from the sight of Willie's being trampled. I watched helplessly as that entire drove of terrorized mustangs continued on to plunge over the sheer cliff to their death.

Silence hung in the air heavy as the cloud of powder dust made by the horses passing.

Only Marybeth's sobs and the distant drone of the airplane could be heard.

I helped Marybeth into the seat of the car, her thin body shaking like an aspen leaf.

"Why?" she managed to ask. "Why are they doing this?"

There was no answer I could give. I handed her my handkerchief and went to look for Willie with a broken heart.

I knew he was dead the moment I saw him. Willie Pavlak was nearly unrecognizable, beaten and torn from the many hoofs that had struck him. All I could do was cover his body. He was far too heavy for me to carry.

Marybeth looked up hopefully when I came to the car. When she saw my expression, she buried her tear-stained face into my handkerchief with trembling hands as waves of despair racked her slender body.

For some reason, I'd put that tent in the trunk of the Packard. I took it out and carted it through the sagebrush to Willie's body and unrolled it for the first time. Once I had the canvas tucked well around him, I began shaking with rage. I sped the short distance to Kitty's, lost in a red fog.

Everything had happened so fast, my mind couldn't comprehend it. One minute we were happily driving to a wedding, the next, Willie was dead and wild horses were being slaughtered by the hundreds.

Theodore Spurgeon, Reece, and two uniformed men, carrying guns, were standing in front of the inn. Kitty, wearing her usual baggy overalls, was sitting on an overturned wooden barrel, staring down the fast-flowing river with vacant eyes. A dead horse was caught in a snag, its rigid legs pointing skyward, bobbing in the strong current. Marybeth ran to her, but Kitty paid no mind. She just kept her blank gaze on that mustang in the river.

"It's C. C. Logan," Spurgeon said loudly when I approached. "He hired the airplane and there's nothing legal we can do to stop him." He hissed the word *legal* like a snake.

"They've killed Willie!" I shouted.

The older lawman, who I would find out later was County Sheriff Ben McKeever, rolled his deep green eyes at me. "Did they shoot him?"

"No," I replied sharply. "He tried to stop a herd of wild horses from running off the cliff and got trampled to death."

"Damn it all," Reece spat, "these blasted lawmen won't let me do a thing about this."

McKeever's face flushed. "Logan's lawyer sent us here to keep the peace. He knew there would be trouble from shooting those mustangs, but there ain't no law against it. If what you say is true, what happened to this Willie fellow was an accident. He should have had more sense than to get in the way of a bunch of stampeding horses."

"He was retarded," Spurgeon growled. "He had the mind of a child."

The sheriff frowned in cold fury. "I'm sorry. I didn't know. I don't like this business any more than anyone. It's just that I have to uphold the law, even the ones I don't like."

The younger deputy nodded toward Reece. "You want me and him to go get the guy that got run over? It's gonna get plenty warm today."

"Just make sure he don't take any pot shots at that plane," the sheriff said with pained firmness.

Reece Morgan watched sadly as a pair of dead horses washed by. "Don't worry about me, it just doesn't matter any more. A man knows when he's beat. I reckon Kitty'll never get over it, though. She's been looking forward to this day for a long spell. Then they go and kill all those wild horses."

I watched as Reece and the deputy left and climbed into the police car. Kitty didn't appear to understand the part about Willie's getting killed. She just kept staring down the river. Marybeth stood behind her, eyes streaming tears.

I swallowed hard. "Then all of this is over Kitty's claim to the ranch?"

McKeever said: "Logan figures no horses, no income. Then Kitty will give up and let him have the place."

"Someone should kill that cold-hearted son-of-a-bitch," I spat out.

"He ain't worth it, son," the sheriff said firmly. "The good Lord will take care of him, eventually."

The sheriff and I watched as Theodore Spurgeon walked over and took a seat alongside Kitty on that overturned rain barrel. Both were staring down the river when we heard a long series of *pops* from atop the mesa. When that red biplane roared over the rim, at least two dozen mustangs plunged over that sheer cliff. Kitty's expression never changed, but, for the only time in my life, I saw a lawyer cry.

The whole town shut down when we buried Wheelbarrow Willie. Even the weather took on a mood of despair. Black clouds hovered over the mountains, blocking the sun.

Marybeth clung to me, crying, as Slabs,

Turkey Curley, and the Bruckner brothers lowered Willie to his rest. Slabs had worked all night to build a coffin large enough to hold the big man.

Once he was in the ground, everyone looked to me. I took the eulogy from my pocket and tried to read it, but the lump in my throat wouldn't let me speak.

Eggs took the paper from my trembling hand and gave Willie a good send off. The Bruckners sang in German while the grave was being filled. When it was over, Marybeth wrapped her arm around my waist and together we walked home in the cold rain that had begun to fall.

Word soon came that Kitty and Reece had abandoned the ranch and moved to Glenns Ferry, a little town on the Snake River. They weren't there long when Kitty passed away. The newspaper said a stroke killed her. I knew better. Kitty Wilkins couldn't live in a world without wild horses.

No matter how bad the storm, there always comes a sunny day and life goes on. Things slowly returned to normal in Jarbidge. Under Tully's capable direction, Elkoro Mines began producing huge quantities of gold.

Eggs, Marybeth, and I were getting the

Miners' Exchange spruced up for a big 4th of July celebration. We had run red, white, and blue streamers from side to side across the ceiling. Tully had a dozen red sticks of dynamite stuffed under the bar alongside Willie's set of dominoes no one would play any more.

Marybeth answered our ring on the wall phone and motioned for me to take the call. It was Theodore Spurgeon.

"I've some good news for a change," the lawyer said in his professional tone. "C. C. Logan's dead."

"I hope he choked on a piece of meat."

"Nothing that simple. He was out irrigating his hay when someone shot him."

"Does McKeever know who did it?" I asked.

"When he gets back from his fishing trip, he says he'll give it his top priority."

"What does this do to the Pavlak mine suit?" I questioned.

"It's all over. Logan's wife's moving back East."

I thanked the lawyer and was in a downright good mood for celebrating when I hung up the phone. Since the sheriff didn't have a clue who had done the shooting, there was a good chance Reece Morgan might return my Winchester someday.

Chapter Twenty-Three

"That vein of gold ore at the Pavlak is richer than Rockefeller's dog," Jackson told me early one afternoon when we were alone in the bar.

"Why don't you and the Bruckners mine it?"

Jackson washed down a mouthful of tobacco juice with a swig of beer. "Milo, I've been at this game for over twenty years. We might make one little blast, and it'll be gone."

I had begun to realize lately there was a lot more to mining gold than I'd thought. "What have you got in mind?"

"The most money in the mining business is made either in stock swindles or selling out to some outfit that wants to run one. A little high grade showing can move a lot of paper."

After my experience with Dave Bourne's stock, he had my full attention. Jackson was acting nervous as a pregnant nun, so I knew he had a plan.

I told him: "You're going to die from tobacco-juice poison, if you don't come out with it."

"Tabaccy juice keeps you from getting worms. Rock dust and the cold from mining gets you dead. There's a company from California that wants to buy my lease. They'd pay a lot more if they was to own the Pavlak."

"We just sell them the mine and have nothing more to do with it?"

"That's the size of it," Jackson said.

"What kind of deal can we make?" I asked.

"They offered me twenty-five thousand dollars for my lease. There's another hundred grand available to buy the mine. I was wondering if I might talk you out of a finder's fee."

"Jackson," I said firmly, "if you can get those fools to part with a hundred and twenty-five thousand dollars cash, I'll split the whole thing down the middle with you."

He got a wad of tobacco crossways in his throat and nearly choked. When he could speak, he wheezed out: "That is more than I'd hoped for."

"I don't suppose I could have sold it for

that much without you."

Jackson managed a grin. "Not likely. To keep everything on the up an' up, though, we best run the deal through Spurgeon. I'll pay his bill out of my share."

It was my turn to smile. I felt better going through Spurgeon, but I also knew how much he charged for his services. If preachers charged as much for using words as lawyers did, heaven would be a mighty lonely place.

"Now that we got our business settled," I said, "tell me what you got planned to do with your money?"

Jackson said with a gleam in his eye. "Inman Searcy and me's been staying in touch. Sylvia and him bought a hotel on the ocean in San Diego. The weather's so dadgum good out there, both of 'em quit drinking."

"You don't have to move to California to quit drinking."

Jackson gave out a chuckle. "I'm going to buy half interest in Searcy's hotel, and we're going to expand the place. You wouldn't believe what people will pay for a stay on the ocean."

Two weeks later, I banked my share of the money from the sale and said my good byes to Jackson Lyman at the train station.

When we had met at Spurgeon's office, I scarcely had recognized Lyman. He'd come to town the day before and visited a barber. His white beard was gone and his hair trimmed short. The snappy suit of clothes he wore, topped off with a brown bowler hat, made the transformation from tobacco-chewing miner to normal human being complete. He looked dangerously similar to a certain lawyer.

I hated to see Jackson leave, but, at the same time, I was glad for him. While most people come to a gold rush town expecting to get rich, only a small fraction actually do. Far more remain entombed in the rocky ground of a cemetery. Others like old Ed Kennison leave broken in health. The more I thought on the matter, the happier I was to see that train chug its way out of the station carrying Jackson Lyman to California.

Marybeth surprised me when she cried her eyes out over getting that money from selling the Pavlak mine.

"It should have gone to help poor Willie," she sobbed.

I gently reminded her there had been a lawsuit against the property that prevented anyone from selling it until after Willie was gone.

She gave me a hug and kiss, then stepped back, leaving the fragrance of lilacs hanging in the air. "Oh, Milo, I know it's not your fault what happened. It's just that I miss him. I can't help but get lonely on occasion."

If she had slapped me, it wouldn't have made a deeper impression. I had been so busy running a business and trying to find a lost mine that I'd overlooked the fact Marybeth didn't have any women friends in town to socialize with. What few women there were in Jarbidge of Marybeth's age either had a houseful of kids to tend or worked down in Cherry Flats.

"Marybeth," I said, taking her hand, "Jarbidge is a gold rush town. The closest most of these miners ever get to a pretty girl like you is when they plunk down a silver dollar in Cherry Flats. We won't be here much longer, but, to help pass the time, Eggs would like to have you help him in the bar once in a while."

"It would be nice to get out some. Do you think we might also be able to spend a day or two in Twin Falls?"

Remembering the last time we stayed in the hotel there, I readily agreed. "Honey, I'll make you a promise. I want to make one more try at finding that lost mine. Then, win or lose, we'll sell the bar and move any-where your little heart desires."

Her eyes sparkled. "Do you mean it?"

"Of course, I do. Where do you want to go?"

"If we could move to where it's warmer so I could plant some flowers, besides peonies, I would like that."

"They have flowers all year long in San Diego," I said.

"I hear it's *so* beautiful there," she squealed in delight, "and I've never seen the ocean!"

"We can stay in Searcy's Seaside Resort until we get a place of our own. It would be nice visiting with people we know."

Marybeth gave me a toe-curling kiss, then pushed me away with a frown. "Milo Theodore," she said with feigned anger, "just how do you happen to know what it costs to visit Cherry Flats?"

"Just bar talk," I answered quickly as I remembered some urgent business I had to attend to.

The rest of that summer of 1917 was a busy time. Elkoro kept hiring more men and the town of Jarbidge grew to 1,500 souls.

"I'm going to make this the number one gold mine in Nevada," Tully was fond of saying. From the frequency bullion was being shipped, escorted by shotgun-wielding guards, few questioned his judgment.

Turkey Curley and I built a large addition onto the Miners' Exchange to handle the increased business. Turkey had been kept too busy to go on a decent drunk. He'd quit shaking and could now hit a nail with the first lick of his hammer. Even with Curley speeded up, it took until the end of August for us to finish.

I nearly didn't make another trip to God's Pocket that year because Marybeth got sick. Every morning she'd head for the bathroom and toss up her breakfast. After she promised to see Dr. Harlan while I was gone, I made another attempt to find the Lost Sheepherder's Mine.

Not having any expensive mules to kill off made for a faster trip. This time I walked, carrying only a canvas tarp to cover up with should it storm, and a backpack crammed with foodstuffs. I didn't have my rifle any longer, so I stuck a little pistol under my belt along with a prospector's pick.

This time I stayed far lower on God's Pocket than Dugan's cabin. To my way of thinking, that area had been gone over closer than a baby's thumb. Besides, Stinky might still have been up there. I had rather sleep in a cold rain surrounded by hungry mountain lions than be stuck in a nice warm cabin with him when he passed wind.

I had been out four days pounding on rocks where God's Pocket Creek runs into Slide Creek when I actually found gold. The weather was beautiful and the sun glinted off a yellow nugget. When I picked up this rock, however, I knew it was the genuine article — dull yellow and soft to a knife point. The only problem was there wasn't any vein to be seen. Just this one lone nugget the size of a flattened hen's egg laying in a stream.

Three days later, I was short of food and hadn't found another speck of gold. The weather took on an ominous tone. Pewter-gray clouds began rolling in and the temperature dropped like a stone. I had lived in the high country long enough to know better than to challenge an early snowstorm. Making certain I had the area well marked, I hitched up my gear and headed for Jarbidge.

It was growing dark and freezing cold when I got home. The first thing I did was grab the nugget from my coat pocket to show Marybeth.

"Have I got something to show you," I proudly said.

"And I've some news for you, too." She

giggled excitedly. "I saw the doctor like I promised. Milo, I'm going to have a baby."

It took a moment before my mind could get in gear and open my mouth. I was both dumbstruck and happy at the same time. I had supposed from all the lovemaking, this could happen someday. I was just shocked it had occurred so soon.

"You are happy about it, aren't you?" Marybeth asked with concern.

I wrapped my arms around her. "Of course, I am. It's just that I'm surprised is all."

She kissed my cheek and whispered: "I really don't know why, especially after those two nights we spent in that hotel in Twin Falls."

It slowly soaked into my head I was going to have a family again. I held Marybeth tight and felt happier than at any time in my life.

"One person in town isn't going to be happy about this," I said.

She wrinkled her freckled brow. "And who would that be?"

"Turkey Curley . . . he's going to have to stay sober long enough now to build a new room on our cabin."

Marybeth's smile fled. "I thought we had agreed to move from here, Milo. This is no place to raise a child."

"Of course, we'll go to California. It just might take a little longer than I thought is all," I said, placing the nugget in her hand.

"You found gold!"

"Just this one piece, but the mother lode can't be far."

"It's so heavy and pretty," she said excitedly. "What is it worth?"

"I guess it to weigh four ounces. That would make it worth eighty dollars."

"And it was just lying there waiting to be picked up?"

I squeezed her hand. "Just give me through next summer then the Goodman family can leave Jarbidge rich."

"There will be three of us by then. The baby should arrive in April, Doc Harlan said. Couldn't we go see Gramma, and then go to California? We can come back next summer, once the snow is gone, and find your gold mine. Eggs can run the bar."

Then I made a fateful decision. "We own a business here, Marybeth. There's a chance someone might buy the bar at a good price if we're in town to negotiate."

She pursed her lips, and I knew she wasn't happy with me. "We'll do what you think is best."

Then I went to the Miners' Exchange to inform everyone about my good fortune in becoming a father. When I entered, Eggs looked at me strangely, then I saw why.

At the end of the bar, humped over on a stool, sat Billy McGraw.

Chapter Twenty-Four

Billy looked pale from all those months he'd spent locked up in jail.

"No one ever told me about what happened to Kitty and Willie," were the first words he spoke.

I sat down beside him.

Billy took a sip of beer. "Bad luck's like a faithful dog. It'll follow you anywhere. I should have listened when everyone told me to stay away from Ben Kuhl."

"I take it they let you off?"

"Day before yesterday, when the jury came in. It's taken me that long to get here. I walked most of the way. All I've got's what I'm wearing."

Eggs had been listening. "What happened to Kuhl and Beck?"

Billy's eyes lowered. "Ben's gonna be shot by a firing squad. The bloody fingerprints on the mail was his, and they proved it. Ed Beck's going to prison for helping him."

I felt gratified Ben Kuhl was finally getting the kind of attention he so richly deserved, but, at the same time, I was sorry for Billy. His only crime had been being dumb enough to loan out his gun. My heart did a double thump when I thought back on where my Winchester had gone.

"Do you have any plans?" I asked.

"I can't stay around here. I just wanted to tell Kitty and everyone how sorry I was." He answered, then pursed his lips. "I guess I'm a little late for that."

Eggs refilled Billy's beer mug and slid it to him. "When was the last time you ate?"

Billy's voice was distant: "A couple of days ago."

"I thought so," Eggs replied, fishing in his pocket for money. "Go to Fong's and get something to eat and rent a room there for the night. Thing's will look better tomorrow, kid."

From the cash register, I took forty dollars and laid it on the bar in front of Billy. "Wherever it is you're heading, you won't have to walk to get there."

"All I done was cause you hurt. I don't understand anyone helping me," he replied, keeping his head down.

I gently put my hand on his arm. "Everyone makes mistakes. You're a free man.

Make the most of it."

Billy slowly took the money, stuck it in the pocket of his ragged shirt, and said: "There's a war on. I'll go sign up for the Army. With my good luck, maybe I'll get kilt."

When a broken Billy McGraw left the saloon that evening, he joined a long list of people who, when they departed Jarbidge, was never heard of again.

The ominous-looking storm that ran me out of the high country and away from where I found gold never did amount to anything. It got cold enough to freeze Marybeth's peonies, then warmed up to give us a beautiful Indian summer.

Bright hues of orange and red were washing up the sides of the jagged mountain slopes when Turkey Curley and I started building onto the cabin. Fall has always been my favorite time of the year. In the high country, the air is so clear and crisp you can almost touch it.

Marybeth began taking on that rosy radiance only a mother-to-be can sport. She wasted no time ordering a crib from Twin Falls, even though Doc Harlan said the baby wouldn't arrive until April.

Jarbidge was deep in snow by Thanksgiving. Not having to contend with Crippen Grade kept people moving around without a lot of problems and the town kept booming.

Elkoro Mines was operating three shifts a day. To accommodate all the thirsty miners wanting to part with their pay checks, Eggs and I began keeping the saloon open twenty-four hours a day. Eggs tended bar from six at night until six the next morning. I took the day shift.

While I was at work, Marybeth kept busy knitting baby clothes and quilting blankets. With one exception she had that new room decked out from stem to stern for our future arrival. I told her it was going to be a boy. She argued against that and wanted to paint the place pink. We compromised and bought both blue and pink paint to await the outcome.

With prospecting and mine expansion shut down for the winter, life slipped into a routine. When our country entered the war in April, Tully had a lot of men quit Elkoro patriotically to join one of the Armed Services. Finding workers became an increasingly difficult proposition for him.

Wars create many different forms of hell. Reading newspaper accounts of soldiers being blown apart or gassed by the thousands in some distant country is one thing. When those who are wounded in body or spirit return home, that's another.

By January of 1918 a few of these poor souls began drifting into Jarbidge hoping for employment and to forget the horrors they had undergone. Tully, in need of any warm body who could work, gave them a job and a place to stay in the Elkoro boarding house.

None of us living in this sheltered little Nevada mountain town ever dreamed one of these men would bring more than bad memories along with him.

It was snowing hard the afternoon of the 15th when Tully came into the bar. He stomped the snow from his boots and went to the stove to warm himself. From the expression on his face I knew something was terribly wrong.

"We just took a man over to Slabs," he said solemnly.

"An accident?" I asked.

"Nope," Tully replied. "He had a headache and the chills this morning. When one of the guys checked on him, after lunch, he was deader than a doornail."

I started to say something, but Tully wrapped an arm around my shoulders, drew me close, and said in a hushed tone: "Doc Harlan looked him over. He's mighty worried that he might have died from the Spanish flu. Pneumonia don't kill that fast. To top it off, he came straight to Jarbidge once he got off a boat that come in from Europe."

Icy fingers of dread played along my backbone. From reading newspapers and listening to people talking, I had heard of this deadly new strain of flu. It was gaining notoriety for killing young, healthy adults in a very short time. I remembered reading an article where, in England, a young woman climbed aboard a streetcar. By the time it arrived at the end of its route, the conductor found the lady dead in her seat.

"It can't be," I told Tully. "The Spanish flu's only really hit in Europe and India. That's thousands of miles from here."

"Doc Harlan says it's caused by a germ. He also said there's been increasing cases on the East Coast." Then he scared the living daylights out of me when he told me just how easy germs can travel, and that a sneeze or even a handshake can infect a person.

"But the doctor's not sure that's what killed your man?"

"Nope, he said he hopes like hell it's not the flu because, if it is, there's going to be a bunch of people get sick around here. The man that died, ate his meals at Fong's, shopped at the Adams's store, and who knows . . . he might have drank some beer here or even visited Cherry Flats."

"What did Doc say we could do about it?"

"Wait to see if people start dying," was Tully's cold, simple reply.

We didn't have to wait long. Two days after Tully and I talked, Doc Harlan had four men in his little eight-bed hospital. All were miners who worked for Elkoro and lived in the boarding house where the first man died.

"If you make it through the first twenty-four hours," Eggs told me, "Doc says you'll most likely live."

Three of the men in the hospital were to make it, one wasn't. But by the time we knew this, Dr. Harlan had set up more beds to care for the growing numbers of sick. There was no longer any question — the Spanish flu had come to Jarbidge.

In those days there wasn't much a doctor could do except force fluids into the patient and try to get their fever down. Mustard plasters, aspirin, and laudanum were administered to ease the person's suffering. Outside of that, a body was either able to fight off the infection or not. With the Spanish flu, there wasn't a long wait to find out.

Dr. Harlan quickly became exhausted tending to the sick twenty-four hours a day. Most people were afraid of catching the disease and refused to go anywhere near the hospital, let alone help him.

Marybeth offered her services, but the doctor took one look at her swelling belly and said: "Young lady, get yourself home and stay there. You've got a baby to look out for."

Much to everyone's surprise, Dumb Dora, the prostitute from Cherry Flats, pitched in as a nurse. Tirelessly she worked around the clock, helping Doc Harlan as best she could. Dora Mays was her real name. After a few days of her caring for the sick or holding the hand of a dying person, this became the only name she would ever be called again. I'm certain if anyone dared call her Dumb Dora ever again, they would have been cheerfully beaten to a pulp.

By the 1st of February, the Miners' Exchange had become nearly deserted. People were afraid to go anywhere. Those who did wore gauze masks to cover their faces and mouths. Most of the freighters refused to deliver anything to Jarbidge for fear of becoming infected. The few who braved a trip to the mountains would leave their goods at the edge of town for us to pick up.

"Minnie Adams died this morning," Eggs said sadly when he came to work the afternoon of the 3rd. "She's the first woman we've lost."

"Damn it," Butt-Block fumed. "If this was something you could shoot, I could handle it. How in hell do you shoot a disease?"

I had no answer for him.

A distant, muffled blast rippled through the silent air; Turkey Curley was dynamiting a fresh grave in the frozen ground of the cemetery. Slabs and he were working long hours. Counting Minnie Adams, so far eight coffins had been put into the ground. No one had a clue when it would be over.

Eggs began coughing and running a fever. I left Butt-Block to tend bar and helped him home. The hospital was too full to hold any more patients. Somehow, Dora found out about Eggs's being sick and came by. She put a mustard plaster on him that smelled strong enough to peel paint.

Marybeth cried when I told her Eggs had the flu. I kissed her and said: "I'm going to stay with him until we see it through."

For over a day, Eggs took turns shivering and burning up with fever. Dora came by a couple of times to change his mustard plaster and dose him with some kind of medicine Doc had given her. He was so sick, it was a chore to get him to swallow it.

Around midnight of the second day, the fever broke. Eggs roused enough to raise his head from the pillow. "What does a man have to do to get a cigar and a beer around this place?" he asked hoarsely.

I had a tear of relief in my eye when I answered: "He can start by getting his lazy butt out of bed and going back to work."

For the next few days the disease seemed to ebb. A few did come down sick, but all recovered. People began moving about again, and business slowly picked up at the bar.

Then Slabs was called to Fong's hotel to take away a body. The dead man was one of the promoters who bought the Pavlak mine from Jackson and me.

While nailing the man into a coffin, Slabs himself took ill. In spite of the doctor's efforts, Slabs Larson passed away that same night.

Turkey Curley had been helping bury folks for so long, the job of undertaking naturally fell on his shoulders.

"I'm gonna get drunk as a waltzing pissant when this thing's over," Turkey grumbled as I helped him with the sad task of laying Slabs away. "And it'll be soon, too, 'cause we're using the last coffin in town."

I glanced around the undertaker's parlor and saw he was correct.

"What happened to them all?" I asked. "There hasn't been *that* many people pushing up daisies."

"Folks building bought them to use the lumber. They make real good shelves and such. There never was a need for all those coffins he kept around" — Turkey Curley's voice trailed off — "until now."

Marybeth insisted on accompanying me to the cemetery when we went to bury Slabs. Slabs Larson was one of the first friends I'd made in Jarbidge.

Turkey Curley and I slid the coffin into the back of the undertaker's shiny black horse-drawn hearse, and drove to our cabin. I went and started the Packard to let it warm up for a while so Marybeth wouldn't get chilled.

Even wearing a heavy fur coat, it was obvious Marybeth was expecting. Turkey Curley climbed down and held the car door open while I helped her inside. Then we slowly joined an all too familiar funeral procession to the Jarbidge cemetery.

Snow was spitting down from a dismal sky when we got Slabs laid away. On our way home, Marybeth began coughing. I got her inside the cabin quickly and stoked up the fire with a worried brow.

"Go to work, Milo," she said happily, giving me a peck on the cheek. "It's just the cold air."

I'd closed the bar for Slabs's burial. When I glanced out the window toward the saloon, I saw Butt-Block and a few thirsty miners awaiting my return.

"You rest up, honey," I told her. "When Eggs takes over for the night, I'll drop by Fong's and bring dinner home with me, so don't worry about cooking anything."

"Anything is fine but the oysters," she said, laughing as I went out the door.

The snowstorm increased its fury the rest of the day. I remember slogging through over a foot of white stuff when I carried home two of Fong's choice butter-fried steaks.

I set them on the kitchen table and called out to Marybeth. I could see her lying on the sofa, wrapped up like a cocoon in a heavy patchwork quilt. When she didn't answer me, I assumed she had simply dozed off. Then I heard her heavy breathing. It was the same raspy sound Eggs had made when he was sick with the flu.

I ran to her and placed my hand on her forehead. It was like touching a stove. She was burning up with fever.

"Marybeth!" I cried out, too shook to think. "Let's get you to bed, then I'll fetch Doc Harlan."

She roused enough to look at me with red, watery eyes. "Oh, Milo, the baby," she rattled through the phlegm filling her lungs.

Quickly I picked her up and carried her to the bedroom. I didn't take time to grab a coat before running to the hospital through the falling snow.

A look of disbelief crossed the doctor's face when I shouted to him Marybeth had the flu.

"Christ, no," he blurted out, grabbing up his black leather satchel. Dora Mays followed hot on our heels as we headed for the cabin.

"Go make a pot of coffee," Doc Harlan told me when he began examining Marybeth. "I'll stay with her as long as I have to."

Even in the kitchen, I could smell the pungent odor of one of those mustard plasters like they had used on Eggs. I desperately hoped it would work as good on Marybeth.

The doctor blew into the hot coffee with a frown. "Waiting is the hardest part of practicing medicine, Milo. I've given her some laudanum. Dora put on a mustard plaster. Now all we can do is place some cold towels on her forehead to see if we can get the fever to break. And pray."

"What can I do?" I asked, listening to Marybeth's ragged breathing.

"Go outside and bring in some snow," Doc ordered. "We'll use it to cool the towels."

A feeling of sheer black fright struck me like a fist to the gut. I knew all too well how deadly this disease could be. I cursed myself for not taking Marybeth to California like she'd wanted.

For the next few hours I carried in bucket after bucket of snow only to watch with growing despair as Marybeth's fever continued unabated.

The rhythmic ticking of the swinging brass pendulum of that big Regulator wall clock Dave Bourne had left behind began keeping time with Marybeth's broken breathing, which now had become a shallow rattle.

Just past one in the morning, the 13th day of February, 1918, the ticking of that clock was the only sound to break the dark silence in that little room.

My Marybeth, my family, was dead.

317

And it was all my fault.

A tear trickled down the doctor's cheek as he sadly drew the patchwork quilt over her face. He tried to say something to me, but his voice broke so badly, I couldn't understand him.

A cold knot of realization formed in my stomach. Somewhere in the cloudy distance I heard a woman crying. Dora Mays's soft hands wrapped around my shaking body.

"I'll stay with him," I heard her sob to the doctor. "You had best get back to the hospital."

The next thing I remembered, I found myself sitting at the kitchen table. Eggs was there, and so was Butt-Block and Tully. From inside his coat, Butt-Block brought out a bottle of whiskey. He opened it, poured a water glass full, and stuck it in my hand.

"Drink," the big man said softly. "There's nothing else left to do."

The next morning, a sun that gave no warmth was hanging in a clear blue sky when I went outside into the snow. There was something I had to do. I wished in vain for the same numbness to return that had enveloped me when my first family had been killed, but this wasn't to be. A pain burned where my heart had been. I knew this pain would never be extinguished.

I trudged to the shed where Turkey Curley and I had stored some leftover lumber from when we had built the room on the cabin for the baby. I laid out some boards on sawhorses and began building a coffin. Tully and Butt-Block came to help, but I ran them off. This was something I had to do alone.

When I was tacking that patchwork quilt inside the coffin for a liner, a muffled boom echoed from down the still cañon; Turkey Curley was blasting Marybeth's grave into the frozen earth.

Eggs tried his best to say the words when we buried her, but he kept choking up. Tully finally took the tattered paper from his hands and did a good job of reading the eulogy.

The Bruckner Brothers sang in German like they'd done for Fred and Willie. Dora put her arm around Eggs and cried her heart out.

I just watched.

Trying to make more money than a man would ever need, I had killed the last person in this world who loved me. I shoved my hands deep into my coat pockets and walked back to town in the cold air, following behind Slabs's creaking, empty hearse.

Then I went to the bar and crawled deep into a whiskey bottle.

Chapter Twenty-Five

When you're using booze as a salve for an aching heart, it takes frequent and liberal applications to achieve decent results. Turkey Curley just *thought* he was successful at being the town drunk. For the next year, I showed him and everyone else in Jarbidge how to get the job done right.

After Marybeth and the baby died, I had no reason to live. At first, I thought God might be fair about this and let me get the flu. That wasn't to be. Hell, I never even caught a cold.

Then, quickly and without reason, the disease left Jarbidge.

After I finally sobered up, I read where the Spanish flu had killed millions. It's strange how little numbers mean unless one of them represents someone you loved.

Dora Mays moved in with Eggs right after Marybeth died. The two of them never took the trouble to get married, but they were happy together for a lot of years. Some of us have far less time together than they did.

If it hadn't been for Eggs and Dora, I would have drunk myself to death. They made sure I ate something on occasion. Once a week, Eggs would haul me inside my cabin and, in spite of every threat I could throw at him, made me take a bath and put on clean clothes.

Eventually I ran out of spending money. I had bled the Miners' Exchange capital down to where Eggs could barely buy stock. There was lots of money in the bank, however.

One morning, while I was still sober enough to do business, I grabbed up my checkbook and staggered over to the bank.

"I can't cash a check for you," Ben Jorgason said firmly. "Your account has been frozen by a lawsuit."

"What do you mean about a lawsuit?" I asked with slurred words.

"The bank can't release any funds to you until the court order is lifted," Ben said with finality.

"I'm going to get my lawyer, Theodore Spurgeon. Then I'm taking my money out of your bank!" I shouted.

Jorgason's eyebrows drew down into a point. "Spurgeon is the one who filed the suit freezing your funds."

I wandered around town the rest of the day under a black cloud of anger, trying to get someone to buy me a drink. Even Tully and Butt-Block refused me. I ranted and raved against lawyers in general, telling everyone how hell was too decent a place to send them.

"You can't win a battle when you're drunk," Eggs reminded me.

I kept my bloodshot eyes on Eggs for a long while. The anger had finally burned away enough grief for me to see he spoke the truth. I slid my mug of beer down the bar to a startled miner and said: "You're right, Eggs. No more drinking until I get this thing straightened out."

"Dora's got a pot of venison stew made up. Go over to the cabin and get something to eat. It'll take a couple of days to clear your head. You've had a damn' good reason to go on a drunk. Now you've got reason to sober up."

Eggs was wrong about one thing. It took me *four* days to quit shaking enough to drive the Packard to Twin Falls.

As my usual good sense began returning, the madder I got. Before leaving to combat Spurgeon, I had slipped that little pistol I'd bought to protect myself from Ben Kuhl into my coat pocket. I'd never shot anyone before, but blowing holes in a lawyer seemed like a great place to start.

My throat tightened when I drove past the cemetery. I hadn't been down that road since. . . . I blinked the mist from my eyes and kept going.

Theodore Spurgeon showed no surprise when I burst angrily into his office.

"Hello, Milo," he said pleasantly. "Nelson called to tell me you were coming."

It took me a moment to realize who he was talking about. I hadn't heard Eggs called by his last name for a long time. Then it struck me — *Why would Eggs call Spurgeon?*

"I'm here about your locking up my money in some damn' lawsuit," I growled.

A knowing smile crossed the lawyer's lips. "Oh, I'd already assumed that much. Would you like a cup of coffee? Then I'll explain everything."

I felt like a mouse eyeing a rattlesnake as I took a seat in front of that huge desk of his, nodding in suspicious agreement.

Spurgeon filled two cups and carefully placed one of them on a coaster in front of me.

"A short time after your wife's death," the

lawyer began while pacing back and forth behind his desk, "Nelson came to visit with me. He said your intentions were to drink yourself to death."

"It seemed like a good idea at the time."

"Neither he nor I agreed. You had a terrible thing happen. Dave Bourne lost his wife, and only three short years ago . . ." — I noticed the lawyer's lip quiver when he took a sip of coffee — "my own sweet Mattie died in childbirth. Life comes with no guarantees, Milo. When a man gets kicked down, he has no choice but to get up and walk again."

"I'm sorry about your wife. I didn't know," I said sincerely, "but what has this got to do with your suing me?"

"Four Roses Mining Company filed against your assets to keep them frozen so you couldn't get at them. I am the president of that company, and Egbert Nelson is secretary. I have personally advanced funds to keep that bar of yours running and pay Egbert's salary. As soon as I receive your word that you are through trying to drink yourself to death and pay me back, Four Roses Mining Company will withdraw its complaint."

I swallowed hard, trying to absorb what the lawyer was telling me. "The whole thing was a set-up."

Spurgeon replied: "Sometimes it's necessary for a man to have something else besides his own pain to focus on."

"I owe you my thanks . . . and an apology. I was mad as hell when I came in here."

Spurgeon shrugged his shoulders. "I'm a lawyer . . . people are always mad at me. All you owe me is money. Dora and Egbert are the ones you need to thank, especially Dora. It was her idea."

I looked at the clock behind Spurgeon's desk. "It's lunchtime. What do you say we go somewhere and grab a steak."

"Sounds good to me, as long as you're buying."

"I'm broke, remember?"

"That's no problem. I'll pay for everything" — he gave me a devilish grin — "and add it to your bill later."

Once I could get to my money, I gave Eggs and Dora a check for a $1,000 as a "getting together" present, and told them to take a vacation.

Eggs received a friendly poke in the ribs from Dora when he said he would take her to Yellowstone Park so Old Faithful could put on another great performance. The last time he'd teased about that, Marybeth had been there. Now that I was off the whiskey, memories flooded in like water from a broken dam. The fact that a lot of them were good memories kept me sober.

For nearly a year I never touched another drop. Then I began to sip on a beer once in a while, like I still do to this day. A little booze once in a while is fine if you can keep it under control. If not, it will surely control you.

"Did you hear about Ben Kuhl?" Tully asked, when he dropped into the bar one evening.

"Nope," I replied. "Did they finally shoot him?"

"It's not going to happen. Governor Sullivan felt there was a reasonable doubt that Fred Searcy might have been in on the stage robbery and commuted Kuhl's sentence to life in prison." Tully continued after lighting a cigarette: "We should have hung that bastard. It's hard for 'em to work up sympathy and get their sentence commuted once they're planted."

For the next several years, things clicked along rather normally in Jarbidge. Elkoro Mines Company finally fulfilled Tully's goal and became the premier gold producer in the state of Nevada, a title it would hold for some time.

I kept going back every summer to look for the Lost Sheepherder's Mine. I scoured the area where I'd found that nugget, but never found another piece.

Butt-Block got fidgety in the summer of 1927 and left to work in a silver mine near Wallace, Idaho. Tully received word only a few weeks later that he had been killed in a rock fall there.

The whole country slid downhill towards the doorway to hell in the Fall of 1929 when the stock market crashed. I even had some money there myself. Theodore Spurgeon had talked me into buying some stock in a soft drink company called Coca-Cola. I figured the entire $2,000 I'd invested was gone like a covey of spooked quail. This turned out to be one of those rare times in my life that I was mistaken about something.

The market crash wrecked a lot of people, however. There were panic runs on banks and wholesale closings of factories causing massive lay-offs. None of this affected Jarbidge much. We waited until 1932 for our very own depression to arrive. That was the year Elkoro Mines ran out of ore and closed down.

"When you take the first shovelful of ore out of a mine, you've begun to kill it," Tully said when he announced the shutdown.

"There's simply no more gold left in that mountain."

Jarbidge grew silent as a tomb when that big Elkoro mill ceased its constant rumbling. Gold had caused the town to be born; now the lack of that metal had killed it. Tully gave everyone some hope when he said Guggenheim was embarking on a drilling program to look for more ore before scrapping out the mill.

None of the 200 odd men who had been working at the mine were needed for this, however. Most headed for places where they'd heard rumors that work was available. Homes wouldn't sell at any price. People simply abandoned them to the tax collector, along with whatever furniture, clothes, or kids' toys couldn't fit into the car.

Charlie Fong closed his restaurant and hotel late that summer. The skinny pig-tailed Chinaman wasn't the least concerned about leaving Jarbidge.

"Me go home to Chinee now," he said happily. "Me have all money Charlie ever need. Get big house and little wife. Never cook 'nother damn' thing for nobody again."

The Miners' Exchange and Stray Dog were the only bars needed to handle the thirsts of those few miners, drillers, sheepherders, hunters, or lost-mine seekers that remained.

When the last whore closed up shop and left Cherry Flats, everyone knew Jarbidge was becoming a ghost town.

Eggs and Dora, of course, kept right on living in that cabin by the river. I had some money coming in from interest and, surprisingly enough, stock dividends from Coca-Cola. Every week, I wrote out a check to him for tending bar, just like I'd been doing for years.

Many days we would open the bar and the two of us would play dominoes for hours, using that set I'd bought Willie so long ago, without a single customer coming in.

"The drilling is over," Tully announced in the bar on a warm July day in 1935. "We found nothing worth mining. Elkoro's going to scrap the mill out and abandon Jarbidge."

I felt like I'd been kicked in the gut.

"Then you'll be moving on," I said to Tully.

He answered me sounding sad as a preacher at a funeral. "Yeah, the Guggenheims offered me a job in Arizona. I hate to leave this place for some damn' reason. It's colder than a witch's tit most of the time, and we're so far back in the sticks you have to use a telescope to see civilization." Tully rolled sad blue eyes at me. "It was quite a time, this last big gold rush. I reckon every party has to break up eventually, but by God it *was* something to behold, wasn't it?"

"No matter what you say, Milo, you don't need a bartender any longer," Eggs firmly told me a few weeks later. "Dora and me are going to San Diego. I've got a job working for Inman Searcy and Jackson Lyman at their resort. Even with the Depression going on, they're making money."

I was more surprised Eggs had a job with the Searcys than the fact he was leaving Jarbidge. Only about a hundred people still lived here, and most of those were working on tearing down the Elkoro mill.

"It's been a while since I've heard from those folks. How is everyone?" I asked.

"Sylvia passed away some time ago. Inman's doing fine, but the problem is Jackson. He didn't get away from the mines soon enough and has consumption so bad it takes him an hour to catch his breath after he passes wind. I'm going to tend bar for them, now that Jackson can't work any longer."

I gave Eggs and Dora that old Model T of mine to drive to California. They made the springs sag when they climbed on, but, without Crippen Grade to climb, I figured they'd make the trip fine.

Dora dabbed at a tear with her handkerchief and said: "Milo, there's no reason for you to stay here."

"You two go on," I replied, "there's still a little business to do here. This town's going to come back someday, you'll see."

Neither would have understood my real reason for staying, even if I had told them.

The Great Depression ended when another world war erupted in Europe. Those Germans sure can start a ruckus when the spirit moves them.

In October of 1941, the government, with their usual lack of common sense, made gold mining illegal. They said it was unnecessary to the war effort. That winter, we had less than twenty residents living in this rugged, snowy cañon.

The atomic bomb had just been dropped on Hiroshima when I received a letter from Inman telling me Eggs had suffered a stroke and passed on. He said Dora took it hard. Jackson Lyman, his letter mentioned, had died three years earlier. This was the first I'd heard of it, and it saddened me as much as Eggs's passing. At the rate my friends were being put in the ground, I would soon be the only one left who knew what had happened here during the big gold rush.

Jarbidge came close to becoming a ghost town, but it never quite made the grade. Hunters and fishermen gave the bar a little business every summer.

There was always some outfit poking around one of the old mines, headed by a big-talking promoter spending someone else's money like it was water. Not a one of them ever shipped enough gold to fill a bad tooth. But it was enjoyable listening to their bullshit. It reminded me of the old days.

Things slid into a routine of short active summers followed by long dead winters, until June of 1952 to be exact. I remember that year well.

It was when Ben Kuhl returned to Jarbidge.

Chapter Twenty-Six

The weather was warm and I had the door to the bar propped open to air the place out when this battered old Dodge car pulled to a dusty stop out front. I thought the lone driver was probably some fisherman and paid him no mind until he came in and sat down at the bar.

I had my usual afternoon crowd of none in attendance. After splattering a green fly with last week's newspaper, I walked around behind the counter and asked the man if I could get him something.

"Just a cold bottle of beer," he said pleasantly, plunking down a fifty-cent piece on the bar.

There was something vaguely familiar in the man's voice. He wasn't much older than me, maybe in his late-fifties, slender with a short, salt-and-pepper stubble of beard covering a decidedly pale face. Then I noticed the dark insolence in his sunken, deep-set eyes and remembered. It was the same arrogant defiance I had only seen in Ben Kuhl.

"Do I know you, friend?" he queried.

"You remind me of someone from a long time ago," I said, inching my way toward the sawed-off shotgun I kept under the bar. "If you are that man, I reckon the *friend* statement won't hold water."

The man's expression never changed as he took a drink of beer and looked out the door toward the distant snow-covered peaks and said: "A snot-nosed, arrogant punk by the name of Ben Kuhl used to live here. He killed an innocent stagecoach driver just outside town. Then he lied about what happened to save his neck."

"I thought he was to spend the rest of his life in prison," I answered as my hand rested on the cold steel of the shotgun.

"He did. All the life that's worth living, anyway. I'm what's left of a man after he's spent thirty-five years behind bars. My name is Ben Kuhl, and there's something I have to do here." Kuhl's pleasant expression never left his face as he closely looked me over. "I know you, but I can't remember the name."

"Milo Goodman," I replied coldly. "I owned this place back in those days, too."

A look of deep sadness crossed Kuhl's

335

face. "Sure, I've thought of you often. We have business that needs to be settled between us."

My hand tightened around the shotgun when Kuhl reached into his jacket pocket. The only thing he took out was a dollar bill. "Could I buy you a beer? When it's hot, they taste real good. For a lot of years I only dreamed about how good a cold beer is on a day like this."

The last time I had relaxed my guard around Ben Kuhl, I'd taken a two-by-four to the gut. "This business of yours, just what may I ask is it?"

"You won't have any use for that gun you've got your hand on. I only came to Jarbidge for one reason . . . I want to see where Fred Searcy's buried and make sure he's got a proper marker and tell him I'm sorry. That's not much to do for a man after you've taken his life, but it's something I need to do."

"You mentioned there was business between us?"

"I doubted anyone I knew would still be here," Kuhl said, "but I'm glad you are, so I can tell you to your face how sorry I am for all the grief I caused."

I'm sure my mouth must have dropped onto my boots. Never, when the memory of

Ben Kuhl had crossed my mind, did the possibility of him ever saying anything like this occur to me.

"That shotgun might have been necessary thirty-five years ago, Mister Goodman," he said in a distant voice, "but I want you to believe me when I tell you all I want to do is clear my conscience before it's too late."

"Are you sick," I asked cautiously, still not trusting him.

"That's why I got paroled. The docs tell me I've got a cancer and don't have long for this world."

I removed my hand from the gun, walked over to the cooler, took out two bottles of beer, and set them on the counter top.

"Your money's no good here," I said as Ben's lower lip began quivering. "And by the way, the name's Milo, not mister."

We talked for a while about the old days. I had never seen a man so transformed as Ben Kuhl was. He took a coughing spell during our second beer that racked his whole body. I noticed there was blood on the handkerchief when he stuffed it back into his pocket.

Mostly he asked about what had happened to people he knew. There wasn't a single one, except Inman Searcy, that I knew for certain was still alive. After a while, he finished his beer and began nervously spinning the bottle on the bar.

"I've got to go see Fred Searcy," he said sadly. "I'd like it if you would come along."

I glanced around the empty bar. "The crowd will just have to wait until I get back," I said while putting a **Closed** sign in the window.

On the way out, I grabbed up two bottles of beer. After I locked the door, we piled into my Jeep and drove to the cemetery.

"Where is he?" Ben asked with a breaking voice when I opened the rusty iron gate.

"Over there." I pointed out a marble stone by the fence. "Next to where Wheelbarrow Willie and my wife's buried."

I stayed behind as Ben Kuhl shuffled to the grave of Fred Searcy.

"He's got a nice stone," he said after a long while. "Who keeps the weeds chopped out?"

"I do."

"Good of you to do that."

"I don't mind."

"I didn't think he'd have such a good marker. My folks left me a little money when they passed away. I'd planned on buying him one. A man needs a good stone, so's folks will remember him."

Ben Kuhl dropped to his knees and began shaking like an aspen tree in a windstorm.

"Oh, my God, please forgive me," he cried. He rocked back and forth as the guilt he'd carried all these years became a maëlstrom of flowing wretchedness.

I had a lump in my throat when I walked away to sit in the shade while Ben made his peace. I knew how he felt for I had done the same thing many times, the next grave over.

After about an hour, Ben came to me with dried tears streaking lines on his dusty cheeks. "I reckon we should go now."

When we got back to the bar, I offered him another beer, but he refused. "I've done what I set out to do. I'd best be heading back before it gets dark. I can't see worth a darn at night."

"You drive careful and come back."

"I'll never be back," he said with finality. "The only thing I ask is that you tell me I'm forgiven for hurting you and to keep the weeds chopped out of Searcy's plot."

"What happened is in the past and forgotten. Keeping up the cemetery's no trouble. I'm there a lot."

He shook my hand and slowly climbed into his car. I stood on the boardwalk in front of the bar and watched the last man to rob a stagecoach in the United States drive away, leaving a cloud of gray-powder dust hanging in the still mountain air.

Epilogue

This book has gotten longer than a telephone wire. I reckon if I had known just how much work it would be, I would never have written the thing. If I hadn't, though, no one would ever know some of those interesting characters who made up the last gold rush.

I suppose that is what I miss most of all: people with some grit in their craw; people who were not afraid to follow a distant star to some place they had never been; people who held hope and love as their most prized possessions.

The ones who did are still here. Many of them, anyway. They reside behind the rusting iron gate that enters into the Jarbidge Cemetery. That is the reason I could never leave here.

Marybeth lies there.

For a lot a years now, I have been the only one to tend that cemetery. Everyone else seems too busy to chop weeds or straighten a tilting headstone. It would not take much time from their busy lives to remember those who have gone before.

But no one does. I am always alone when I go there.

On a summer afternoon, once I have watered the peonies on Marybeth's grave, I rest myself in the shade of a big pine tree.

When the weather is calm and the deer come to drink from the clear, running waters of the Jarbidge River, I swear I can smell lilac perfume.

Some love too little, some too long,
Some sell and others buy;
Some do the deed with many tears,
And some without a sigh:
For each man kills the thing he loves,
Yet each man does not die.

The Ballad of Reading Gaol
Oscar Wilde

Author's Note

The last robbery of a horse-drawn stage-coach actually occurred December 5th, 1916, just outside of Jarbidge, Nevada. Ed Beck and Ben Kuhl were the last ones to rob a stage in the United States. Bloody palm and fingerprints left at the scene were used to convict them in court, one of the first times forensics were employed to solve a crime. My fictional narrator, Milo T. Goodman, becomes acquainted with many historical characters and events, including Kitty Wilkins and the machine-gunning of wild horses from airplanes to run her off of her ranch.

Gold caused Jarbidge to be born in that remote area where snow can reach depths of thirty feet in the wintertime. When the rich veins became exhausted, this once proud boom town almost, but not quite, became a ghost. It is estimated that as many as fifty hardy souls still live there year around.

The lost Sheepherder's Mine is a well-known legend that has drawn treasure hunters and adventure seekers to these rugged mountains for many years. It remains as lost as ever.

When I visited the decrepit cemetery outside of Jarbidge, I found one lone grave surrounded by a newly painted white picket fence. The headstone was missing. In its stead lay a bouquet of pink peonies. I never learned who is buried there, or who placed those flowers. But love often outlasts flesh and bone.

About the Author

Ken Hodgson was born in the shadow of Pike's Peak in 1945. His grandfather mined gold in Cripple Creek, Colorado, and fueled his imagination at an early age with tales of lost mines, ghost towns, and characters of the old West. He attended Metropolitan College in Denver and was a professional prospector and miner for many years. He has written numerous articles for magazines such as *True West, Rock and Gem, Lost Treasure*, and the *International California Mining Journal*. Three of his Western novels are: *The Hell Benders* (1999), *Lone Survivor* (2001), and *Hard Bounty* (2001). *Fool's Gold* (Five Star Westerns, 2003) tells of a gold rush to Oregon. His short stories have been included in various anthologies. He resides in San Angelo, Texas, with his wife Rita and their ill-tempered cat, Penelope.